S0-ARO-799

The
Erotic
Writer's
Market
Guide

The Erotic Writer's Market Guide

Advice, Tips, and Market Listings for the
Aspiring Professional Erotica Writer

Compiled by
The Circlet Press Collective

Circlet Press, Inc.
Cambridge, MA

Table of Contents

SECTION ONE
Advice for Erotic Writers

SECTION TWO
Market Listings

SECTION THREE
Resources/References

The Circlet Press Collective

This book began almost ten years ago as the brainchild of David Laurents, one of Circlet's regular stable of erotica writers and a real write-a-holic under multiple pseudonyms. Laurents as writer, poet, and anthologist is prolific to say the least, and to this day is still cooking up ideas for books faster than he, or anyone else, can write or publish them. For a while he worked on the book alone, then with the help of Cecilia Tan, Circlet's publisher and editor. When they faltered, another talented erotica writer and editor, Rachel Kramer Bussel, made significant additions but the task proved too large for her as well. Many other hands have since worked to shape, fact-check, update, and otherwise polish the finished product, including Rob Hill, Nick Richardson, Kelly J. Cooper, and others of Circlet's authors, employees, and interns we call The Circlet Press Collective.

We are working erotica writers, editors, and publishers, and it is this collected expertise that makes this book unique. We hope it inspires you to join our ranks.

SECTION ONE
Advice for Writers

Chapter One:
Writing for Publication

Many people dream of publishing their erotica. Some start writing it for a particular reason—for a lover or to explore their own fantasies—and then feel ready to make the next step: publication. Others write for the same reasons people start writing other forms of fiction, for creative fulfillment and self-expression. We've written *The Erotic Writer's Market Guide* as both a way to help you get started writing erotica and as a guide to assist you in getting published. The rapidly changing erotic market has undergone many shifts since we began this book and it continues to evolve. While working on the book, we saw many publishers close or change the focus of their business while various small presses focusing on erotica have sprung up.

The erotic writing world is also constantly evolving with the times, both in content and in style. You can now find specific erotic writing to fit almost any particular fetish, and if it is not already out there, you can create your own (witness the recent anthology *Best of the Best Meat Erotica*, only nominally a parody about sex and meat). The Internet has been a boon to erotic writers, providing new markets and drawing in new readers while allowing readers privacy in reading and ordering books, easing any potential embarrassment. Also, many mainstream magazines regularly publish articles about sex, the porn industry, and even some erotic fiction. *Cleansheets.com* editor Susannah Indigo recounted in an article at *Salon.com* her uncertainty when a copy of men's style magazine *Details* arrived for her teenaged son with an erotic story of hers printed inside!

Erotica has reached the masses, which is good news for you as a future erotic writer. Literary authors such as Marge Piercy, Bret Easton Ellis, Dorothy Allison, Aimee Bender, and others have appeared in the widely read and well-regarded *Best American Erotica* series. And erotica seems to be blooming given the number of calls for submission that cross our desks. No longer considering erotica as something to be hidden away in a bedside drawer, authors are using their real names and proudly penning erotic works that are thought-provoking, political, and literary, as well as hot. When you sit down to write erotica, you are joining a long tradition of writers who've found inspiration in the world of sex, and these days you may even gain some measure of respect for it.

This book is designed to give you an overview of the world of erotic writing, from what types of writing are encompassed by "erotica," through how to deal with potential disapproval (as well as eager readers and fans) of your writing, to how to go about getting your work published. The chapters are followed by market listings for book publishers, magazines, and websites that are seeking erotic works. We've included publishers interested in sex-related nonfiction as well as erotic fiction, though the focus of this book is erotic fiction (with a smidgen of poetry). The resource list at the end of the book offers other sources of information that should prove useful to you. Please bear in mind that while the topics and markets covered are current as of this writing, things change often. Although this guide may point you at certain appropriate markets for your work, please double-check that their information has not changed before sending off a submission. Almost every market now has a website that makes it easy to get their most current guidelines and submission preferences.

Writing for publication does not have to be a daunting task, though it will take effort, dedication, and professionalism. This book is not a handbook on "how to write a story," since there are dozens of good books on that subject as well as hundreds of writing classes, worskshops, writers' colonies, and college degree programs. What we have included are some basic thoughts on writing, particularly on writing erotica, with publication in mind. Writers tend to work in one of two ways. Some look at the markets available to them and then sit down and craft a story that will fit one or the other. Others write things as the ideas come, shaping and crafting them over time, then look for a suitable place to publish after the piece is finished. Whichever style you employ, the writing is still the most important part of the process.

Generally, it is best to focus on the actual writing while you are writing. If you are thinking about whether Editor So-and-So will like your story, or how your name will look in print, or whether your sister will be upset by the content of the story, you may find yourself sitting and staring at a blank page or screen. Don't create writer's block before you've even started. While they are valid concerns, the time to worry about them is after you finish writing a specific story, not during.

Regularly dedicate yourself as best you can and find a period of time—be it an hour or a day—to devote solely to creating the best writing that you can. If you are constantly getting up to check the stove or answer the phone, your mind will be distracted from the task at hand. If there is something in your personal life that is worrying you, you may find that it works its way into your story (which could be a good or bad thing, depending on what you're writing). When you write, you are tapping into areas of your subconscious. If you are too distracted, or too self-conscious, you may find you can't reach that wellspring of inspiration.

For writers of any genre, but especially for writers of erotica, it is very easy to get distracted by worrying about how the story will reflect on you and your own sexuality, on how others will react, and on other outside pressures. What you need to focus on is whether the story works for you, whether it sounds plausible, whether the characters would actually sleep with each other, whether the erotic tension that you intended comes across in the work. The same things that make a non-erotic fiction story work also make an erotic story work. Create vivid, believable characters, put them into interesting situations, and involve the reader emotionally in the outcome. If you write fiction which satisfies you as a reader, chances are there is a readership for you out there who will feel the same.

Try not to critique your work while it is coming out. Let it flow and see where it goes. Sometimes your characters will surprise you. But eventually you will reach a point where you have a piece in hand that you feel is "done."

An excellent way to proofread your manuscript is to read it out loud, as if in front of an audience. This will tell you where certain words and phrases work, and where they don't, where something that looked good on the page falls flat when read aloud. Every time you stumble while reading, chances are you could work on that sentence to make it better, smoother, tighter. It should go without saying but we'll say it anyway for emphasis: the story must have correct grammar and punctuation. But beyond that, it must make sense in a larger context. Did the story have a beginning, middle, and end? Did you express yourself clearly?

Before sending the story out, you must make sure that the story meets your own personal standards; have you written the story you wanted to tell? Then, after proofreading it, you might want to share it with a friend, writing partner, or trusted advisor. When you are new to writing, or new to erotica, some feedback can be helpful in letting you know whether you have communicated your ideas effectively.

Most of all, you have to give it your all. Writing erotic fiction is similar to any other kind of writing in that it works best when your full attention is devoted to it. Though there are plenty of money-making opportunities, if you are only in it to make a quick buck and couldn't care less about erotica, that will show in your work. Everything you write doesn't have to be deeply felt, but if you want to write the best stuff you can, you need to believe that erotic writing is something worth pursuing. We hope this book helps you get off to a roaring start.

Chapter Two:
Overcoming Your Inhibitions

If you've bought this book, chances are that you're already on your way to unleashing your erotic imagination on the page. However, you may be nervous about doing so. Many questions arise when writing erotica that may cause concern: what if someone finds out, what will this kind of writing mean about me, will it affect my love life, and more. This chapter will give you some tips for getting over fears that keep you from writing erotica.

Sex is a natural part of our lives, and it is a natural subject for us to want to write about—and read about. Most people end up looking at or reading some sort of "dirty" book or magazine during their teen years—whether it is a smuggled copy of Hustler, a furtively passed copy of Judy Blume's Forever, or a book like Terry Southern's Candy. And that doesn't include any number of other erotic classics or naughty magazines found in bookstores, parents' rooms, or borrowed from friends. Even though young adults are curious about these "forbidden fruits," they quickly pick up on the fact that these materials are not deemed acceptable and should be kept hidden away. From having to hide these desires and interests early on, you may have entered adulthood unsure of what to do with your impulses towards erotic writing. But rest assured, there are thousands of people writing erotic fiction who enjoy unleashing their fantasies and learning about their own desires. And there are also plenty of people reading these kinds of works—on the web, in magazines, and in books. The erotic fiction market is booming, which should tell you that for every person telling you that you shouldn't do this, there are many more who approve of and even enjoy this type of writing.

Fear of the law, your family, how your employer will react, whether your rabbi or minister disapprove, etc. are all reasons that can make people nervous about writing erotica. Indeed, this is a major internal struggle. You may not know the potential reaction of these people and may not want to find out. First of all, you should know that nobody has to see your writing if you don't want them to. You can begin writing even if you're not yet sure whether you want to publish your stories. But as this is a book aimed at writers who want to publish their work, there are other options, such as using pseudonyms (see Chapter Three: Care and Feeding of Pseudonyms).

You may have bought this book simply looking for insight into the working life of someone who writes this kind of fiction for a living. Maybe you want answers to questions such as "Does the writer of erotica need to be turned on while writing?" Or perhaps you are looking for a better understanding of what makes fiction sexy. Maybe a friend bought this book for you as a gag gift. Maybe you've written steamy love letters to your lovers in the past but are looking for another outlet for those writing impulses. People come to erotic writing via many different paths and for many different reasons.

Censorship and Self-Censorship

Many people are familiar with some level of censorship of pornography. Censorship comes in the form of retailers refusing to carry certain publications (like Wal-Mart dropping the "lad mags" Maxim and FHM) they find objectionable, to publications limiting the content of what they will buy or publish.

Stories on certain subjects, including underage sex and bestiality, are illegal to publish in the United States and in much of the English-speaking world. Other forms of sexuality may be considered extreme, but are legal to depict, and there are markets that serve them—though they may not be easy to find.

The debate over what should and should not be allowed, as well as the place of sex in our lives and in our society, is important and not everyone is comfortable with every piece of porn or erotica out there. You don't have to be, but having an open mind about sexual variance and sexuality can only help a writer. If spanking turns you on, you might enjoy writing spanking fantasies, but if it leaves you cold or scratching your head wondering what other people see in it, then it's not the genre for you. By reading the various types of erotica (see Chapter Four: Forms of Erotica), you can figure out what you enjoy most and perhaps what you'd like to start writing. As social mores change, what was once extreme may now be acceptable or commonplace in some places, but still taboo in others. Various forms of erotic expression do still come under fire.

Almost every day, newspapers are filled with stories about obscenity battles or social disapproval from those who dare to express their erotic impulses, whether in fiction, nonfiction, or in their daily lives. First amendment advocates and others work to make sure that our rights to free speech are retained. As an erotic writer, you do not have to personally take part in these battles for the freedom to express ourselves sexually, but you certainly will benefit from the efforts of many brave people who are arrested, imprisoned, fined, harassed, and otherwise penalized for demanding the cultural space for sexuality that we all benefit from today. (If you are moved to fight this fight, the ACLU, the Free Speech Coalition, the National Coalition for Sexual Freedom (NCSF), and the Comic Book Legal Defense Fund (CBLDF) would love to hear from you.)

Although you may not be in court fighting censorship, the prospective erotic writer must confront one important type of censorship: the unconscious censorship that springs from our cultural upbringings and the emotional baggage we may carry (without even realizing it) about sex, sexuality, pornography, and other related issues. Self-censorship is the daily hurdle we must overcome.

We may absorb many cultural attitudes about sex, often without recognizing them until years later, and then only after much introspection, self-examination, and confrontation. Almost all English-speaking cultures still have strong cultural taboos about seeing the naked body, sex in public, and talking about (or writing about) sex, which is another way to be public with your sexuality. You will have to confront these taboos, at least within yourself, when you begin writing about sex.

Many people fear feeling exposed and vulnerable when writing their sexual fantasies down. This may feel too raw, too emotional to face, especially if you don't usually spend a lot of time consciously thinking about what your sexual turn-ons and fantasies are. You may be afraid of being rejected—and if the fantasies you are writing are very personal, this can feel like a rejection of your sexuality (see Chapter Nine: Coping With Rejection).

How can you disable these multiple internal censors in order to write comfortably about sex?

You must first acknowledge these fears and censors. Confrontation is the only way to know what you are afraid of and how you might get past it. Sit down and ask yourself about your own views on sex, sexuality, and pornography: What turns me on? What are the fantasies I play in my head? Where do they come from? Am I ready to share them? Be honest with yourself. If you are not able to be honest with yourself, you will not be able to write with conviction about sexuality.

This does not mean you must be "out" about your sexual

desires to your family, friends, or co-workers. Some of the best erotica writers today are "closeted." But these writers still have an internal understanding of where their desires come from, or how to mold their unrequited desires into fiction.

If you are embarrassed now, in private, when thinking about the things you like, you should know that these reactions will probably come up again when you sit down to write, again when it's time to show your erotic stories to an editor, and again when they are published for a wider, anonymous audience. Keep these fears in mind as you work through them; they may be interesting fodder for an erotic story (the protagonist is worried about her lover finding her erotic stories, he does find them, and then…). And the only way to overcome fear and embarassment is by repeated exposure to them. These are two emotions that lessen their impact with time. Like a scary movie that loses its ability to frighten when we watch it over and over, internal fears will lose their power as well.

People Are People

As a beginning erotic writer, you may find it easier—especially at first—to think about actual people as you write. If you do this, maybe fantastizing about the girl next door, be careful to avoid including any conclusively identifying details in your work to protect yourself from libel suits. While some folks are tickled or flattered to find themselves in an erotic story, many more people tend to take the opposite view. Using the people that you yourself fantasize about as characters can lend an immediacy and involvement to your fiction—a charge which comes across clearly for the reader. And you may use yourself, or someone very like you, in your story too.

Using the people you fantasize about as characters in your erotic fiction is not the same as simply writing down your erotic fantasies. While it is probable that if you're having an erotic fantasy about something, others will likewise share the fantasy, creating effective erotic fiction for the reader to enjoy and respond to requires more background and buildup—i.e. the craft of fiction—to be effective. Compare your task as an erotic author to that of actors in visual porn: the position that porn stars have to get into in order for the cameras to have the best angles for the viewer's pleasure are not usually the most comfortable positions for the actors themselves. In other words, you will have to take your reader through the many levels of your fantasy. You'll need to write not only what you want to do with person x, but who person x is, who you are, why you are fantasizing about them, and so on. You will have to expand the fantasy to create a realistic whole. But you can begin at any point, and if the heart of your fantasy is what gets you going, by all means, start with that. You do not have to start at the "beginning" of a story necessarily; you can jot down notes or details that you may want to incorporate, or keep a running file of sexy scenes, people, body parts, character traits, etc., and use them as you need to.

Instead of real people you know, it may be easier to use movie stars or actors who you find sexually appealing, because they're distant and unavailable. You can project your fantasies onto them in a safe and nonthreatening way and easily get a picture in your head of what they look like. The clerk at the greengrocer's shop who you've got a crush on might feel too "real" to use effectively as a cipher in your erotic piece. You may be resistant to changing details you know to be true about him or her, even though the story may call for it. But if you've never met Michelle Pfeiffer or Mel Gibson, and you are writing a character who is loosely based upon them, you can imagine them to be a few inches taller or shorter than they actually are, or nicer or nastier, so that they are a better "fit" with the hero or heroine of your tale. Or when you suddenly realize that you've described all the women in your story as blonde-haired and blue-eyed, you can decide to change the color of their hair or eyes even though, in real life, that's what they look like.

The actual details of these people's lives are immaterial; you are using them simply to recall that physical attraction you feel when you see them or an image of them in a magazine or on a movie screen.

Another reason to think of an actual person when writing erotica is that it helps to remember that there's a whole body involved. And if you're using someone familiar, it makes it easier to remember all the details about a body (and persona/personality) that makes your character unique.

If you are having trouble getting started, a tactic that may get you writing is to do the opposite of the above; if it makes you nervous to write about things that are too close to home, you can start with something totally outside the realm of your real life. This way, you at least know that there is no confusing you with your characters. You can start by creating someone who is totally different than you, your opposite in every (or most) ways, and go from there. This can be a fun and interesting way of challenging yourself and stretching your erotic writing muscles far beyond your own fantasy life. (For more about this, see Chapter Five: How To Write About Something You've Never Done (Yet).)

One of the conventions of erotica is that all characters are sexually of interest, meaning your characters are all desirable and beautiful or handsome in one way or another, and usually they're perfect in all respects (at least physically). One way to differentiate characters is through your descriptions. Since variety is the spice of life in erotic fiction, you want to make all of your characters at least somewhat different from each other, to help the reader remember them and to highlight what makes them unique. You want them to come alive, not just to be faceless bodies having sex. If you make your characters memorable, people will remember your story long after they've read it, even if they don't recall every detail. This sort of attention to creating differentiated characters will pay off, especially when you're working on an erotic novel where you've got to maintain the reader's interest for a much longer period of time. It can also be useful if, at a later time, you want to create another story featuring the same character.

Finding Your Erotic Voice

Ultimately, the decision whether or not to pick up the pen is your own. But if you find yourself coming back to this desire to write about your sexual fantasies, shunting them off will probably only lead to their haunting you later on. You can always tear up what you write, but getting it out of your head and onto the page will most likely feel freeing and energizing. Once you get these pressing thoughts and images onto paper, you are free to do what you like with what you have written. You are not obligated to keep writing or to always write about sex or anything else. Or, as mentioned earlier, in the process of writing down a specific sexual fantasy, other ideas may occur to you, or you might find that a fictional character who shares your own personal sexual fantasy comes to mind. There are many things you can do with a certain story, fantasy setting, or sex scene; they do not always wind up where you originally intended them. What started out as a short story may take on a life of its own and become a novel, and the woman you thought would live happily ever after with her doting husband may run off and have wild affairs while traveling across the country.

You have the autonomy to make your own decisions; you shouldn't feel that you have to seek out publication for every piece you write. The main point we want to emphasize is that there's nothing wrong with writing about sex. Many of the finest writers in literature have incorporated sex into their work. While they were not always lauded for their efforts, some of these are noted classics read in schools and universities to this day. Some authors such as D.H. Lawrence, who were persecuted in their day, are now recognized as major figures in the history of erotic writing. Some characters or phrases, such as the "zipless fuck" of Erica Jong's *Fear of Flying*, become part of our sexual lexicon.

If what is holding you back is your own fear, the best way to confront it is to start slowly, writing what is most compelling to you at this moment and assessing your feelings about the writing as you go. If there is a recurring theme when you start to write, go with that. There is no obligation or pressure on you to continue once you've started, but seeing your thoughts on paper will likely help you figure out what it is you're really getting at, and can foster greater creativity. You may be genuinely surprised what comes from your pen once you make the decision to start writing. There is nothing lost (except perhaps time) by putting pen to paper (or fingers to computer keyboard), and you may find that if you do not write out that fantasy lurking about in your mind, it will continue to plague you at all hours of the day, begging to be written down. The most important thing to remember, especially as a beginning writer, is that you are in charge of your own writing; you do not have to show it to anyone, and nobody else but you has to know about it. Keeping this in mind should help you get started, and from there, anything goes.

Chapter Three:
The Care and Feeding of Pseudonyms

Why Use A Pseudonym

While writing erotica has gained much more respect and mainstream attention in recent years, many people still choose—for a variety of reasons—to use a pseudonym when publishing erotic work. Although we know many writers who use their real names, there are various reasons to choose a pen name.

Sometimes the pseudonym is dependent on the kind of story being written. Some writers might use their real name for most of their work but choose on occasion to use a pseudonym because of something relating to the content of the story (safe sex, gay vs. straight writing, creating a different persona) or when working with a specific publisher. They may have a separate writing career on a completely separate topic, such as children's books, and don't want the two to be associated with each other. Or they may have another career outside of writing and don't want colleagues (or neighbors, family, etc.) to know about their erotic publications.

Sometimes, a writer will want—or need—a pseudonym to disguise his or her gender. For instance, gay erotic magazines are familiar with women writing and submitting gay erotic stories; almost all of them have published stories written by women. However, a woman writing gay erotica may need a male-sounding name to publish her work in the gay men's erotic magazines, because the audience for these publications wants to believe that these stories are actually written by a man who has first-hand experience in the hot and sweaty gay sex depicted. Usually, the same goes for men looking to write lesbian erotica, with the exception of certain writers who are very prominent in the field. There is a similar long tradition of men writing romance novels under female names.

Some prolific writers, who are only writing erotica to make a quick buck, don't care what their pseudonyms are and will make up a new one for each story. Some magazines even insist on picking pseudonyms themselves, randomly, to prevent libel suits. When it comes to publishing stories in some magazines, it is very difficult for writers to keep editorial control over their work; this is a fact of working in the industry. Magazines need to be able to cut any references to illegal or taboo activities that can cause their publication to be impounded, stopped at national borders, or otherwise cause them to come under legal action. Quite often commercial erotic magazines have a heavier hand at editing than one will find in other genres. The overworked people who work for the magazine conglomerates simply have to produce as many titles per month, as cheaply as possible, while still satisfying the needs of the marketplace.

There are reasons other than privacy to create a pseudonym. One reason "David Laurents" continues to use that name even though he is "out" about his writing, is to prevent himself from overpublishing. If you have too many books, especially too many erotica books, set to publish in a given season, you dilute the possibilities for review attention that each of these titles may attract. Your books may compete against one another for readership, shelf space, and publicity attention. By putting one of the books under a pseudonym, it removes that conflict—at least in the public eye.

The needs of the public sometimes outweigh those of the

author. While you may have written in a wide variety of genres and sexualities, it is often useful to choose a different pseudonym for each type of writing just to help your readers find what they want. The reader of erotica wants, in general, more of the same thing from an author. This helps readers find material that will interest them, based on their past enjoyment of a particular author's work. Using only one name can create a vast and confusing array of material. Readers looking at stories and books under the name "Cecilia Tan," for example, will find heterosexual, lesbian, and gay erotica, as well as science fiction, fantasy, horror, mystery, etc. making it difficult to single out one genre or type of writing.

David Laurents also keeps his pseudonym because of his personal morality. He strongly believes that safer sex guidelines should be mentioned and followed in erotica; everything published under his own legal name therefore follows this moral position. However, some of his regular magazine editors disagree on the assumption that pornography is fantasy and their readers shouldn't be distracted by real world concerns. They claim that the mention of condoms and other safer sex awareness is a "downer" that ruins the reader's enjoyment of the fantasy. On those stories he uses a pseudonym.

Rachel Kramer Bussel is one writer who hadn't had a reason to use a pseudonym until recently. Sometimes an editor will want to publish two of your stories, but wants each one to go under a different byline. In these cases you could be asked to publish one under a different name. Rachel recently agreed to this, because the other option was to have one story cut from publication. You always have the option of using a pseudonym (or conversely go from using a pseudonym to using your legal name and publicly "claiming" your pseudonymous work) at a later date. During her early writings, Lisa Palac went by "Lisa Labia," but later switched to her own name.

Whether you use a pseudonym or not is a very personal decision, but at least it should be an informed decision. One drawback to a pseudonym, unless you are willing to own up to it being your pseudonym, is that you are not able to use any credits you publish with your pseudonym as your own; you are not able to "claim" those works. Yet, if you are open about using your pseudonym, you can list these credits on your resume, noting that they are "Written as ____." Vampire book author Nancy Kilpatrick wrote a series of erotic horror novels under the name "Amarantha Knight." She eventually realized that the readers of her vampire books were likely to enjoy these books too, but they had no way of knowing they were written by the same person. When the books were reprinted recently, the covers were changed to read "by Nancy Kilpatrick, writing as Amarantha Knight."

Some authors may wish to use a pseudonym for a period of time, for instance while their children are still living at home, and later in life may wish to claim those stories as their own. They are welcome to do so. Pseudonyms can be temporary or lifelong, but keep in mind that once you start using a pseudonym and build a reputation with it—such as with lesbian pulp author Ann Bannon—the name will take on a life of its own. You will likely want to continue publishing under the pseudonym even if you no longer feel the same qualms about using your name you once did. And if you do have qualms, by all means pick a pseudonym. Getting your work out there (if that is your goal) is better than not publishing due to fear.

How to Pick a Pseudonym

You should give careful thought to what name you choose, since this is a new identity you are adopting. Names have power; some names we find very glamorous, some we'll remember because they're so catchy. We definitely come to associate certain writer's names, pseudonymous or not, with their stories, sometimes remembering them years after we've read them, even if we may have forgotten the story's name. Sometimes what people remember is the byline that the story is published under, especially if they are inclined to seek out more of the writer's work based on their enjoyment of a single story.

Should your pseudonym be male, female, or androgynous? If you want one "all purpose" name, then something androgynous like "Chris Martin" might work for you, but this particular name is also bland and boring—and therefore not memorable. Some pseudonyms seem designed to make the writer seem almost anonymous, but if you are trying to "make a name for yourself" and build reader recognition, you might want to pick something that stands out more. The last name can add a touch of glamor if you are trying to stick with a gender-neutral first name. How about "Chris Versace" instead?

Using initials, instead of a name like "Chris" or "Pat," along the lines of "J. R. Gilbert," or even "M. Christian" (the actual pseudonym of a well-known erotica writer and editor) may read as male to many readers. For years, female science fiction writers would use their initials to appear masculine on book covers, where the male readership would assume the author was also male. (This is no longer *de riguer* for female writers since science fiction is not as male-dominated a field as it once was.) Initials used in an all-lesbian anthology would probably come across as feminine. But in mixed markets, initials still tend to read as male.

Writers of Victoriana often choose upper-crust British-sounding names, like "Virginia Huffington." Gay male writers often tend toward the hypermasculine, like "Jim Ford." If you plan to stick to only one sub-genre, this tactic may work, but if you think you may write in many categories, you might want something less aesthetically matched to one type of fiction.

Porn star Jenna Jameson chose her stage name for Jameson's whiskey, so you might choose a name that evokes a certain air by association with a product or brand. But be careful if you think your name might infringe on a trademark or copyright. A rap star using the name "Luke SkyyWalker" was forced to cease using the name because, despite the unique spelling, he was infringing on George Lucas's character name from *Star Wars*.

Some writers will choose their names based on an in-joke or pun, like "Palm Olive" or "Stu D. Muffin." Generally we'd only recommend those for one-shots and not for your best work. You don't want to be saddled with a joke name for years to come when it will no longer be funny.

Some writers will anagram the letters of their real name, or choose some part of their name to reverse, modify, or otherwise use in their pen name. Romance writer Nora Roberts chose the pseudonym "J.D. Robb" when she started a new book series that differed from her previous one. Anne Rice wrote the "Sleaping Beauty" series under the name "A. N. Roquelaure," and the more modern *Exit to Eden* under the name Anne Rampling.

For some writers, the name they choose helps them dip into their creative well, the way a character's name can help an actor take on a persona. Others have more practical concerns of privacy or business matters.

Correct Use of A Pseudonym

Even when writing under a pseudonym, you will need to provide your legal name and an Employee Identification Number (EIN) or (if you are a US resident) Social Security Number (SSN) to publishers in order to receive payment. (See Chapter Seven: The Business of Writing.) Although some writers set up bank accounts that can accept payments made out to pseudonyms, national security concerns have made that more difficult than it was in the past. As a legal entity you are still known by your real name, and it is this name that you should use to sign contracts. Both names should appear on your manuscripts to prevent confusion. Put your legal name and address in the upper left hand corner of the first page of the story and your pseudonym centered below the title, as indicated below:

```
Rachel Kramer Bussel
Prince St. Station
P.O. Box 39
New York, NY 10012
```

```
            "The Fabulous Palace"
               by Arriana Green
```

If you want to keep your pseudonymous life as separate from your personal life as possible, you can arrange to create an alternate address at which correspondence may be received.

You can rent a mailbox at your local post office or at any of the various privately-owned mail services if they are available in your town. You can have up to five names listed on a Post Office Box. The price of a P.O. Box will vary depending on location, availability and size. For instance, one writer we know rents her post office in downtown Manhattan for $60/year for a small size mailbox. A medium-sized box at The UPS Store in Boston, MA costs closer to $300 for the year. The Post Office will often ask for identification when you pick up packages; since you probably won't have identification for your alter ego/pseudonym, you can arrange with the post office for an alternative. Another advantage to a post office box for writers is that you can list it on your business cards or give it out as a contact and not reveal your personal residence.

Another way to create a separate identity for your pseudonym is to create an email address under that name for correspondence related to your erotic writing. If you are using a service provider such as AOL, you will need to provide your real name and credit card information to the online provider, but then you will be able to send and receive mail as your alter ego—which can be especially useful when trying to disguise your true gender. Many online providers such as AOL allow you to create multiple screen names, making it simple to add an account for your alter ego to an already existing account or one which you can use for other purposes. Free email providers, such as the commonly used hotmail.com, yahoo.com, and excite.com, also allow you to create anonymous email accounts and are very convenient for exchanging email and storing information.

One final note to bear in mind. While the risk of being revealed accidentally is very slight, you should know that nothing is foolproof. Publishers sometimes do make mistakes, and you must be prepared for the eventuality that your real name may be mistakenly mixed up with your pseudonym and published in a book or magazine. We know several writers who discovered, much to their chagrin, that their real names appeared somewhere (like on the back cover) even though their pseudonyms were otherwise used correctly throughout the rest of the book.

Chapter Four:
Forms of Erotica

When you think of "erotica," many different things may come to mind—the Marquis de Sade, Anais Nin, anonymous short stories, *Penthouse Letters*, literary collections, classics, smut, and more. All of these are forms of erotica, and this chapter will outline the primary types of erotic writing and what they mean.

Before delineating the categories, we'd like to note that you do not always have to know what form your writing will ultimately take when you begin. You might start out writing a quick, dirty porn letter that might wind up as a short story, or attempt a short story and wind up with only a brief vignette. This is perfectly acceptable. You can always keep these parts of stories or in-progress pieces and use them when inspiration strikes; you don't always have to have all the answers in your head right away. You can write the sex scene that happens last in the story first, and work backwards from there.

Sometimes you may write a story specifically in response to a call for submissions; these can often be useful in jogging your brain into action, providing a theme around which you can set your next story. But don't force a story about cowboys and sex, for example, if what you really want to write about is a teacher/student fantasy dependent on the milieu of British boarding schools. In general, you should concentrate on writting the best story you can, without regard to marketability. Then, when the manuscript is completed, edited, and polished, try to find a buyer for it.

Short Stories

Short stories are by far the dominant form in the erotic field. They are simple, easy to read, and leave the reader with enough information to get them aroused and thinking, but not so much that they can't read it in a single sitting. The wide market for short stories makes this an ideal one to focus on. If you note that certain characters or situations keep recurring, you may later want to create a novella or novel out of a short story. In addition, you can bring characters from an old story into a new one, thus keeping them alive in your work. Short stories are published in magazines, books (both multi-author anthologies and single-author collections), on websites, and sometimes as stand-alone chapbooks.

Short stories can vary in length, from 1,000 words or less (considered "short shorts") up to 10,000 words, with the average range being 3,000-5,000 words. Always read guidelines very closely, because many editors and publications will only consider stories that fall within a certain word count. Even if your story is brilliantly told, if the piece is too long or too short then it won't work for that publication. That said, you should ideally write the story you want to write, first; you can always edit it later to fit a certain publication's style or length requirements.

Novels

Erotic novels can fall under a number of categories. If you are writing for a specific publisher, they will often have detailed guidelines about plot, number of sex scenes, and other requirements. But an erotic novel doesn't just mean sex scenes or stories strung together; there needs to be an overarching plot tying the narrative together. Your best bet is to try to find a plausible, interesting, and compelling setting that will give your characters the opportunity to have a lot of sex. Stranding your character alone on a desert island wouldn't really work very well, but stranding him or her with a band of lonely explorers, or something similar, could work nicely. In addition to believable characters the reader wants to follow and get involved with, you need to make sure there's enough potential for sex to happen quite often in an erotic novel. Consider varying the types of sex that take place in a novel; it wouldn't be very interesting, for instance, to read about a female lead character who has sex with 20 men throughout the novel, but in exactly the same position each time (unless perhaps this were an integral—and interesting—part of the plot).

Letters

"Letters" are a genre of erotic writing popularized by magazines such as *Penthouse Letters* which feature anonymously written (though given a fictional byline and location) first person tales of erotic adventure. Each publication will have its own guidelines for this type of "story," and generally the sex should comprise the bulk of the story, especially if you only have around 800 words to tell your tale. The best way to get a feel for how they want their stories told is to read the publication. This is true in particular with letters magazines, where you need to read at least one issue (preferably two or three) to see what type of slant there is on the pieces they consistently publish. Letters magazines each have a unique "voice." Writer's guidelines can tell you a lot, but they do not say everything. These letters are different from short stories told in the epistolary form (i.e. "Dear Kim, I remember the last time we made love like it was yesterday..."). These are more like fictional recollections (though they are usually billed as nonfiction). Part of what makes letters work for the reader is that they seem so believable and immediate. They are usually written to sound convincing, like they could have really happened, and some magazines only take letters on certain themes, like "girl/boy next door," "first time," and the like. Letters are usually written in a down-to-earth, colloquial style ("aw shucks") and always in the first person ("here's what happened to me...").

Poetry

Poetry is distinct from prose (stories, essays, etc.) in that a single poem is an artistic representation that cannot be replaced by paraphrase. Unlike a story, a poem's individual words are the substance of the work, separate from their meaning. The placement of the words on the page, their meter, whether they rhyme, et cetera, are all part of the creation of a poem. Poetry, being the most literary of all the creative forms, is also the most difficult to sell. This is true whether your poetry is erotic or not. Erotic poetry, though, if written to high literary standards, can sometimes be published in erotic publications and sometimes in literary journals. What makes a poem erotic? Since poems do not always have narrative flow to create erotic tension the way stories can, a poem that has sex as its subject matter may or may not be "erotic." The erotic markets that do take poetry generally pay by the word, and generally pay very little, but that may be preferable to the literary journals who do not pay at all (and who may take a whole year to reject or respond).

Sometimes a publication or web site may ask specifically for naughty limericks, erotic haiku, or sonnets for a special issue, but in general non-rhyming free verse is the dominant form.

"Non-Fiction"

There is a Catch-22 in erotica. Sometimes we write fiction and sell it as if it is "true life" stories (as with letters), and sometimes we use our real experiences as material for "fiction" stories. Sometimes works billed as "erotic fiction" are culled from the author's own life. You will not necessarily know this when reading, and many erotic stories are written in the first person, drawing the reader in and making them think the story is autobiographical. Some authors who have owned up to a few of their supposedly fictional stories being autobiographical include Carol Queen, Michael Lassell, Rachel Kramer Bussel, and David Laurents. Many others have surely written stories that contained elements of nonfiction, but they have not told which these were, and it is not the author's obligation to reveal this.

But there are some markets which specifically seek out erotic stories about real-life events. Anthologies such as *Guilty Pleasures, My First Time, Some Women, Faster Pussycats*, etc., draw on the allure of "voyeurism—a glance at real sex," to get readers interested in these sexy stories that have really happened.

To write about something that really happened may be easy for some people; rather than crafting characters from a blank slate, you have your memories available. If you are submitting to a general anthology, you have the added bonus of being able to tweak your story, adding or subtracting relevant details to further the plot. If the call is specifically for nonfiction, you have less leeway. Nonfiction, although in one sense "true," is always going to be subjective; you may remember a certain night of passion in one way, while your lover may remember it differently.

Some publications may publish "real-life" stories that are about sex and sexuality but that are not erotica. Alternative weeklies, newspapers, and mainstream magazines may all be interested in sex how-to or first person essays about sex, but where the purpose of the piece of writing is to inform, rather than to arouse.

Erotica Plus

Though there may be a category called "erotica" on the bookstore shelves, this doesn't mean that all "erotica" must be about sex and sex only. Many authors of contemporary works of erotica blend it into other genres, such as erotic romance, erotic horror, and erotic mystery. They are creating works that are sexy and arousing while also working in another genre. The erotic horror genre has taken off and is its own thing, spawning anthology series such as *Hot Blood*. Many romance novels feature explicit sex scenes, and romance lines like Harlequin Blaze and the Secrets series specifically look for these kinds of tales. Of course Circlet Press' speciality is erotic science fiction. Literary fiction can also feature well-crafted sex scenes that can encompass "erotica;" authors such as Dorothy Allison and Marge Piercy have had their work published in the *Best American Erotica* series even though their work is generally labeled "fiction." The category of "erotica" can be a slippery one, and as you'll see in the market listings section, encompasses a very wide array of publications and genres, with much crossover potential. Sex obviously doesn't only appear in "sex books," and many readers of other types of fiction, especially genre fiction, enjoy sex scenes that conform to the genre's general standards. You probably aren't going to read a heavy S/M scene in the average romance novel, but the characters certainly may get down and dirty.

Chapter Five:
Writing About Things
You Haven't Done (Yet)

People often ask erotica writers if their erotic stories are based on personal experience. There is an assumption that anyone who writes erotic stories must have a hedonistic, deviant lifestyle. Often there is an element of envy involved in this question: the reader may think if reading about it was good, doing it must have been *great*. All of the questioner's history with pornography—all those orgasms realized as a result of erotica—are for the moment transferred onto the writer, the person responsible for the experience. Sometimes there is an element of sexual interest expressed with the question: do you do these things and can we do them?

The first person, diary-like nature of some porn also encourages the assumption that a pornographer must be a "trained professional" at sex in order to describe such things. This is the seduction of well-written erotica; it draws readers in, makes the stories believable and the authors seem incredibly sexually aware. And while most good erotica writers should be knowledgeable about various kinds of sexual activity, it certainly doesn't mean that they have each engaged in all of them—or even any of them.

For many readers, what they want is the vicarious thrill, the titillation, the erotic curiosity of a glimpse into a voracious sexual life. They equate the sex lives they see and read about in pornography with the producers of pornography. As a writer, you do not have to admit or deny any of your own behavior, but you will, most likely, be challenged to write about acts you yourself may not have performed.

We each draw on our own sexual histories to add verisimilitude to the descriptions of our stories, but after that, fiction takes its turn. We may modify a sex scene from our own lives into a wildly different scenario, or a feeling we had before, during, or after sex into an entirely new realm.

Rachel Kramer Bussel reports that even when she is writing about something that actually happened, because the story is "fiction," she is able to embellish, adding or subtracting details that will make the story more interesting or exciting, or including what she *wished* would have happened. Even when you are writing about an act that actually occurred, it is good to remember that there is no absolute singular truth. What it felt like for you may not have been what the other person experienced; thus, we are always inserting our own subjective feelings into our memories about sex, giving even nonfiction erotica our own personal spin.

But you certainly do not have to experience a given type of sex firsthand in order to write about it. If that were the case, much of the porn out there would never have been written. First of all, one does not need to be a man to write about gay sex, or a woman to write about lesbian sex. In the recent anthology, *Set in Stone: Butch-on-Butch Erotica*, a first of its kind collection of lesbian erotica, only two authors had more than one story in the book, and both were men: M. Christian and Thomas S. Roche. All four contributions were outstanding. If you're looking for an example of such a story, study theirs and others like these, which will show that you cannot always guess the gender of a writer from their writing. They are two of the more prolific men writing in the genre of lesbian fiction, but as Lawrence Schimel and Carol Queen's anthology

Switch Hitters: Lesbians Write Gay Male Erotica And Gay Men Write Lesbian Erotica demonstrated, many authors can successfully tackle erotic writing that is outside of their direct experience. Carol Queen has excelled at writing gay male erotic fiction, and so have many others. See Thea Hillman's story "Close to Coming" in the anthology *Quickies* for an example of a touching, tender, and hot story about gay male sexual longing.

Writing about things you've never done isn't only about crossing gender lines. There are a seemingly infinite number of sexual practices and fetishes out there, and it can be interesting and arousing to explore some of them, even if they are ones you don't particularly share.

For example, you're writing a story about "golden showers," perhaps because you think it might be sexy, you've heard that it is a popular fetish, or you just want to explore a character who is into piss play. Maybe you got a call for submissions from an editor who needs a story on the subject. You don't have to actually partake in golden showers to write about them, but you do have to consider what the participants get out of the act, why they do it, and why they enjoy or don't enjoy it: is it dominance and submission? Do they enjoy the taste, touch, smell, feel of piss? Is it a special sacred act between one set of lovers or would the character do it with anyone? What does it feel like as your pee hits your lover or goes in their mouth? (If you're looking for an extremely hot, well-written tale of piss play, check out "The Balm That Heals" by Tsaurah Litzky in *Best American Erotica* 1999. The story features an excellent buildup of erotic tension and a very special release, all summed up in the last sentence.)

Asking these kinds of questions about any sex act you want to explore will help you think more about what your characters are doing and what you want them to do. And as a fiction writer, you get to answer these questions yourself. You may find that you don't know all the answers right away, and that's okay. You can work through them as you work on your story, perhaps trying out different scenarios, talking to people and doing research to figure out whether the story works and whether the characters' actions are believable the way you've explored them.

There are also some parts of sex that, no matter the participants or their actions, are almost universal. Certainly, when you write about a caress during the afterglow the first time you've had sex with a new partner, it almost doesn't matter what piece of flesh is being touched or what the genders of the participants are, there's a certain universality of feeling underlying the moment that applies to all such situations. That's part of our own experience that we tap into when we're writing, translating it into the needs of the story. You may use this type of description in more than one story, but it will read completely differently in each case.

In many ways, it is easiest to tap into these common elements of sexuality when writing something radically different from your own sex life, because then it is easier to use only those aspects of the experience that actually contribute to the story at hand. You don't have the luxury (which in itself is a double-edged sword) of slipping back into your own sexual history. Instead, you are forced to fantasize and create characters and sex scenes that are outside your experience and then humanize them.

If you want to write about something you've never done, and want to know, physically, how it feels, talk to your close friends. If they are comfortable with answering such questions, ask them what it is like when they have an orgasm, what their favorite sexual experience has been, their worst, what it's like to go cruising, and so on. You can either incorporate their descriptions or emotions into your stories, or simply use your imagination, taking their comments as a starting place from which to work your own magic. Talking to friends or others about sex can also highlight aspects of sex that may not have occurred to you before and can help even when writing about the kinds of sex that you may have actually had. If you're on good terms with them, talking to past (or current) lovers can also give you insight into their perceptions of sex, and you might be surprised at their responses and reactions. You can then incorporate their suggestions and hopefully show them the finished product to make sure it reads with the ring of truth and that there aren't glaring errors in how the sex would normally take place.

Another extremely useful tool for learning about all kinds of sex is pornography in the form of sexually explicit videos. In porn videos you get to see the action up close and personal and can use the scenes in porn films to help you work out the logistics of certain sex acts. You can challenge yourself by watching a sex scene in a video, then writing out a story using the same act but with a different plot than what the video offered. The video provides clues as to what is happening on the outside. As a fiction writer, you provide what is happening on the inside.

You can also be inspired by other erotica writers, but be careful that you do not end up just trying to copy someone else. In addition to the possibility of plagiarism, you want to avoid having your own voice tainted with the influence of another writer, no matter how good they may be. Finding your own voice will ultimately serve you better in your career than trying to sound like Anais Nin or using the themes of Anne Rampling again and again.

Remember, too, you do not always need to go into explicit detail about every single miniscule motion. If you were writing a book in which a person rode on a train, you wouldn't necessarily spend two paragraphs describing how a train's engine works. Though a large part of erotic writing is the description of sexual acts, that is not the only thing going on in erotica. Sometimes subtlety can have more of an impact than explicitness. We've all seen examples of the latter, where every other sentence is filled with body parts doing things to other body parts, and without enough human emotion in between. If there is something you want to write about but are not sure of every detail, you can talk about the sex in others ways. However, when writing about something highly specific, such as certain BDSM practices or complicated sexual positions, it is wisest to research the actual practice, perhaps observe it in person if you aren't experiencing it yourself, in order to get the logistics of the situation correct.

Research materials in this case could certainly include the many sex how-to manuals published every year. Whether it is tantric sex or sadomasochism, there are plenty of books on the shelf to satisfy your curiosity and provide you with the details you need for a convincing story.

Simply describing your actual sex, no matter how satisfying it was for you, does not always result in satisfying erotic fiction. The intentions are different. It may have felt incredible, wonderful, and earth-shattering, but you will have to convey that somehow to the reader instead of just telling them how good it felt. Why did it feel good? What were you thinking? What made it different from other times you'd had sex?

Two characters (or people for that matter) may be engaging in the same physical act together, but for different reasons and with different sensations. If you are a straight woman, you do not know exactly what it is like for a straight man to have sex, even though you've done it with straight men. One exercise is to write a sex scene and describe it from all the various participants' points of view, in order to find out whether you truly have a feel for what your characters are doing and why.

Though you don't have to write about differently gendered characters or go outside your own experience, you benefit as an erotica writer by being able to describe sex that you yourself may not have had. It challenges your writing skills and can also lead you to new avenues, settings, and scenarios for your stories, while bringing a welcome diversity to your work. You can reach more markets and you also grow creatively. As exciting and hot as your writing may be, if every single story centered around, for instance, a man and a woman having doggie-style sex, you can get into a rut. Though there are certainly a multitude of ways to continuously write about similar acts and make them all thrilling, if you always hit the same note even the most exciting sex can become monotonous and repetitious.

If you don't end up using the scene with the sex act you've never tried, you may return to that particular act at a later date or use a portion of your description for something entirely different. There may be a minor character in one of your stories whose sex life is relevant to the plot and the scene fits with his or her personality. Exploring various kinds of sex acts can help you think about and delve into how various acts are alike in how they make us feel, physically and emotionally. That said, if you only talk to one person or watch one porn video, you will not find all the answers. Not every man experiences getting a blowjob in the same way; everyone has varying reactions to different kinds of touch and sensation. You can play and work with these human variations, contrasting, for instance, two characters' reactions to the same kind of sex. Exploring things you've never done in your writing can give you insight into various sexual practices as well as allowing you to expand your erotic writing repertoire.

Chapter Six:
The Basics of Submission

In order for your work to be published, you must send it out. To give your story the best chance at being considered, you want it to look its best, and you want to send it where it will be most welcomed.

Many aspiring writers, caught up in the heady rush of having written a story, make the mistake of sending their work out before the piece is actually ready. It is often helpful to put a story aside for a week and then reread it with a fresh eye to see if it needs rewrites or corrections. If you have a trusted writing friend or writer's group, or even a nonwriting friend or roommate who would be willing to read your work over for content and style, this can be invaluable in catching mistakes or typos, and also in making sure that the story comes across the way you intend it to.

Some writers have the opposite problem, wanting to do "just one more draft" before they're ready to let anyone else see it. If you think like this, you may never finish anything. If you want to publish, instead of merely write, there comes a time when you must send the story out and let others read it.

Once you reach the point where you are sending your work out, there are various steps you must take to insure that you represent yourself professionally and are treated professionaly in turn.

Manuscript Preparation

Many would-be writers spend far too much time worrying about how their manuscript should look, instead of putting their efforts into improving the quality of their stories or researching prospective markets. Although we will go into proper manuscript format in a moment, let us stress that market research is in many ways a bigger contribution to a story's successful placement than you might think. *Make sure you are sending to markets that are not wildly inappropriate.* You will save yourself time and money by properly researching your markets—which is the whole point of this book.

Circlet Press is a specialty publisher—our niche is erotic science fiction. Yet we regularly receive manuscripts of how-to books, children's books, do-it-yourself legal advice, conspiracy theories, and much more. Sometimes the author has gone to considerable expense to copy the manuscript, ship it express mail, and include return postage. We don't even read these submissions, which aren't appropriate for us. No doubt there are gardening publishers out there getting erotic science fiction, and children's magazines getting home-improvement articles and, like us, they dump it directly into the trash.

It is just as bad to send erotica of one kind to publishers of another kind. Gay male stories should go to gay male publications, fetish stories to fetish publications, and so on. If you truly have a story that doesn't fit any recognizable category, you should not send it to *Penthouse Letters*. Find a publication with more open-ended needs—many are in the market listing section in the back of this book.

Now, assuming you have chosen an appropriate place to send your story, you must conform to standard manuscript formatting.

The rules for manuscript preparation are quite simple, and once you go through the process a few times, it will become second nature. While presentation is extremely important, you shouldn't spend more time worrying about your margins than about the content of your writing. By following these rules, you will ensure that your writing reaches an editor's desk in the most professional manner possible.

Following these rules is not a secret formula or guarantee that you will get published. Stories are not bought because they are presented well, but they are often discounted when presented poorly. It may be a cliché, but editors are genuinely overworked; they do not have the time or patience to bother with difficult or complicated submissions. And, because they spend all day reading, they do not need the extra eye-strain of trying to decipher submissions that are handwritten, typed on colored paper that is hard to read, done without a clean type-writer ribbon, or that did not have enough toner in the print-er, and so forth.

You do not want to do anything that will encourage an edi-tor to reject your story without reading it, or to make yourself stand out as unprofessional. Why? Because there are plenty of other manuscripts that are presented in standard fashion, waiting to be read. Editors drowning in a sea of submissions will not waste any extra minutes trying to read your poorly formatted submission or figure out information that should be readily available to them.

Your work must be submitted in as clean and readable a for-mat as possible. The presentation of your work should be unmemorable, so that the editor can focus on its content.

When submitting hardcopy, prose should be typed, double spaced, on only one side of an 8 1/2 X 11 page. Use standard white paper—colored paper will only mark you as an amateur in the eyes of an editor, and is distracting and harder to read.

You should leave wide margins of at least an inch on all four sides. This gives the editor room to make corrections, write notes to you or to the typesetter, and so on, if he or she is interested in publishing your story.

You should use a standard font, such as Courier, Times, or Palatino, in 12 point size. Script fonts and other ornate type-faces are difficult to read and will not endear you to any editors.

Using Computers

At this point, very few professional writers are using type-writers instead of computers, and many editors insist on receiving electronic copy of stories if they are bought, even if they accept hardcopy submissions. Some pay a lower rate for stories that are not available on disk or via email, so if you want to earn top dollar, a computer with email access is an absolute must. Some writers are holding out, sticking to their old typewriters, but they are finding it harder and harder to compete with the writers who have instant communication with editors. And more and more of the markets are online markets.

A computer is much more than a fancy replacement for a typewriter; you can easily save and store your work, make revisions, send stories via email, keep track of your work and submissions, do research on the Internet, and communicate with editors and fellow writers. Writing and storing your work on a computer will ultimately make revisions and future submissions easier for both you and your editor. You never know when you may need to call up a story you wrote last month, last year, or even long before that. You can compose stories or scenes and leave them in a folder marked "Possibilities" or "Starts" or something similar, and come back to them later when you're in need of a few paragraphs or to jog your brain for ideas. Having them handy on a computer or disk will save you the hassle of trying to locate hardcopy of your work at a later date.

A few years ago, when David Laurents was editing a series of erotic anthologies, he found himself reluctant to purchase work from an author whose submission he liked and whose career he wanted to support, because she used a typewriter. As he was required to deliver the anthologies on disk, buying from this author would have meant that he would be forced to type the manuscript himself or pay to have it typed. Neither possibility seemed worth the effort, especially since there were other comparable stories available from computer-literate writers.

Exactly what kind of computer you use makes little difference, unless you are using archaic software. These days, most word processors are able to translate files from other programs, or output your file in pure text in the format of another program. So whether you choose Macintosh or Windows-based PC, or use a high-powered Unix or Linux-based text editor, you should still be able to submit.

Unless a market specifically solicits submissions via email, you should send a hard copy printout of your work via regular mail ("snail mail"). It is usually a waste of time to enclose a disk with the text of the story, unless the guidelines for this market specifically request that you do so. Disks are often not compatible from machine to machine and email is a much more reliable way to transfer the story.

You should carefully note the guidelines of the places you are submitting to, especially whether they ask for snail mail or email submissions, and conform to any specific formatting requirements given by the editors. Many editors resent being sent unsolicited work via email, for numerous reasons. Some do not read submissions at the computer, so submissions sent via email must be printed before being read, adding both cost and hassle to the process. Some, fearing computer viruses, delete all attachments unopened. Others are the complete opposite, and only want submissions in email, reducing their office clutter. Many email addresses listed in guidelines are the personal accounts of the editor, or accounts used primarily for correspondence, and submissions may get lost or accidentally deleted if the editor is not expecting them. Even when they *are* expecting them, be sure to follow exactly the procedure regarding labeling your story in the subject line of your email; often editors will only read submissions marked specifically for a certain project, and others may get deleted. And, of course, the rules can change. The only way to know these facts is to carefully read the guidelines, and if you are unsure or have a question, ask! Most editors would rather answer a question beforehand than deal with an improperly formatted submission later.

Again, remember to follow the specifications of the guidelines exactly! Some editors request two hard copies, or a specific format, or certain information in the cover letter, and it behooves you to follow their directions lest you find yourself out of the running before the editor even gets a chance to look at your story. Also, make sure to send your story, a cover letter, a self-addressed stamped enveloped (SASE), whatever postage is requested, and that's all. Do not send photos, personal letters, gifts, bribes, or anything else. This is extremely unprofessional and will mark you as an amateur.

Manuscript Layout

In the left hand corner you should type your real name as it would appear on the check you may receive if your work is bought. Below that type your address.

Some books of writing suggest putting your SSN; we recommend against that as it will increase your exposure to identity theft. You will need to provide your EIN or SSN if your work is accepted, but you can send it along when the contracts are signed.

In the right hand corner (or beneath your address) you should type an estimated word count for your story; the quickest way to determine this is to choose Word Count from the Tools menu, if using Microsoft Word, or a similar tool in another program. You can round this number to the nearest hundred. Because there are so many variables of font and line spacing that affect how many pages your story is this number will be a better indicator for the editor as to how long the story is. The editor will use this number to determine if the work fits within the space he or she is trying to fill.

One double-spaced page of text typed in Courier 12 point averages 250 words. Use this rule of thumb if from some reason it is difficult for you to get an exact word count from your software.

The pages of your submission should be numbered sequentially, though it is not necessary to number the first page. It is also helpful to include a header or footer that has your name or the title of your story on each page, in case they accidentally become separated from the rest of the manuscript. Do not staple or otherwise bind your submission, and don't bother to attach a paper clip.

Please note that on some occasions, editors will ask that your name not appear on the actual manuscript, but only on the cover letter. This is sometimes done for contest entries where they do not want the judges to be prejudiced for or against a name they recognize. Be sure to follow these instructions as they are requested for a reason.

The Cover Letter

With your submission, you should include a cover letter addressed to the editor. Leaving one out can come off as arrogant and at the very least may seem unbusinesslike.

The cover letter should be brief; some editors don't even bother to read them until after they have read the work itself and decided they are interested. But no letter at all can leave a weird impression, so even though the letter is short, it still needs to be included.

What should go in the cover letter? As little as possible.

Until you have a relationship with an editor, the cover letter is not the place for chatty banter. Nor is it the place to enthuse over how much you're sure the editor is going to like the story. Likewise, you should not talk about how the story brought your lover to multiple orgasms, even if it did. Keep things simple and professional.

Many writers have the urge to synopsize their short story in the letter. Resist this urge. When submitting a novel, a synopsis is a must, but for a short story, a recap of the story's premise is more likely to prejudice the editor against the story than it is to pique interest. The content of the story should only be mentioned in context if it is relevant, i.e. "Since your guidelines asked for more stories from the female point of view, here is my story about a female tour guide in the Himalayas."

Cover letters should not be used to threaten the editor if he or she does not buy your work. Nor should cover letters be used to offer bribes to editors—although it depends on what you're offering, what you're asking for, and how strong the scruples of the editor in question are. (This is a joke. We do not know of any editor who has accepted a bribe offered in a cover letter to publish someone's manuscript. Many editors, however, have ridiculed the submissions of people who offer them bribes, both in public discussion, panels at writers conferences, and in private conversations with their writers and other editors.)

If you have previous publication credentials, this is the place to put them. If your publication credits are in a vastly different field—technical writing, for instance—or under a different byline, you may think they are irrelevant to your current submission. They are, but at the same time, the fact that other editors have considered your work publishable may stand in your favor. Previous credits, depending on what they are, can indicate that you are familiar with the process of publishing, that you are able to work with an editor on revisions, that you can meet regular deadlines, and so on. If the editor decides to accept your work, he or she can be fairly sure that your expectations are in keeping with the usual publishing standards.

Some editors will request a short (3-4 lines) biography in the cover letter for inclusion in the publication if your submission is accepted; you can include your publication credits in the bio as an alternate option to simply listing them.

If the manuscript is disposable, you can state this in your cover letter, but it is better to say so directly on the first page of the manuscript.

Cover letters should be used to state the obvious. "Dear Editor—enclosed please find my tale, 'Hot Story,' which I hope you'll find suitable for publication in SEXY MAGAZINE. Sincerely, Hopeful Author." Simple and redundant as that seems, this is enough.

Why should an author bother with a cover letter?

The cover letter is often used as a tracking device for the publishing house. They may keep it on file to show that they did receive your submission and may mark on it what was done with the manuscript (accepted, rejected, etc.). Make sure you include your full contact information (name, address, phone number, fax number if applicable, email address) on the cover letter so the editor can easily access this information.

The managing editor for one erotic book publisher once told David Laurents that the cover letter was nothing more than an extra barrier between her early morning cup of coffee and your story. Think of cover letters that way and spend your time on more useful things, like writing your next story. Do not write urgent pleas or important information about your manuscript in your cover letter; the editor may have an assistant opening their mail and may never even see your actual cover letter or may simply flip through it to get to the manuscript.

Mailing Your Work

When you are submitting to a place that accepts hardcopy, or even prefers it, always use regular First Class Mail if you and the market are within the Untied States. Regular airmail is best for overseas. Unless there is a very tight deadline, do not send Fedex, DHL, UPS, or other specialty carriers.

Do not use certified or registered mail because editors don't have time to stand in line at the post office to sign for them and will usually view this as an added encumbrance when reading your story. Many editors, after having stood in line, mark the envelopes "Return to Sender" and hand them right back over the counter, unopened and unseen.

If you crave verification that your manuscript arrived, you have two choices. One is to enclose a stamped self-addressed postcard. Write on it whatever tracking information you want, which should always include the title of your submission and the name of the place you sent it to. You may leave blanks to be filled in by whoever opens the mail—some writers we know ask for the date to be written in "Manuscript received on ____." However, the less whoever opening the mail has to write, the likelier they are to drop it directly into the mail back to you, confirming that your submission has indeed arrived.

This postcard is NOT meant to tell you whether they liked the story or not and are considering it; you must wait a while to receive notice of that (see below). But some editors may not even open your envelope until they are ready to read your actual story, so the "postcard method" is not foolproof.

Another choice you have these days is to send your manuscript via Priority Mail with Delivery Confirmation. This is a service of the United States Postal Service, and is a form of glorified first class. A manuscript that might cost around $1.50 to mail via regular first class would be closer to $4.00 Priority, but you can add a "Delivery Confirmation" option that gives you a tracking number for your package. You can then track the package by calling a special phone number or looking it up on the World Wide Web. "Delivery Confirmation," unlike certified or registered mail, requires no signature and no standing in line.

Use a SASE (self-addressed stamped envelope) so the editor can respond to your submission. Editors may ask that you add enough postage for the return of the full manuscript; they request this so that if they have corrections or would like you to resubmit your work, they can mark their notes on your manuscript and return it in the envelope provided, at no cost to them. If this is requested and you do not provide sufficient postage, you are likely ruining the chances that the editor will read or accept your submission. Always enclose some sort of SASE, unless the editor has noted that they will be responding by email or phone. For most, a regular letter-size SASE is sufficient.

If you are mailing to an editor in Canada or overseas, regular US postage will not work for the SASE. You can buy a Postal Reply Coupon at your post office instead.

What You Do Not Need

You do not need an agent. Most short story sales are made directly between authors and editors.

You do not need to register the copyright on your story.

Your work is automatically copyrighted from the moment you write it. Registering the copyright is generally useful only if there has been an infringement. Moira Allen of Writing-world.com notes in an article there that if you are worried about protecting your material, you can add "Copyright © 2006 by (your name)" to your submission, but there is no actual need to do so as your work is copyrighted whether you add that statement or not. Many editors look upon the copyright notice as a sign that the author is a novice. When submitting to credible editors, there is little chance that they will infringe on your copyright, and if a publisher buys a story, it will bear the copyright date of its publication, not the date you wrote it.

It is extremely rare for your unpublished submission to be stolen by someone else and passed off as their own work.

After Sending Your Manuscript

After submitting your work, you should not contact that editor again until a reasonable time has passed (six months). It is best to be patient and move onto other works and wait to hear from the editor at their convenience.

You may hear back from an editor anywhere from a month to two years later about your submission, although usually you will hear in several months. For anthologies, deadlines often get extended and the reading of submissions can take longer than expected. If an editor has listed a date by which he or she will be responding to submissions, and that date has passed (even if it is sooner than six months), feel free to politely inquire, via email or snail mail, as to the status of your sub-mission. But do not inquire more than once, once you've found out that your submission has been received. Editors at small publishing houses are often overwhelmed with multiple book projects and cannot respond to every curious author. You will in all likelihood hear back in due time.

Waiting for reply is one of the hardest parts of the submis-sion process. But as you start sending out more and more sub-missions, you will be too busy to worry after you've sent in each one.

Create a spreadsheet, use another database, or even just keep a paper log book to keep track of your submissions. For each submission be sure to note:
- Date of your submission
- Title of your story
- Name of the market and the editor's name

- Type of submission (story, poem, etc.)
- Expected deadline or date of publication, if known

And make room to fill in the following when additional information comes:
- The editor's response (yes, no, still thinking...)
- If yes, how much they are offering
- Date contract received
- When payment is expected
- Date payment received

You would think that keeping track of contracts and payments would be the editor's job, not yours, but it is all too common in the publishing business for the writer to have to issue reminders and invoices in order to get paid. Publishers are typically not mailicious in being slow to pay, but writers must be firm, and sometimes bold, in order to insure the money they are owed is paid out in a timely fashion. If you do not have this information well-documented, you may later find yourself in the position of not being paid for work you did. (More on this topic in Chapter Seven: The Business of Writing.)

Some editors may only notify those writers whose work has been accepted for publication, so please keep this in mind. If you have not heard back from an editor within a reasonable amount of time (9 months to a year), even after following up with them, you can assume they will not be using your work and feel free to submit it elsewhere. Waiting as long as possible and being patient can pay off; the editor may in fact want to use your piece over a year later, and if you've sold it elsewhere, that not only may kill your chances of having that piece accepted, but may jinx your future relationship with that editor.

Always keep careful track of your submissions so you know

how much time has gone by between your submission and the editor's response—or lack of one. When corresponding with editors, be polite. For all you know they may not have received your submission; they may have overlooked it or missed it through innocent error. Editors are not usually malicious by nature. They work with writers because they care to. The worst that can happen is that your story is rejected and you can then send it out elsewhere, which in the long run may work out quite well for you. (See Chapter Ten: Coping With Rejection)

Chapter Seven:
The Business of Writing

If you are going to make writing a part of your income, you will need to think of your art in business terms. For some writers this is difficult, but keeping your business interests in mind can help your career to grow and succeed on both artistic and financial levels. Much of the information in this chapter will apply to any freelance writer, whether or not they are working in the erotic field. The specific details may or may not apply to the writing you do. You may be able to deduct the cost of that lap dance if that is part of your research, but the overall rules apply to any kind of working writer.

Get Organized/Get Paid

One of the most important aspects of being a businessperson as well as a writer is keeping accurate records of the money you are owed. A mentioned in Chapter Six, keep a chart of your submissions. Mark each entry on the chart with the date you sent it out, and the reply. For each story accepted by an editor, mark the expected payment and the expected date of payment. Keep track of whether you signed a contract or agreement, when you mailed it back, and always keep a copy of it for yourself.

Some writers do this using a notebook as a log, others use a software spreadsheet. The most important thing is that you use a system that works for you. If spreadsheet software is hard to figure out and you struggle with it, you probably won't keep up with the log and might miss some important data. Perhaps a word processing document that you update each time you have a change would do just as well or better for you. (If you do keep your log on a computer, make sure you are making backups of your files! Computer hard drives are like tires on a car—for most of them it's not a matter of if they will go flat, but when.)

Remember, the most important things to log are:

- Date a story was submitted and where to
- Date a story was accepted and the terms
- Whether a contract was received and returned
- Whether payment was received

When you do receive payment, mark how much you received and the date. There are two reasons to keep this information up to date. One, you will need this information to file your taxes each year. Most publishers do not send out a 1099 form (the freelancer's equivalent of the W-2) to every author, so it is up to you to keep track of your income for reporting purposes. (More later on taxes for writers.) Two, you will need to follow up with publishers if they do not pay you in a timely fashion.

It may seem odd if you are accustomed to receiving a regular paycheck, but as a freelancer you will sometimes need to remind your editors to pay you. In fact, the majority of writers report that they must nag for payment on a regular basis. If a long time goes by without payment, always ask when the editor expects to pay you. If too much time goes by (three to six months after your payment was due), you may want to demand immediate payment. If you are worried that the publisher may be trying to weasel out of paying you, or if you do not want to make the confrontation yourself, you might consider joining the National Writers Union. A union grievance officer would be happy to make the collections call. There are other writer advocacy organizations, as well, such as the American Society of Journalists and Authors (ASJA), the Author's Guild, and the PEN American Center. Generally speaking, late payment is not intentionally malicious, but the author who spoke up may be the one who gets paid before the author who remained complacent. Some markets may have such bad bookkeeping that they are not even aware of the fact that you have not been paid until you remind them. Writers lose hundreds of thousands of dollars a year in money they are owed simply because they do not follow up.

In short, get organized to get paid. Only you have the ability to look out for yourself in this manner.

Incorporation

Some writers choose to incorporate as a business. Whether you do this will largely depend on whether you are pursuing writing full-time or as a side business and how much money you are making. Most writers do not need to incorporate, but it is an option that confers certain protections, but also incurs certain costs. If you are interested in incorporating, we suggest you speak to a professional certified public accountant (CPA) about the tax implications, liabilities, and advantages.

An alternative to incorporating is creating a DBA (Doing Business As), although your town may call it something different. This requires registering with your town, usually for a small fee, that you are a business. You could even register using your pseudonym. You then apply to the IRS for an Employee Identification Number (EIN)—you can apply online at http://www.irs.gov. Look to the IRS website, various books on small businesses, and CPAs to help you understand the requirements.

Agents

Many working professional writers will retain the services of a literary agent if they are writing books. Agents work on your behalf, selling your work and then taking a commission (usually 15%) on your earnings. They search out the publishers, pitch the projects, negotiate the contract terms, and collect the payment for you. Because the amount of money to be made from short story sales is so small, most agents will only do this for book projects such as novels, anthologies, or collections, but there are some exceptions.

Until you hit the relatively big time, you probably won't need an agent, but they can be useful. As you'll see in the market listings section, many major publishing houses will only review book manusripts that have been submitted to them by a literary agent. This is a pre-screening process for them, ensuring that they will not have to read a huge slush pile of barely intelligible manuscripts. An agent can not only negotiate on your behalf, but can also tell you whether your proposed work seems marketable. They can advise you which publishing houses would be advantageous for your career, and an agent who fits your work well will already have professional relationships with editors who are interested in the type of work you do.

We will warn any prospective writer, though, to beware of the "wannabe" agent. Any person with an entrepreneurial spirit can hang out a shingle (or put up a web site) saying "I'm an agent." Sometimes these are well-meaning individuals who think they are going to help their writer-friends get published by doing the leg-work for them—but in reality they are no better off than the authors themselves at getting the attention of a publisher and no more knowledgeable about contract negotiations! These agents may even pump up the ego of the writers, telling them how many houses they have submitted the work to and how publishable it is, while the publishing houses are tossing the manuscript into the same slush pile they would have if the authors had sent it themselves. At worst, these types of agents are sometimes scam artists preying on the weaknesses of hopeful writers, charging them reading fees and other fees to make their money while never actually selling any of the authors' works.

How can you avoid a scam agent? First, make sure your agent is either a member of the Association of Author's Representatives (A.A.R.), or subscribes to the A.A.R. canon of ethics, whose rules include charging no more than a 15% commission, no reading fees, and that authors be paid within 30 days of receipt of their monies from a publisher. The A.A.R. also requires its members to make their living exclusively from selling books, so you will not find people in other lines of work who think agenting is a good "side job" in the A.A.R. This is important because you and your agent are, to some extent, financially dependent on each other. You depend on the agent to protect your interest as if they were his or her own.

Finding an agent may seem even harder than finding a publisher, but it is often a worthwhile step if you are writing novels or creating other book-length work. Network through writers organizations, at writers' conferences, and look for agency listings in *Writer's Market* and *The Literary Marketplace*, both available in most public libraries. One helpful resource for much more information on the subject of agents is *The Insider's Guide to Getting An Agent*, by Lori Perkins, published by Writer's Digest Books.

Self-Publishing

Many authors are turning away from traditional publishing routes in favor of the independence and control of self-publishing. It used to be that self-publishing was almost solely in the domain of "vanity publishing," meaning paying a printing press to publish a certain number of your books so that you were a "published author." The drawback to being your own editor and publisher, though, is that you lack another knowledgeable person perusing and refining the manuscript as a professional editor would do.

Nowadays, the self-publishing scene has changed a good deal. "Vanity" publishing has been taken over by "print-on-demand" and e-book publishers who do largely the same thing. But self-publishing is seen as a way to get work out there that may have otherwise fallen through the cracks of the marketplace. Author M.J. Rose made a huge splash when she self-published her erotic novel *Lip Service*, building word-of-mouth awareness and sales via Amazon.com, before the book was picked up for publication by Pocket Books. Even Susie Bright, editor of the *Best American Erotica* series and a well-known writer, chose to go with Booklocker.com, an e-publisher, for the first version of her book *How To Write a Dirty Story* (then called *How to Read/Write a Dirty Story*). The book was such a success that Fireside, a division of Simon & Schuster, later published the book with some slight revisions.

The Internet can also be a boon to self-publishing, allowing authors to create their own websites or webzines to promote and publicize their work, direct fans to where their pieces can be found, as well as allow people to read their writing for free, thus building up an audience. Be aware, though, that self-publishing is a lot of work. You will have less time to focus on the art and craft of your writing because you are dealing with the minutiae of having your own publishing company. You will have to deal with printers, distributors, and other businesses in the process of publishing your own work, and this can be time-consuming and frustrating. On the other hand, you will have the freedom to publish and edit your own work, have complete control over content and artwork, and will be taking a truly hands-on approach to your writing career. Some writers thrive on this kind of involvement, while for others who simply want to write and do nothing else, it is an added burden.

Tax Deductions for Erotic Writers

Which kinds of tax deductions you will be able to take will depend on various factors, and you must investigate which of the myriad deductions will apply to you. Find an accountant who has other clients who are writers. An experienced accountant can advise you specifically on deductions you can apply. Writers, musicians, and other "artistic pursuits" have similar types of deductions available to them.

If you are a full-time writer making your living off of your writing, you will be entitled to more deductions than if you write part-time. If your writing is only a side hobby, you can only deduct as much as you make in income. But if you've shown a net profit for at least three out of the last five years, you will generally be thought of as running a business rather than a hobby.

You can deduct all writing-related expenses like office supplies: pens, paper, printer cartidges, computer parts, disks, envelopes, etc. You can deduct the cost of communicating for business, which includes your Internet Service Provider fees, email and web connection fees, cell phone and long-distance phone charges, stamps and postage. As a writing professional, you can also deduct the cost of any book, magazine, or newspaper you buy, and any periodical subscriptions including online subscriptions. If there are specific items you have used as research for your work, such as porn video rentals or sex toy purchases, these can also be included, but they must be actually used in the furtherance of your writing career. Just because you are an erotica writer does not mean you can write off every trip to the strip joint (or every tip you gave a stripper), but a specific excursion there for an article might be allowable.

You may also be able to take a home office deduction,

which would include a percentage of your rent or mortgage payments, utilities, and home repairs. A tax accountant can advise you on the percentage.

And how about your car? Did you drive to that writers' conference in Quebec? You can deduct that mileage, the cost of gas, and so on. You can deduct car/tansportation expenses for trips to the library for research, to bookstores to do readings, to meetings with editor or other writing-related events. Keep track of your mileage, parking costs, and/or the fares you paid.

Other travel for writing can also be deducted. Did you attend conferences or classes? The registration fees can be deducted, along with a portion of your plane fare, hotel room, and meals. Check with your accountant as to what portion of your meal expenses to deduct. You might use your actual receipts or you might use the IRS guidelines of per diem food allowance. You and your accountant should try to make sure that your deductions are reasonable in nature so as not to raise red flags with the IRS. As of now, a log of your expenses is considered as good by the IRS as actual receipts, but the tax laws can change at any time.

One trick some writers employ is to have a credit card they only use for deductible expenses. That way they do not need to keep receipts and their bills serve as a complete log of deductions.

As mentioned before, an essential thing that all writers must do is keep track of all of your payments. We recommend keeping copies of all contracts and payments (you can photocopy any checks you receive) and keeping these in a secure location. Record keeping is vital to taxes and to tracking stories. It's something you should get used to from the start. Beyond the specific issue of taxes, keeping a chart or other list will be useful in making sure that you do get paid in a timely manner, and will allow you to easily follow up with an editor or accounts payable department if you do not.

In order to prove that you have been working, keep a notebook or diary and jot down what you worked on each day. Even if you did not complete a story or send in work, if you did research, wrote, edited, took a course, interviewed an expert/author/editor, attended a lecture, etc., note it as part of your writing business. You know which parts of your day-to-day activities are actually relevant and a part of your writing. If you need your computer in order to write and it breaks down, getting it repaired would be considered part of your daily business operations. Whatever you note must be something that is necessary for you to conduct your business. This does not mean that just because you listen to music while you're working (unless you are reviewing the CDs) you can deduct the price of the CDs from your taxes.

An excellent resource is CCH's *Tax Guide for Journalists*, usually available for free by emailing mediahelp@cch.com or calling 847-267-2038.

Chapter Eight:
Rights and Contracts

One concept many beginning writers do not grasp is that when you sell a piece of writing, you are not selling the piece, you are selling the *right to publish* the piece. Or the *rights*, if you are giving the right to publish it in English and in translation, for example. Any story, poem, novel, etc. has many potential publishing rights associated with it, and publishers are more interested in some rights than others.

As a general principle, you want to make the most money possible from each story, poem, or piece you write. That means you will want to sell it again and again. You can sell it in English, sell audio rights, sell it for Spanish translation, sell it for movie adaptation, and so on. You may have only received a hundred dollars for it when you initially sold it, but if you kept the rights to sell it again, a single story could earn ten times that much over the course of your life.

The more copyright you retain on your work, the better off you are; you then have that much more control over your work and can sell and re-sell the rights to other publishers. Even though you may never think that your story could wind up published in another language in another country, and that signing away your foreign rights may be of no concern, you never know what can happen. An editor could stumble across your story in a magazine and want to reprint it in an Asian or

European or Asian anthology; it may perfectly fit with their theme. Wouldn't you rather be the one to control the permission (and income) from such sales rather then allowing the original publisher to reap the benefit? The point is not whether you personally plan to pursue sale of other rights, but rather that as the creator of the work, you should be the one to retain these rights for future potential, not a publisher who only publishes in one language, or in one area of the world, or in one medium.

At first, you may be so overjoyed that a publisher wants to use your work that you are willing to give them the moon and the stars in addition to your story, but don't give in simply because they hold the power of the paycheck. Some writers who write in multiple genres are also more willing to sell off all rights to their erotic writing because they feel their erotica is somehow less worthy, and therefore worth "less" than their writing in other genres. Don't make that assumption! Even if, in your estimation your sex-related writing is artistically inferior to your other work, don't underestimate its earning power.

If you have an agent, his or her job is to help you negotiate better contracts and deal with publishers on your behalf, but many agents do not handle short stories, poems, or short nonfiction pieces. And if you are just starting out in the erotic writing field, you probably don't have an agent yet. It is up to you to go over your contracts and make sure the terms are acceptable to you. If there is something that you don't understand or are unsure about, find out what it means before signing. Once you sign a contract with a publisher, you cannot go back and change it.

All Rights

Once you sell "all rights," you no longer have control over your material. The publisher may, if they decide to, publish only part of your work, publish it in various pieces, never publish it, published it under a pseudonym, publish it multiple times without paying you again. If you sell all rights, you no longer control any of the work and may not be entitled to any further payments, even though the publisher can sell your work again and again.

Selling all rights means that you cease to have any decision-making power when it comes to your story; you are selling them the story and the right to publish it (or not) in whatever form they see fit, usually for a single fee. (Some contracts will demand all rights, but provide for additional payments if the rights are exploited further by the publisher, but this is rare. The publishers who are trying to grab "all rights" are usually also trying to get you to do it for a single payment. And even those who promise additional payments may never make the additional payments. If they sell Korean translation rights, are you likely to find out? Remember how you had to harangue them for the money you knew about? How will you collect on sales you don't even know about?)

As an example of "all rights," if you sell a magazine all rights to a story, and later a book publisher wants to include it in a collection of your stories, you will not have the automatic right to use the story in the collection. You or the publisher will have to get that magazine's permission and also pay the magazine for the right to use it, if you do!

Many "standard contracts" demand all rights. But the boilerplate contract is just a starting place for negotiation. If an editor tries to tell you "oh, that's our standard contract; everybody signs it," respond with what your concerns are regarding the terms. Sometimes publishers will reduce what rights they demand if prompted. Other times they might offer a higher fee than the original deal in order to appease you. If you still feel they are asking for too much and paying too little, you have the right to walk away from the deal and look for another publisher.. *Penthouse Variations* pays $350-$400 for an erotic story, but they buy all rights. You will have to consider whether the work in question is one you may later want to resell or retain copyright to, or whether the financial compensation is sufficient to grant the publisher all rights. One writer we know was dismayed that the contract sent her by Simon & Schuster for inclusion in the *Best American Erotica* anthology, which offered her a single payment while S&S retained the right to sell the story again in translation, for ebooks, audio, and so forth without ever compensating her further. When she complained about this to the editor, S&S upped their offer by a couple hundred dollars and the author signed the deal.

There's no single answer that works for everyone; rights are something that need to be looked at and negotiated each and every time you make a sale, because your actions now will affect the future of your writing career and your stories. It would be painful if you sold all the rights to a story only to have an editor decide later that it was brilliant and ask to include it in an upcoming anthology, but because you were unable to grant access to it, had to leave you out of the book.

Works for Hire

Work for Hire is the extreme case of "all rights," in which the author has no right to the writing in the first place. This may happen because you are ghostwriting a novel or story, or for various other reasons, but in essence it means that you do not own the copyright. You may not even get the right to have your name on the work. In work for hire situations the writer is usually get paid a lump sum with no future royalties, and the writer cannot use the piece of writing again in the future. The publisher can decide how they want to use the piece and once you've sold them a work for hire, you no longer have any say in how the piece is used. You might also have to sign a non-disclosure agreement (NDA), which limits whether you can even tell anyone you wrote it.

One Time Rights

At the other end of the spectrum from all rights we have one time rights. One time rights means exactly that; the right to publish your work one time and one time only. After that, you are free to do with your story as you wish, since you retain all other rights. You can sell the story again, reprint it, sell the translation, the audio tape rights, the web or electronic rights, etc. since the publisher paid you once for a single use. This is the ideal rights situation for an author.

First Time Rights

First time rights is a special type of one time use: the first use. If you sell first time rights, you are stating to the publisher that yours is an original work and has not been previously published anywhere. Some publishers only want first time rights within their medium but do not care about other media, i.e. first appearance in a magazine, first appearance on a web site, etc. You must check with the editor as to their needs before you can affirm that they are the first.

Many authors these days have a personal web site where they may post stories or works in progress. Some editors and publishers will consider that "published" and if they are seeking first time rights, they would not accept a story that had been posted. Others are not so stringent. If you want to avoid this situation, hold off putting any work on your site until it has been published and no longer eligible for "first time" sale. (Make sure, of course, that you have retained the right to self-publish the piece in this manner!)

First North American Serial Rights

First North American Serial Rights (often abbreviated FNASR) is the most common form of first time, one time rights requested by magazines publishing in English in the US and Canada. "Serial" rights are the right to publish in a periodical, i.e. a newspaper, magazine, journal, or other regular publication (not a book). Since it is a kind of first rights, you must be able to promise the publisher that the work in question has not been previously published in any book, magazine or newspaper in North America. With FNASR, the timing is very important; if you are selling FNASR to a magazine to be published in March 2004, and also have the same story slated to be published in a book in November 2004, you're fine; you can sell FNASR to the first venue and reprint rights to the second. But if for some reason the first story were to be delayed by a year until March 2005, you would no longer be granting FNASR because the story would be published in November 2004. If a piece has previously appeared somewhere and a magazine wants to buy it, they would then ask for "second serial rights" or just "serial rights."

Reprint Rights

Reprint rights is the general term for selling the rights to a story that has previously appeared somewhere. When you see calls for submissions for anthologies, you will see some asking for "no reprints." Those editors want first rights. Others are happy to use reprints to find material that fits their theme. Some pay more for first rights then they do for reprint rights.

Online Rights

Online rights are what a web magazine like *Clean Sheets* or *Nerve.com* would buy. Since online rights is a fairly new area, it may not appear on standard contracts you sign for print pubishers. If you're unsure when signing with a print publisher, make sure you inquire whether the publication in question has plans to use your work online also, and if so, ask that you be compensated, and add this in writing in your contract.

Many e-zines and websites do not use contracts with writers, but others do. Often, a website will ask for a certain time period (such as 90 days) of exclusivity and the opportunity to archive your work on their site; after the exclusivity period expires, you are free to sell your work elsewhere. Sometimes this exclusivity may only apply to other websites, other times it will apply anywhere. If you are giving permission to a book publisher or magazine to carry your story, if nothing is stated about electronic rights, find out for yourself; you may want to sell or grant use of your story or stories to websites for payment and/or to promote your book or magazine credit. Some publishers will try to include online rights when buying an article or story, and you must either grant them the rights, try to negotiate for more money, or retain your online rights to possibly sell your story to another market.

Media Rights

What about books on tape, radio plays, movie adaptation rights, and so on? Many publishers would love to get a piece of the action if a piece they publish is turned into a hit in some other medium. You can see their reasoning: without the publisher, the work never would have reached the public and caught the eye of that movie producer, audio book company, etc., so they feel entitled to a piece of that future profit. But they do not usually expect to pursue the sale of these rights actively. If you have an agent who would pursue these rights sales, you should try to keep these rights for yourself.

In the area of mass media we are seeing many publishers doing a "rights grab" by putting clauses into their contracts demanding the rights to all forms of media adaptation "forever, including media not yet invented" which applies to online rights. Some landmark Supreme Court cases have recently been won on the part of freelance writers who found newspapers and magazines who had purchased the print rights to articles were also selling copies of their articles online without offering any additional payments to the authors (Tasini vs. *New York Times*). To prevent this sort of situation in the future, publishers are trying to bully writers into signing away not only all rights, but all rights that might be created in the future by new technologies, rather than offering contracts that provide for continued payment of authors.

We caution you against signing any contract asking for future rights "forever" that does not provide for future compensation. The principle is simple: if the publisher earns additional money on the work, the author should get paid again.

For more information on contract negotiation, reasonable pay rates, and author's rights, contact a writers organization like the National Writers Union (NWU), American Society of Journalists and Authors (ASJA), or the PEN American Center., listed in our resource section.

Chapter Nine:
Coping With Rejection

There is an essential element of optimism involved in sending your writing to a publisher. You have faith that the editor will read it, love it, and decide to publish it.

No one likes to have that faith shattered.

Rejection letters, however, are one of the facts of a writer's life. We know writers who have published hundreds of books (yes, hundreds) who still get rejections. And many books that are now considered Classics of Literature received their share of rejection notes before finding an editor who had faith in the work and decided to publish it. Even *New York Times* bestselling authors have gone through rejection after rejection before getting their big break. Many authors have said they were tempted to give up and let their novel reside in their desk drawer, but kept submitting it until they finally found a publisher who believed in their work.

Receiving rejection letters can be one of the most depressing things about being a writer. Build up a personal support network to help you cope when you get them. This could be a sympathetic friend who you call up to complain about how stupid the editor was not to buy your story, or a newsgroup or writing list where you can compare notes about rejections with fellow authors. You might also want to write about it in a journal, or find another way to let out your feelings about the rejection. As you get more rejection letters and meet other writers, you'll learn that often there are various issues—be they financial or editorial—that might be the cause of your rejection, rather than the merit of your piece. That may not sound fair, but it is part of the publishing process.

We all still get rejections, even from editors we've sold work to before. Some days, rejections affect David Laurents terribly, and he gets depressed. More often, he's already caught up in some new project he's excited about, which takes the sting out of the rejection because his focus is now elsewhere. This does-n't mean he's lost interest in the work that was rejected, but because he's no longer so caught up in that particular piece of writing, he can consider it and why it was rejected in a more objective frame of mind. Maybe he'll decide the editor was right and the story needs more work. Or he may decide it is exactly the way he wants it, and send it off to another venue that seems more appropriate.

Rachel Kramer Bussel likes to make an analogy to her chess playing career. She used to compete in chess tournaments quite frequently, but before she had any wins, there were lit-erally hundreds of losses. She began playing chess against her father, and for the first few years she never won, not even a sin-gle game, which was especially demoralizing at a very young age. But there was a turning point, where she did win one game against her father, and the hope and joy of that win were monumental. That helped sustain her over the next period of losses, until the time when she was winning chess games, against her father and others, on a fairly regular basis. So it was with her first acceptance, for the anthology *Starf*cker: A Twisted Collection of Superstar Erotica*, edited by Shar Rednour. Getting the news that Rednour wanted to use the story was extremely exciting—so much so that Bussel saved the message on her answering machine for several weeks so she could play it every time she listened to her messages. She was especially pleased with this acceptance, because she was also receiving many rejection letters at that time, and it gave her hope that there would be more acceptances along the way.

As you begin submitting your work more often, you'll begin to learn just from looking at your mailbox whether the news is good or bad. A thick envelope usually means a rejection, since they've returned the story to you in your SASE, although sometimes this means they are asking you to do revisions. Acceptances are usually thinner, containing only a congratulatory letter from the editor and perhaps a contract. Some publishers use their own letterhead to send out acceptances, instead of your SASE. (Sometimes they'll return your SASE, other times they keep them on file or trash them. Just chalk up the lost stamps as part of the cost of doing business as a writer; after all, you can deduct them from your taxes.)

And sometimes a rejection actually opens the door to something better. Cecilia Tan sent a story to a small press editor who had asked her for something, and was shocked when the editor turned it down. She sent it out the next day to a major mainstream anthology where it was bought immediately, and the story was later picked for *Best American Erotica*, as well. In that case, it was a good story that just didn't fit the first place it went.

Develop a Thick Skin

It is important to remember that your writing, no matter how personal, is separate from you. Especially as an erotica writer, you may feel as if your sexuality or lifestyle is being rejected, and not merely the work that was submitted.

David Laurents developed a thick skin back in high school, when he joined the cross country team his freshman year. At the time, there were no other freshmen or even sophomores on the team; he was competing against runners who were older and taller than he was, and he lost every race he competed in.

The truth is, he is not an especially fast runner, although he has the stamina to run long distances. He learned to be pleased just to finish each race, especially as the races got longer and longer—3 miles, 5 miles, 8 miles. This was an accomplishment in and of itself. By setting goals for himself, he was able to gradually improve as well as prove to himself he could accomplish what he set out to do. The same can be said for writing. By setting goals, and actively pursuing them, we move closer to achieving them. The truth is that your work cannot be rejected if you haven't finished and submitted it; getting to that point is an accomplishment in and of itself, and means that you have a completed piece in your possession. If it gets rejected, you can submit it elsewhere, revise it, put it away to be examined at a later date, or use parts of it in other stories.

To reiterate, there is an essential optimism involved in submitting your work to publishers. You must simultaneously be confident that your work will be accepted, while realizing that not everything you send out will meet the editor's tastes. It will at times be emotionally difficult to keep sending your stuff out and having it rejected, but the best way to assuage your hurt over rejections is to follow them up with acceptances!

So much of placing a story will depend on the whims of the editor or publisher, the financial reality of the market, as well as the positioning of your story *vis a vis* other submitted stories. An editor may love your story about an erotic chef, but if she just bought another story about an erotic chef (it could happen!) she probably won't take yours, no matter how good it is. But if she liked it, she might remember you in the future and perhaps want to use that story or another one of yours for another project.

You may lose faith—in yourself as a writer, in a particular story, or in the publishing process. If this happens, take some time off and focus on something else. When you return to writing, make sure that your writing is as sharp and brilliant as it can be, and then start sending it out again with your own internal knowledge that it is worthy of publication.

You may find it heartening to read the book *Rotten Rejections* edited by Andre Bernard.

A thick skin will come in handy later, as well, since once your story is published you may receive other forms of feedback. You may get fan mail. Or you may get an email or a letter sent in care of the editor from a reader who thought the story wasn't erotic. If you publish a book, critics may give it negative reviews. All of these things may happen, and while it is a positive sign if people are reacting to your work, you will have to learn to insulate yourself and your ego from these types of reactions.

Types of Rejections

The standard rejection letter, in any genre, is the Form Letter. Because of the volume of submissions most publishers receive, it is easiest for them to have a preprinted form that they can use to reject work that is inappropriate or which they are not interested in.

A form letter is usually a short, anonymous note along the lines of:

```
Dear Writer—
    Thank you for submitting your work to
us. We have read it carefully and have
found that it does not meet our present
needs.
    Sincerely,
    The Editors
```

Don't think that merely because you received a form rejection the editor is "blowing you off." For a magazine that receives thousands of submissions a year, a form letter is a reasonable way to respond to work that is definitely not what they are looking for, so they can spend more time replying to the manuscripts that are. If editors really wanted to blow you off, they wouldn't respond at all—and you will find that happens sometimes, too.

Some publishers use a Checklist Rejection. This is also a pre-printed form, but an editor (or usually, an editorial assistant) will check off one or more reasons why your work was reject-ed. This could be a technical reason, such as your submission exceeded the maximum word length the magazine considers, or it could be for content reasons, such as the subject matter wasn't what they were seeking. Sometimes you will also get a short (possibly even a few words) written comment specific to your story, like "nice characters but ending made no sense," or "present tense didn't work."

And then there is the Personal Rejection.

When an editor has taken the time and energy to write you a personal note, it generally indicates that something in your submission caught the editor's attention enough to merit this special effort.

David Laurents would much rather get a fast anonymous note than a personal rejection that will take longer to receive. As an established writer, he is not hanging on editorial feed-back and would prefer to send the story on to someone else right away. He is more impatient than when he started writing because he is used to working with editors who are expecting his work. At the same time, he remembers how excited he was the first few times an editor took the time to give feedback on his work, and how valuable those experiences were. In fact, he still has those letters in his files.

For Rachel Kramer Bussel, the first few rejection letters were the hardest, because it seemed like they were all that was coming in the mail. But now she has learned to appreciate them for what they are and to move on. She tries to glean any insights from personalized rejections, but tries not to focus on the rejections for more than a day or they tend to distract her when she has other writing to do. While a personal rejection can feel more painful, it really is a sign that your work stood out enough to get a handwritten note; after all, the editor did not have to take the time to write a personal note.

More on the "Good" Rejection

People who have never tried to sell their writing are often confused when they hear a writer tell another writer how happy they were to get a personal rejection from an editor. *What could be good about a rejection?* You might wonder; all it means is that your writing wasn't bought.

Sometimes rejection letters can point you in a direction that you would not have imagined on your own. They can point out flaws that you overlooked or bring up suggestions that you may find will improve your writing. Also, just because an editor rejects your work doesn't necessarily mean they did not like it. Editors usually receive many times more than the number of ideas or stories they can use, and you do not know, until you see the final product, what competition you were up against.

For Rachel Kramer Bussel, a rejection that is well-written, sincere, and thoughtful can even leave her feeling good about her writing. For instance, she submitted a personal essay to *Nerve.com*, and got a note from the editor saying that while she enjoyed it, it wasn't quite what *Nerve* was looking for; it was too straightforward and *Nerve* was looking for something a little more "sideways." This rejection was useful because it encouraged her to submit the work elsewhere, while also giving a clue as to what type of story *Nerve* sought. The essay was later accepted at another website. This type of rejection gives more information than is available in a set of writer's guidelines, and can guide you in future submissions. Plus the editor will probably remember you when you submit work to them again.

Sometimes an editor may also be brutally honest about deficiencies in your writing. Do you over-write, using too many adjectives and weighing down the prose? Are your characters too shallow? Did you fail to establish a central point of view and instead meander around from character to character? If an editor gives you feedback like this, think of it as pure gold. There are manuscript evaluation services you can pay to critique your stories; if an editor tells you something they think needs work, that insight is valuable. It can help you not only improve that story, but improve your writing as a whole. It may sting at first, or seem embarassing, but you'd want a friend to tell you if you had spinach in your teeth, wouldn't you? Instead of getting angry at that friend, or that editor, do what you can to fix things and move on.

How to React to a Rejection?

The most important thing when you get a rejection is to bounce back from it and not let it hinder you.

Getting angry can help give you energy, but don't write a nasty note to the editor telling him or her what a fool they are to have passed on your writing. This is not only a waste of your time, but also burns a bridge you may need later on. The world of erotic writing and publishing is very small and it won't help you to fire off scathing missives to editors telling them why they're wrong to reject your work. They're not "wrong" simply because they have the power to accept or reject your work. Also, editors are not infallible, and often face extremely difficult decisions when deciding which pieces to accept and which to reject. They are not trying to make you feel bad by rejecting your work, but trying to create the best, most cohesive publication they can. An editor who has rejected one of your works may accept a different one, and editors often move to other publishers. You may feel better after writing an angry letter, in which case go ahead and do so, but then tear it up once you've gotten it out of your system.

Instead of sending letters, do something constructive with your anger or upset feelings. If you still think the work deserves publication, find another market to send it to. It may take years of submitting a given story, but you may eventually find the right home for it. Success is the best revenge.

A friend who has received multiple rejections from the same editor has strengthened her determination to keep submitting to the same editor; instead of discouraging her, the repeated rejection has made her more determined to crack that market. Rejections are all in how you look at them, and we can state very strongly that wallowing in your rejections and letting them affect the quality or quantity of your output only does you and your writing a huge disservice. We've heard of many authors submitting their work to a publisher or magazine again and again, trying different writing styles or simply being persistent, and eventually achieving success. Just because an editor didn't like some of your writing doesn't mean they won't like any of it. Also, sometimes a piece may, for instance, be too short for a given publication, but just right for an anthology or magazine looking for shorter pieces.

Often there are things you can learn from a rejection letter which can help you make future sales. If you have submitted repeatedly to a certain magazine and keep getting rejections, perhaps instead of banging your head against the wall, you should try to find someone who has written for them and figure out what you are doing differently. Or move on to submitting somewhere else for a while and perhaps try the previous venue again in a year or two, when an editor may have moved or your writing style may have changed. Many editors are pleased to be able to accept work from an author they had previously rejected, pleased at either an improvement in the writing or whatever circumstances have changed to make the work fit with their publication.

Too Personal

Although most writers appreciate honesty from editors, there is no need for an editor to attack you personally or your writing style in a rejection. For example, if someone writes back, "You must be sick to write this kind of material," or "This is the worst piece of trash I've ever read." Mark that editor as someone you'll never work with again. Warn your writer friends not to submit to this market as well. Some editors' style may seem abrasive, but they are not necessarily trying to be cruel to you. If you get work back with a "No" written on it, that may have simply been shorthand for an editor deciding amongst a pile of submissions. You cannot always expect an individualized critique of your work, and should not seek one out from an editor unless they have indicated they are willing to provide such a critique. Find a writing group for that sort of feedback before sending your work to an editor. But if you truly feel an editor has crossed the line into insulting you or attacking you, don't share your work with them again.

Some Final Words On Rejections

The book *Rotten Rejections* is a most amusing read for anyone who has ever attempted to get their writing published; few of its contents were more amusing, though, than the rejection memo to an undisclosed author from a Chinese economic journal, clearly an indication of a cultural adherence to politeness, unknown in the world of western publishing:

> We have read your manuscript with boundless delight. If we publish your paper, it would be impossible for us to publish any work of lower standard. And as it is unthinkable that in the next thousand

years we shall see its equal, we are, to our regret, compelled to return your divine composition, and to beg you a thousand times to overlook our short sight and timidity.

Even though it is difficult, remember that everyone, including the top erotic writers, get rejections; it is part of the life of a writer. What you do with the rejections is up to you. It is all too easy to let them eat at you and feel like they are the be-all and end-all to your self worth, but that won't advance your writing career one bit. Step back and realize that you can submit that same story to another editor, and another and another, until you get an acceptance, or at least until you're satisfied.

Chapter Ten:
Telling the World What You Do

When we say "telling the world what you do," we mean everything from telling your family members to attracting a following of readers. Before you begin your erotic writing career, you will have to decide how "out" you want to be about this endeavor. One of the most important aspects of this is deciding whether or not to use a pseudonym (see Chapter Three: Care and Feeding of Pseudonyms). If you use a pseudonym, you will have more freedom about whether to let people know that this is "really" you. But even if you use a pseudonym, issues may still come up regarding your fame and your family life. Many writers choose to use their real names on their erotic work.

Family Affair

One of the most common questions we get asked is whether our family knows about our writing and what they think of it. Different people will have different responses. According to Susie Bright, editor of the *Best American Erotica* series, her father is her biggest fan. In Rachel Kramer Bussel's case, her immediate family is aware of her writing but only a few have read her work. To some extent, you can control what those close to you know about your writing—you can boldly give them copies of magazines and books with your writing in them, or not mention it at all.

But the truth is, when your name is out there, you really don't know where it will wind up—in reviews of your work, in promotional materials from the publisher, on book covers, in advertising, etc. So you do have to be prepared for co-workers, family, friends and other acquaintances to find out about your writing. Anyone can Google your name and find out you're in an anthology that Amazon.com sells. One thing to keep in mind is that if they are reading the book or magazine or website where your writing appears, they are already disposed to like that sort of work. Another way to think of it is they are as "guilty" of reading erotic materials as you are "guilty" of writing them, so any potential censure from them comes with their own interest in the subject. You may also be surprised, in a good way, at who is reading your work. Rachel got in touch with a relative she hadn't heard from in many years when her cousin came across her writing in lesbian porn magazine *On Our Backs* and contacted her through the publisher.

Also, depending on how common your name is, you do not necessarily have to claim ownership of your writing. But if you are serious about a career as an erotic writer, part of your job will be spreading the word about your work, making a name for yourself. Your friends and family could be an important network for self-promotion. Suppose you have written an erotic story about playing tennis, and you are in a local tennis league; your fellow players may be interested in your story. There are an infinite number of ways you can get the word out about your work, from public readings (see Chapter Eleven: Meeting Your Readers) to emailed announcements, mailing lists, and newsletters.

One of the best ways to react to disapproval from your family or friends is, first of all, not to be defensive about it. By being defensive, you are buying into their way of thinking that there is something bad, something you ought to hide. There is nothing wrong with exploring sexuality, which is a natural part of human experience, through fiction or writing. We know one writer who received a phone call from her mother, where her mother confronted her.

"I just saw you had a story in Penthouse magazine!" her mother said in outraged tones.

The writer had to think fast. She could have played dumb: "Oh, that must be another person with a name like mine." She could have reflected the outrage back: "Oh, did you find Dad's stash hidden in the bathroom? What the hell were you doing reading Penthouse, anyway?" Or she could have reacted, as she did, with effervescent delight, ignoring her mother's anger.

"Isn't that awesome!" she exclaimed. "I'm finally getting somewhere as a writer. They paid me almost a thousand bucks for that piece and I bought a new computer with the money."

Once the mother realized that her daughter was going to express neither guilt nor shame over the story, her harangue was robbed of its power.

Probably the most important thing is for you to get over any feelings of guilt or shame you have about sex writing. If you are proud of what you do, if you feel it betters the world and makes people happy, then what right does anyone have to criticize you? If you are enthusiastic and open about what you do, your friends and family may have little choice but to accept you as you are and support your choices—just as they would a relative who came out as gay or who is transitioning from one gender to another. Not all families, of course, deal with "coming out" in a reasonable fashion. Being disowned or suffering violence or abuse are always possibilities. But mainstream families who respect variations in sexual orientation and/or who support creative and artistic endeavors can come to see erotic writing as a valid activity. (Some people have no problem with the erotic aspects, but they frown on writing as a "waste of time." The only way to convince them is to earn a living!)

Telling the "World"

Being proud enough of your work to push it in public is, to some extent, a necessity for a long career. Telling people what you do goes beyond your circle of family and friends. You want to build an audience for your writings, a following that will eagerly want to buy and read your work every time it is published. Being visible on the Internet with a personal web site has become a key tool in promoting writing and getting the word out. Personal web pages are relatively cheap (you can create a website hosted by a free server such as Yahoo or pay one of a number of companies for hosting and creating your own domain name and website) and your page will be easy for large numbers of people to access. This means anyone in the world, from your mother to your next door neighbor, can type your name in a search engine and pull up your site.

Use your website to let people know about your writings and appearances, to post new work, or to get feedback from readers. You may be surprised at just who is reading your website; Rachel Kramer Bussel is constantly amused at the web searches people reaching her site have performed (her favorite is "nude Jewish princesses"). Cecilia Tan writes both erotica and baseball and so sometimes readers of one are shocked to find mention of the other on her page, but generally both audiences are supportive.

You can increase your traffic by linking to the sites of other erotic writers and asking that they do the same for you, and by joining a web ring such as The Authors of Literary Erotica Web Ring (http://www.mindcaviar.com/literotica.html). You may want to create an informal email newsletter to let people know about your writings and activities, or start an online journal or weblog ("blog"). You don't have to make it simply an advertisement for your work; you can give people a glimpse of yourself as a whole person, sharing anecdotes about your life, perhaps giving a "behind-the-scenes" look at what it is really like to be an erotic writer. You can share the inspiration for a certain story or answer questions from readers; it is up to you, so be creative! Susie Bright has many useful suggestions for spreading the word about your work in *How To Write a Dirty Story* (see Resources).

Getting your name (or pseudonym) out there, whether by doing public readings, writing for websites and other publications that receive a lot of traffic, or networking with other writers, will pay off. People will start to recognize and remember your name, and if they like your work, may invite you to submit to special issues of publications or anthologies. Often editors may need to fill some slots in anthologies at the last minute, and are likely to turn to those whose work they know and with whom they've had good experiences in the past. You'll feel very gratified when someone says "Oh, I know your name, I've read your work." While we started out this chapter telling you that you don't have to shout your writing career from the hilltops, if you're willing to do just that, you will likely find interest all around you. Almost anyone you meet at a party or other social event will want to know more when you tell them that you're a "sex writer." Make some inexpensive business cards to give people you meet a way to get in touch with you and find out more about your work later if they are too embarrassed to ask you on the spot.

But people are naturally curious. Most have read at least some sort of erotic writing and they may want to know what you think of other erotic works, or what your writing process is like. Talking with people is also an interesting way to see how erotic writing is perceived; some may wrinkle their noses while others may take your arm and corner you, begging for more information.

Another way to spread the word about your work is in your "contributor's note." When a piece of yours is published, you are almost always given the opportunity to include a short biography; use this to let people know where they can see your work by listing magazines, books, and websites where your work has been published.

If you're part of a writers group, you can support the other members and they will in turn support you. You can talk up each other's books, offer tips on local places to post notices about events, and much more.

Many mailing lists, newsletters, and other publications will post announcements of published work. This doesn't mean you have to tell every single person you meet about your latest story, but you can selectively spread the word to those you suspect might enjoy your work. You may not see an immediate payoff, but your career advances when people read your stories. This doesn't mean everyone will like them, but that's not something you can control. Each time you get work published or get a mention in the media, you increase your visibility as an author, which can be advantageous in future dealings with editors and publishers (not to mention an ego boost when you're struggling with writer's block or a recent rejection). There is no single formula for how to promote your work, but you should try to identify what is unique about you and your writing, and what it is that you want people to remember. You may want to create a tagline for yourself, such as you would for a business, letting people know in a phrase what they'll get when they read your work.

Publicists and Publicity

When you publish a book or if you are published in an anthology, you may find yourself in touch with a publicist at the publishing house. A publicist's job is to spread the word about a book through the media: newspapers, radio, magazines, television. "Publicity" is any form of media mention which was not paid for (paid mentions are advertising). This may sound terriffic to you, but the sad truth of the publishing business is that very few books are publicized beyond a bare minimum of mailing out the review copies.

Publicists are overworked. While you are focused only on your book and making sure every possible promotion is exploited, the publicist is in charge of many titles. As a rule, publishers—even the large mainstream houses—don't spend adequate effort or money on publicity; the resources simply aren't available, and the return on their investment just isn't enough. Many erotica publishers don't even have a publicist.

A rule of publishing, no matter the genre: No one is as invested in the promotion of your book as you are. Certainly the publisher wants it to do well so that they make more money too. But for the publisher yours is only a single book in their line of many titles. Ultimately, the job of making your name know is yours. As such, you need to be your own publicist to some extent.

One advantage to being your own publicist is that you can arrange to cross-promote. If you have stories coming out in several magazines at once, or you have published more than one book with different houses, the publishing companies are unlikely to work together to publicize multiple works. Publishers only act in their own self-interest; it is rare for a publisher to promote anything but the books which they themselves published. Some publishers will not even list titles you may have published with other houses in your book. But you are the common denominator. You can draw the various threads together to create something greater than the sum of its parts.

By having a hand in your own publicity, you can promote all of your work, thus enhancing your name recognition and potential profits. For some advice on getting all that you can out of publicity, see *The Guerilla Guide to Marketing* by Michael Larsen. At minimum, for your own publicity purposes you will want to prepare the following things:

1) An author photo
2) A one page biography of yourself
3) A complete list of all your publications and credits

This miniature press kit will be very helpful to you when a reporter calls you out of the blue and says "We're running a special Valentine's Day story in the Arts & Leisure section about local erotica writers." Yes, this happened to Cecilia Tan. She had been in an erotica anthology and the newspaper writer went to the local bookstore, looked through all the erotica books on the shelf, saw in her contributors note that she was from the area, and looked her number up in the phone book. She was able to send him the press kit and the local newspaper followed it up with a brief interview. The result was a short feature article, even though she had only a few stories to her credit at that point. Then a local radio station read the article and asked her to be on a local talk show. Once you start getting the word out, you never know how far it will go.

Chapter Eleven:
Meeting Your Readers

Now that erotica has gained a level of respectability in many circles, it is quite likely that you may make public appearances as an erotic writer once you have been published (even if you're writing under an alias). You may seek out these events in order to publicize a recent publication or to test out new work on an audience before sending it off to a publisher. Or someone may approach you.

For instance, a fan of your work might write to you in care of your publisher, asking you to give a reading or talk before a local group of some sort. We know many erotica writers who've been asked to read at or speak to leather clubs, writers' groups, book reading groups at bookstores, and so on. You might be called on to sign autographs, talk about your work, speak on a panel, or to read your work aloud to an audience. There are many types of public appearances and we will discuss some of the more common ones.

Speaking at Colleges and Universities

You may even find yourself invited to speak at a college or university. For instance, Conversio Virium, a student group at Columbia University for students interested in discussing S/M, regularly invites erotica writers to give presentations of their work on campus. Other universities, such as Wesleyan and

NYU, have similar groups, or may sponsor special talks featuring erotic writers as part of a program.

Check out possible opportunities in your area by contacting local colleges or seeking out students who might be interested in hosting such an event.

If you write lesbian or gay material, you can approach the Queer Student Alliances of local colleges, offering yourself as a guest speaker. Most student groups have limited funds available for such events during the year, but many of them do have a lump of money set aside for their Gay and Lesbian Awareness Days or Pride festivities. Ranging anywhere from a week to a month at different campuses, these programs usually fall in April. In general, speakers are arranged a few months in advance, so you might want to contact groups at the beginning of the Spring semester, in late January, if not earlier.

Similarly, many colleges have funds set aside for special events celebrating Women's History month in March. A few years ago, Rachel Kramer Bussel helped bring writer Lisa Palac to the New York University campus, where they then paired her with performance artist Karen Finley. Their speeches played to a packed audience, paving the way for future programs of a similarly erotic nature. The school's program board had a specific budget and it was enough to cover the fees of both of these artists.

Once you have published, you could be invited back to your alma mater to speak at an alumni career forum. Whenever you publish something, send an announcement to your alumni magazine's "class notes" section to spread the word to fellow alums.

Out Loud

David Laurents has given readings of his erotic stories in places as offbeat as temples and sex clubs, and as traditional as bookstores and coffeeshops. (One writer we know was invited on a cruise ship with a special S/M theme to read her work during the voyage!) No matter where you do it, reading your work aloud is one of the most common types of public appearances for any author.

When many people think of being published, they dream of being paid a large advance and being sent on an extensive tour by their publishing house. In reality, very few authors are given this treatment, but giving public readings is an integral part of the process of being published, even if you have to set up your "tour" yourself. Readings are one of the things that many fiction writers expect to do, whether they write erotica or not.

A reading is a unique opportunity to reach out to readers who might not otherwise crack the pages of your book. Some people who may not think of themselves as being into erotica might hear you read and be enthralled. It is a different experience for your audience to be read to than to read words on the page for themselves, and if you can cultivate a compelling voice while reading, you may draw in new erotica fans.

However, no matter how much you write and publish, you may be uncomfortable speaking in public, or speaking in public about sexual matters. This is not unusual. Some people are able to write the steamiest text, but are squeamish about standing up in front of an audience of strangers—or worse, people they know!—and reading about graphic sexuality. Please remember this; you don't have to subject yourself to what feels like torture in the name of promoting your work. If you are truly uncomfortable reading your work or making this type of appearance, you do not have to.

We attended one reading of contributors to an anthology of erotic science fiction stories. One of the writers was unable to make herself say out loud the words for certain body parts, even though she had written them in her piece; she had been brought up never to utter those words. She warned the audience before beginning that there were certain words in her story that, try as she might, she was unable to say; she made a sort of gesture every time she came to one of them in the text, and the audience was able to figure out from the context what was going on. She had published many other non-erotic stories and enjoyed giving public readings, so she was able to get through the experience with good spirits. But if this experience would be emotionally painful for you, you can simply decline any invitations to speak in public and choose not to seek them out.

Finding A Place To Read

The most common places for public readings are in bookstores, hip coffeeshops, or bars. The establishments hosting the event are looking to sell something, whether books or drinks. They're hoping that your event will draw potential customers.

Many of the more literary erotica journals regularly feature public readings by contributors to celebrate each new issue. To promote anthologies of erotica, often the editors will arrange for readings by contributors at bookstores where the books are available for sale. Or, as a contributor you can suggest a regional event, especially if you are not in the same geographic area as the editor. With the editor's and publisher's permission, you might organize your own reading, thereby promoting your own work and the anthology.

You do not need to have published a book of your erotica in order to participate in these kinds of events. You can seek out venues, monthly reading series, or one-off events that are looking for readings. Or you could talk to people in your local community about organizing your own erotic reading. You don't always need to have been published at all to take part in some public readings; you may be able to submit a sample of your writing to the curator of the event and have them base their decision on this sample. Often, coffeeshops will have an open microphone session where people sign up on a first-come, first-served basis. If the series is not specifically of an erotic nature, you should probably notify the host of the nature of what you plan to read, and also preface the work to the audience. Most performance poetry venues expect raw and edgy language and themes, however, so graphic sexuality is not out of place at many of these events.

Good Vibrations, the sexuality boutique in San Francisco, hosts a regular erotic reading circle where patrons of the store (whether published or not) can present their work and get feedback in a supportive sex-positive environment. An anthology of stories and poems from the group has been published by Down There Press (the publishing branch of Good Vibes) called *Sex Spoken Here,* edited by Carol Queen and Jack Davis.

Check out what options you can find close to home. Does your town, or nearby city, have a sex-positive sexuality boutique? Would your local library host something? What bookstores do you have in the area and do they have writers groups or book clubs who invite speakers? Do you have a GLBT community center? Where do the "poetry slams" happen in your area? The venues available to you will depend on where you live; read local newspapers, especially alternative weeklies, to find out what is going on already. If you can't find anything, you might start your own erotic reading series, ensuring you plenty of public reading opportunities and a chance to meet and hear from fellow writers!

To get invited to a reading series at a coffeeshop or bar, it usually helps to attend some of the other events in the series and introduce yourself to the host.

Be polite and be patient, because the host will be preoccupied with the evening's presentations. Don't expect to be offered a slot right away. You may be asked to submit samples of your work if the host is not already familiar with it.

One of the best ways to get invited to read for a series is to give other readings. The people who host reading series usually keep up on the scene by attending events at other venues and checking local listings to see who is reading.

Bookstores

If you are promoting a book, the book's publisher may have a publicist whom you can ask for help in setting up events. Typically the contacts they will have will be with bookstores, and not with the more alternative venues like coffeeshops. But setting up bookstore events is very low on a publicist's priority list, and you may be better off approaching bookstores on your own.

Start with your local bookstores and find out which ones are carrying the book. Call on the phone and ask for the name of the events coordinator. If he or she is not on shift at the time, you may have to call back later. Try to find out when to call back, or when you should drop by the store.

Some bookstores may be leery of the erotic subject matter, even if they do sell your book. In this case, don't push them to host you. Instead, offer to autograph their stock (the term for the copies they have on hand) and try to set up an event at a different bookstore.

Always get permission from the bookstore before signing your book. Most stores are happy to have you autograph them, even if you are just passing through or doing some shopping of your own! Just approach a clerk and announce yourself as the author. If you do not first obtain permission, you're defacing their property (how do they know you're really the author, especially if you're writing under a pseudonym?) The clerk may be able to help you gather up the books to sign (they may be shelved in more than one place)and will often sticker the books "Signed Copy" and may move them to a more prominent shelf. An added bonus is that signed books usually cannot be returned to the manufacturer.

If you're going to be traveling to a certain city, either for another engagement or a vacation, and are interested in doing a reading, find out where the local bookstores or other reading venues are. If you have friends in the area, ask them about readings they've attended and any contacts they may have. If you have a publisher, ask them about readings they may have booked or can arrange. The bookstores in that area may be happy to have you do a reading on a rare visit, and you will be able to meet new readers and broaden your horizons, plus build contacts outside of your immediate living area. This also looks impressive when listing your credentials—instead of saying you've read in every bookstore in Houston, you can say you've read in Houston, Miami, Boston, etc. As an added bonus, while local crowds may have seen you read dozens of times, those in a far-off city will have the pleasure of hearing you for the first time.

Are Public Readings Worthwhile?

Public readings are not usually cost-effective, in that you probably will not sell enough copies of your book at an event to earn much in the way of royalties. If you yourself are selling actual copies of your book outside the bookstore setting (in a coffeeshop for example), you may make a bit more, but you have to deal with the hassle of dealing with money directly, which some people don't like to do. Even with the author discount of 40% to 50% you can get from the publisher, you may not make enough back to pay for your expenses if you traveled far or stayed overnight.

Bookstores do not pay authors to do events. If you are reading at a bar or cafe that charges a fee to listeners, you may get a share of this money. Sometimes, all of that money is used for publicity for the reading series, and the readers participate simply for the chance to be in the public spotlight. You might get an honorarium speaking at a college, but you might not.

Why, then, do authors bother to do public readings?

Some people like performing in public. Writing is a very isolating business; often there is only you and the computer (or typewriter) for long periods of time. Then there is the delay between selling your work and seeing it in print. Getting to meet people who have read your work and liked it enough to come meet you can be exhilarating. Also, public readings are a completely different kind of interaction with your audience than writing, because their feedback and responses are so immediate.

Aside from this emotional gratification, what public readings and events give you is exposure, which can be invaluable.

If you are promoting a book at a bookstore, it is a chance for you to interact with the clerks at the store. Always be polite to the people who work in bookstores; if they like you, they can promote your book to customers who come in and ask for recommendations. They may be more likely to notice when they've sold all the copies of your book and decide to reorder. They can move it to the display tables at the front of the store.

Doing a reading or autographing can even sell copies to people who did not come to the actual event. Most bookstores will order extra copies for the event. Books can only sell when they're on bookstore shelves instead of in the publisher's warehouse, so the more copies that are ordered, the more you have a chance of selling. Many bookshops will feature the book in the store in the weeks beforehand. And after an event, most bookstores will ask you to sign any remaining copies, which they may sticker as "autographed copy" or "signed by the author" to attract attention to the book.

Media outlets are always looking for "news." The mere existence of your book is not news, but your bookstore event is. Hopefully, your event will be listed in the local papers in their calendar section. Check with the bookstore to see if they will handle this—you might want to provide copies of your minipress kit (See Chapter Ten: Telling the World What You Do) to be sent to the newspaper as well. Sometimes you can even arrange for your book to be reviewed in connection with a public reading or event, or you can contact a local alternative or college radio station which might interview you. Many mainstream papers won't review erotica, but alternative weeklies and regional gay and lesbian papers will. The fact that you're giving a reading in a bookstore also helps add "legitimacy" to the book in the eyes of many newspapers.

If you are traveling, doing an event in the city you visit can turn a vacation trip into a tax deductible business trip, as well as bring you a new audience for your work. Refer to the Chapter Seven: The Business of Writing for more information about tax deductions. (And remember to keep your receipts!)

Tips on Reading Aloud

Before you give a public reading, practice practice practice. Stand before a mirror and read to yourself. If you have a trusted friend or roommate who is willing, read your work to them and ask them to be brutally honest about what works and what doesn't.

When you read your work aloud, you may find sections which are awkward to say, or which you keep stumbling over. You can edit these sections to make them easier to pronounce (even if the work has already been published). Many writers read their stories aloud prior to submitting them for publication because it helps them improve their writing. Reading aloud exposes the "speed bumps" in the prose that need to be smoothed out.

When you give a reading, it is always a good idea to stand, even if you're nervous. You'll project your voice better if you are on your feet. Many bookstore settings will not have a microphone so you will need to supply your own volume.

No matter how fast you read, read slower. The slower you

read, the easier it is for the audience to hear and comprehend what you're saying. The funny parts will get more laughs, the serious parts more gasps, as you slow down and give the audience a moment to absorb each word, each sentence. They will not be bored because you are reading slowly—they will be riveted. If you read too fast, on the other hand, an audience can easily lose patience and become distracted because they are not allowed the time to absorb the details. Reading slowly is an especially good style for erotic fiction, where a slow deliberate pace matches the speed of a seduction.

If you are worried that your story will take up more than your allotted reading time, talk to the moderator or host before you go on about your anxieties. Don't race through your story to fit it all in. It is better to read slower and end sooner. You do not have to read your entire piece; in fact, giving only a teaser from your work has its advantages—the audience must buy the book or magazine to find out how things end, and you've just made another sale! Often, as part of a group reading of erotic stories, when allotted only a few minutes, some authors we know will read a sexy excerpt from the middle of a story. They may not actually read a sex scene, but the provocative bit leading up to one. If you are nervous about reading the more graphic parts of your story, perhaps teasing the audience with the build-up would be a good strategy for you.

Humor usually works well for public readings, so if there is an applicable section of a story, choose that to excerpt. Humor often relaxes an audience, and makes them feel more comfortable. But it also depends on the audience. Some lines that get a big laugh in Seattle might fall dead in Chicago. Don't worry if they don't laugh out loud, just keep reading. If you are going to read a piece that is humorous, you might want to tell a brief funny anecdote to loosen them up before you dive into the piece. The anecdote does not have to be about the piece—it can be about the crazy cab driver who dropped you off at the store—but it will help disarm the crowd and get them laughing in advance. You might even try this technique if you are reading a serious piece.

You want to give the audience the best chance of being able to "enter" your story. When reading an excerpt, you might want to set the scene, explain very briefly who the characters are or where they are, how they know each other, etc. If you're reading work in the voice of a character whose gender is different from your own, we recommend that you announce this before you begin. This helps the audience orient themselves, because people tend to assume that all first person voices are the same gender as the speaker/author. This happens even on the printed page, but is especially true if the audience sees and hears you as one gender, but your character is another gender.

"Will You Autograph My Chest?"

Writers don't get the on-the-street recognition that actors do, but David Laurents gets asked for his autograph more often than some of his friends who are actors on Broadway or in movies.

Especially if you've written a book, you will likely be asked to autograph it at some point. Sometimes, depending on the event and the type of people attending, you may be asked to autograph other items, which may include the poster or flyer for the event, an autograph book, bookplates, a cast, or something nontraditional.

Obviously, you'd prefer that people buy your book for you to sign, but you should try to be gracious about such other requests. There are many reasons someone may not buy your book right then and there, and being too cheap is only one possible reason. They might not have the money, they might already have a copy they forgot to bring with them, etc.

Some people ask for autographs not because they have any

particular interest in an author's work, but because they think an autograph from anyone famous enough to have published a book must be valuable. With erotica, sometimes people assume that the author must be or have been a porn star in films and videos.

You never know why someone wants your signature, and it is usually best to just give them your John Hancock on whatever they want, so long as the request is within reason. If someone asks you to autograph a body part and you're uncomfortable doing so, you can always say that you're only signing books. If they persist in crossing whatever boundaries you feel are appropriate, you should notify personnel from the bookstore or venue and ask them to intercede. (Hopefully the events coordinator or host is already keeping an eye on you.)

Most writers we know have never had any problems at any of the events they've given or attended, and some even befriend fans who've come to readings, but you never know who might show up and what oddball ideas they might have. In the introduction to *Best Women's Erotica* 2001, editor Marcy Sheiner recounts a reading done for the previous year's edition of the anthology series, where author Cara Bruce was asked whether she is a misogynist and was grilled by a particularly persistent attendee, much to everyone's discomfort. Sometimes audience members may have a political axe to grind. Cecilia Tan has been challenged by some who claim erotica is anti-feminist, or who disagree with her stance on the difference between erotica and pornography (she thinks there isn't any, really), but the belligerence has always been purely intellectual and never physical or dangerous.

Being a public figure does expose you to these sorts of encounters. It also creates the possibility for public confrontations with the likes of religious fanatics or anti-porn crusaders, who might protest your event. (A lot depends on where you're holding the event.) These are, in all likelihood, quite rare occurrences; most likely, your interaction with individual people at events will consist of just signing your name in their book. Perhaps you'll add a short note or a line that has relevance to the book if you want to personalize it.

Personalized Autographs

David Laurents always freezes up when someone asks him to inscribe their copy of one of his books. If you think this may happen to you, we suggest you spend some time before your book comes out thinking of things you might write. He finds it easier to write the book than something personal in it.

When in doubt, there is always "With all best wishes." David generally tries to think of something cute or outrageous that pertains directly to the theme of the book. For instance, for his anthology *Wanderlust: Homoerotic Tales of Travel*, he could sign "Hope you enjoy these sexy tales for the armchair traveler." If, like him, you live in a part of the world which has a winter season and are signing during it, you can always write something like "Hope this book heats you up tonight!"

Some people will ask that you just put your signature while others will want you to address it to them by name, or to a friend. Always ask how to spell the name, no matter how short and simple it may sound. Is it Kathy or Cathy? Tom or Thom? Marianne or Mary Anne?

We recommend signing with any color pen other than black. It doesn't have to be a fancy color; blue is fine. Black ink can too often look like the signature was preprinted. At a reading in Los Angeles for *Best Lesbian Erotica 2001*, Rachel Kramer Bussel was amused to note that four of the authors had brought the same purple pen for signatures, and thus dubbed it the "lesbian writing pen."

If you know you are going to be doing a public event, bring your own pens. Always bring more than one, otherwise fate will conspire for your only pen to run out of ink at an inopportune moment.

If you are writing under a pseudonym, it is customary to sign with the name that is on the book. If it is for someone you know, you may choose to sign with your real name followed by a parenthetical statement (writing as [pseudonym]). For instance, when David Laurents gives copies of his pseudonymous works to friends he signs:

Lawrence Schimel
(writing as David Laurents)

If you are signing stock for a bookstore, it is generally best to sign only the name that is printed on the book. This way readers who pick the book up will believe you really visited the store and held that very copy. You may need to practice signing your pseudonym beforehand until you can write it as smoothly and naturally as your own name.

Bookstores have different policies, but these days most bookstores require that the customer actually purchase a copy of the book before having you autograph it. If you've inscribed it to someone, and suddenly Joe or Diana decides not to buy it, the bookstore is going to have a hard time selling that copy to a different customer. Most bookstores will try to arrange people in an orderly fashion, lining them up at the cash register first and then sending them to you. If your mob of fans is too chaotic, ask the bookstore clerks to wrestle them into a line for you!

Fan Mail

Your interaction with your readers need not be only through public events. It can happen without you even leaving your home.

One of the most validating moments for a writer occurs when you get your first piece of fan mail. It doesn't matter if you've published dozens of books or only a single story—there's no telling when your work will strike enough of a chord in a reader that you get a note (or even a gushing letter). It might come care of the publisher, or it might be an email through your personal website.

You can easily forget, even if you publish regularly, that there are many people out there, strangers, who are reading your work. David Laurents is always delighted to get mail about his work, because it helps him feel like he's not writing in a vacuum. For him, writing is communication, and getting fan mail is the strongest proof that his words connected with someone on the other end.

So now you understand why getting fan mail might be exciting. But the important question remains: Do you need to answer your fan mail?

The answer depends on many personal factors such as how much mail you get and what the letter actually says or asks. Obviously, whoever wrote to you would like a response and generally does expect one.

Postcards are a convenient way of acknowledging that you've gotten someone's note, without requiring you to say much of anything. They're useful for responding without winding up engaged in an ongoing dialogue you lack the time or interest to pursue. You can also send them without a return address.

David Laurents found that his first fan letter was the hardest for him to answer; in fact, he never did write back, and always regretted not doing so. (There reached a certain point when too much time had passed for him to feel comfortable writing back.) These days he generally tries to give any sincere letter a response of some sort or another.

However, you are under no obligation to respond, in whatever way, to the people who write to you. You will have to judge for yourself if it is worthwhile to reply, depending on your time, the content of the letter, and your own personal feelings.

We should warn you that not all the mail you receive about your work may be positive. In fact, the people with complaints are usually the ones with more incentive to write and take you to task. Writing you an angry letter complaining about a stereotypical portrayal of one of your characters or an inaccuracy of a detail is a way for them to feel like they are taking action of some sort. That's their way of exorcising their personal demons. You can simply toss the letter and try to ignore it, unless you think it bears some truth or has useful criticisms which you want to apply to future works or revisions of the piece in question if it is ever republished.

For most readers of your work, their happy orgasms are the only thanks you get. And even if you don't hear from them, knowing that is enough.

Stalkers

Some of the people who write to you may be confusing the author with the characters in your work. They may write to you wanting to meet you in person, wanting to have sex with you, or similar suggestions which cross a boundary of propriety or comfort for you.

It is hard not to let these sorts of letters disturb you, but you should try to ignore them unless you think you are in personal danger. If you feel threatened, notify the police immediately and let the authorities deal with the situation.

Actual threats are very rare. None of the erotic writers we spoke with had to deal with someone actually stalking or harassing them in person. (The writers we know who have had these problems are all fantasy and horror writers, especially authors who write about vampires.) One publisher of gay erotica had to unlist his phone number because of harassing phone calls from the religious right.

What about getting an unlisted phone number? This is not a bad idea, but not usually not necessary. Many writers in other genres, who don't write erotica, decide not to give their fans the option of calling, and unlist themselves. This is a decision you'll have to make based on your own history.

Some of us have certainly had our admirers who are regulars at public readings and events, even if we might wish otherwise. This is one of the downsides of celebrity—if you're doing a public, publicized event, you can't know or control who shows up. Several writers tell stories about ex-lovers cornering them while they were trapped behind the autographing table; obviously, one of the reasons they were exes was their lack of tact and understanding of appropriate behavior. This is a possibility if you do public events, but for most of us, the good feedback outweighs the bad.

Sometimes strangers at events will seem creepy to you or take too active an interest in you. They may even be trying to pick you up, figuring that an erotic writer must be sexually adventurous (some are, some are not). They may be so turned on by your story that their judgement or normal social graces are impaired. They may try to monopolize your time. If there are other people waiting to talk to you, you might try first politely asking them to step aside to let other people have a turn. If there is no crowd and they persist, you might excuse yourself to the bookstore's restroom or ask the clerk if you can take a break in the back room. If your fan is still waiting for you, you might want to drop mention of your boyfriend, girlfriend, fiance, or spouse (even if you don't have one), as this will sometimes burst their bubble. Eventually, sometimes, you may just have to come out and say "You seem to be very interested in me, but I'm sorry, it's my policy not to get involved with people I meet at readings."

Chapter Twelve: Making a Career

So, you've sold some erotic short stories, perhaps with the help of this book. Maybe you've even sold a book. You can definitely consider yourself an erotica writer. Now what? Can you actually make a career out of writing erotica, or writing in general?

The actual number of people in the United States who make their living exclusively from writing fiction only numbers about 3,000. That 3,000 includes Stephen King, Anne Rice, and other bestselling authors. Part of the reason that number seems so low is that many of our most gifted fiction writers also have other jobs. Toni Morrison is also an editor at a publishing house. Tom Clancy used to be an insurance broker. Others also write nonfiction, teach in college writing programs, or have other writing-related jobs. Many of those people we would consider as "making their living from writing" even though the sales of their stories and books alone may not be enough to live on.

When you move from writing as an ambition to writing as a career, you will want to do several things for yourself. We've already talked in earlier chapters about retaining your rights (selling the same piece again and again to different markets), about keeping organized with regard to things like taxes, and even how to "make a name for yourself" through publicity to ensure that new writing prospects continue to come your way. But there are things that you need to do to ensure your creative longevity as well.

Like an athlete who has made it to the Major Leagues on the basis of talent, you as a writer may find that you sell a bunch of stories right away, or land a book contract. But like the athlete, who has to continue to practice, lift weights, and eat right in order to maintain his career, the writer needs to "stay in shape" as well.

Staying in writing shape means first of all, staying fresh. Some people have a limitless capacity to write the same thing over and over again, whether it is endless rehashings of a romance novel plot, or repeated versions of the "girl next door blow job" story. But most of us find that always writing the same thing gets old and we can get burned out. The marketplace might demand certain things of us; you may get a reputation for being good at a certain kind of story or a certain narrative voice. You will receive accolades and positive feedback (and money) for doing so. As such, the impetus to keep doing the same thing will be quite strong.

But if you are sick and tired of repeating yourself, you will have to find ways to keep yourself fresh. That might mean working on other projects (perhaps under another name) in-between your usual things. It might mean trying your hand at other genres, nonfiction, or maybe even blogging—something else to exercise your creative writing muscles but which isn't the same old, same old. Think of it as cross-training for your brain.

Another important thing to remember is that your creative wellspring is sourced subconsciously from your life's experiences. That includes the input you give your brain in the form of literature, movies, and other entertainment, as well as the real life experiences you live day to day, like the relationships you form, the places you visit, the conflicts you face, and of course, the sex you have. Make sure you keep reading. Find other writers who excite you—whether intellectually or erotically—and read them. They might be writing about art history or sports or crossword puzzles, they might write spy thrillers or memoirs or children's stories, but make sure you keep reading. The input will be part of what refines your style over time, and your own mastery of your craft.

Several friends we know, who all write or edit erotica, joke half-seriously about needing to start a club for "pornographers too busy to have sex." Don't neglect the real thing. Some erotica writers write almost entirely from fantasy and get their erotic fulfillment purely from writing and not from other people, but they are rare. Most of us need some real sex and erotic charge in our lives and our batteries can run low if all we do is tap that power source for story ideas. Recharge the batteries when you can. And that means not just sex, but recharging your overall creative batteries through travel, taking classes, and meeting people.

Some writers find the most wearing aspect of writing the fact that we always do it alone, in a vacuum. Writer's conferences, local writer's conclaves, writer's groups, and the like can help a writer break that isolation and feel positive that writing is a valid choice for something to do. Sometimes talking with other writers about the process of writing can be illuminating and energizing, as you learn about yourself, how your creative process works, and how the hurdles are all surmountable.

As the numbers show, most of us will not ever "retire" on our fiction writing alone, but finding a lifestyle and a way of living that feeds rather than saps our creativity is a must. Some writers only write on weekends, early in the morning, late at night, when their kids are in school, or only in the summers and they still manage to produce a lifelong body of work that is impressive and worthwhile. Whether you do something other than writing to augment your income, or depend on the help of a spouse or family member, or find ways related to writing to earn your keep. If writing is going to be a lifelong pursuit for you, you will need to find that balance.

Erotica writing, and writing in general, is a worthwhile lifelong pursuit and we welcome you to join us in it.

SECTION TWO
Market Listings

How To Use This Book

Almost every publisher or market listed in this guide has a set of "writer's guidelines" that runs anywhere from a half a page of text to twelve pages, single spaced. Yes, some of them are that picky and that specific. If we reproduced verbatim every publisher's guidelines, this book would be five hundred pages, and yet even then it would be inaccurate. When editors move from place to place, addresses change, or when needs change, the guidelines change.

What we have done here is give a thumbnail sketch of each market: who they are, what type of market, and what type of material they seek. Where possible, details about pay rates, rights, and the like are included, but bear in mind these are subject to change. The best way to use this book is to identify potential markets for your work, and then follow up by contacting the appropriate publishers yourself for their own detailed and up-to-date version.

Also remember that new markets are springing up all the time. Entrepreneurs start new websites. Magazines spin off sister publications. Book publishers start new imprints. We have listed here a section of resources that will help you find these new markets in the future.

Meanwhile, if you would like to correct, update, gripe about, or add to the listings here, we welcome your comments by email at editorial@circlet.com or to

Circlet Press, Inc.
Cecilia Tan, Editor
1770 Mass. Ave. #278
Cambridge, MA 02140

Book Publishers

A few notes about book publishers. Publishers run the gamut from operations with only one or two employees to those with thousands, and they range from those who specialize in erotic books to those who handle every kind of popular fiction and nonfiction with only the occasional erotic book. Editors may change houses frequently, so once that editor leaves, the company may no longer buy certain types of stories that the editor favored.

Each publisher has its own preferences about submissions, whether they prefer to see the whole manuscript, a synopsis and three chapters, or if they will only accept submissions from agents. As always, check with each publisher before submitting and try to find out the correct editor to submit to. For clarity's sake, we also list some well-known publishers that are no longer in business so you won't waste your time trying to hunt them down.

AK Press
674-A 23rd Street
Oakland, CA 94612
(510) 208-1700
Fax: (510) 208-1701
akpress@akpress.org
http://www.akpress.org
This left-wing small publisher focuses on political material, though they have published the occasional sexual treatise such as the feminist pro-pornography anthology *Tales from the Clit*. They are not actively looking for sex-related nonfiction, instead focusing on political nonfiction. They do not accept fiction.
Erotic Titles: *Tales from the Clit* edited by Cheri Matrix

Akashic Books
P.O. Box 1456
New York, NY 10009

Akashic7@aol.com
http://www.akashicbooks.com
Publisher: Johnny Temple
Akashic is a small, independent press specializing in unusual fiction and political nonfiction, run by Johnny Temple of the band Girls vs. Boys. They publish an eclectic, often unpredictable mix, and notable titles have included *Kamikaze Lust* by Lauren Sanders and *The Fuck-Up* by Arthur Neresian. Akashic books are often political, sometimes queer, but definitely non-mainstream works. They feature many up-and-coming authors in their diverse catalog. They are much more likely to publish a novel or other work with some smoldering sex in it that furthers the plot than a strictly erotic book, and are known to publish unusual, edgy works.

"Akashic Books is a Brooklyn-based independent company dedicated to publishing urban literary fiction and political non-fiction by authors who are either ignored by the mainstream, or who have no interest in working within the ever-consolidating ranks of the major corporate publishers."

Erotic Titles: *Kamikaze Lust* by Lauren Sanders, *The Fuck-Up* by Arthur Neresian

Alyson Publications
6922 Hollywood Blvd.
Suite 1000
Los Angeles, CA 90028
http://www.alyson.com
Editor-in-chief: Angela Brown
Editor: Nick Street
Alyson publishes books related to the lesbian, gay, bisexual, and transgender community, and is starting to also branch out into general erotic fiction. They publish approximately 50 titles a year, aimed at both men and women, as well as non-sex related nonficition and fiction of interest to the GLBT community.

According to the publisher, "Alyson Publications is the leading publisher of books by, for, and about lesbians, gay men, and bisexuals from all economic and social segments of society and of all ages, from children to adults. In fiction and nonfiction format, Alyson books explore the political, legal, financial, medical, spiritual, social, and sexual aspects of gay, lesbian, and bisexual life and the contributions to and experiences in society of our community."

Alyson considers queries only for books with gay, lesbian, and/or bisexual themes. No unsolicited manuscripts. "Each query will be reviewed and a response sent to you within two to four months of its receipt. Please do not call to check on the status of your submission." They do not consider individual short stories or poetry. To submit a short piece for an anthology, send an SASE to receive the latest guidelines for open anthologies and to be placed on the mailing list for future calls for submission. Many of the calls for submissions for anthologies are also posted on their website (click on the "Call for Submissions" section on the bottom of the page).

Erotic Titles: *Musclebound* by Christopher Morgan, *Skin Deep*, *My First Time* edited by Jack Hart

Anchor Books (Doubleday)
Division of Random House.
1540 Broadway
New York, NY 10036
http://www.randomhouse.com/anchor/
This general trade publisher does occasional upscale erotic books and anthologies for the general bookstore market. Submissions are best made through an agent.

Erotic Titles: *On A Bed of Rice* edited by Geraldine Kudaka

Arcturus Publishing
Unit 26
151-153 Bermondsey St.
London SE1 3HA
ENGLAND
(44)(0)2074079600
Fax: (44)(0)2074079444
info@stopwatch.co.uk
Arcturus Publishing is a general interest publisher that accepts erotica. Query with a SASE and include a proposal package, an outline, and one sample chapter.

Arsenal Pulp Press
103-1014 Homer Street
Vancouver BC V6B 2W9
CANADA
(604) 687-4233
Fax: (604) 687-4283
contact@arsenalpulp.com
http://www.arsenalpulp.com
Publisher: Brian Lam
Arsenal Pulp Press is an independent Canadian publisher, well-known for its books on cultural studies, regional titles, gay and lesbian titles, and cookbooks. They have two ongoing series of gay and lesbian short erotica, and have published other literary titles—both fiction and verse—with erotic content, including Michele Davidson's pansexual anthology of sex in public spaces, *Exhibitions*. They only consider man-

uscripts by Canadian writers. Anthologies are exceptions and welcome submissions from anywhere in the world. They are not considering poetry manuscripts at this time.

"Submissions should include a covering letter, a synopsis of the work, and a sample (fifty to sixty pages is usually enough). If our editorial board is interested, you will be asked to send the entire manuscript. We will try to respond within three months of receiving your material. We do not accept submissions by fax or email, and we do not have sufficient time to discuss concepts over the phone."

Erotic Titles: *Exhibitions* edited by Michele Davidson, *Quickies 1-3* edited by James C. Johnstone, *Hot & Bothered 1-4* edited by Karen X. Tulchinsky

Artemis Creation Publishing
100 Chatham E.
West Palm Beach, FL 33417-1817
President and acquisitions editor: Shirley Oliveira
Artemis Creation Publishing publishes four titles per year for the FemSuprem Books imprint, trade paperbacks, and original mass market paperbacks. Pays 50% royalty on retail sales for eBooks.

Seeking nonfiction with strong feminine archetypes on various topics, including sex. Submit with SASE: an outline, three sample chapters, an author bio, and a marketing plan. They are also seeking erotic fiction. Submit a synopsis with a SASE.

Atria Books
1230 Avenue of the Americas
New York, NY 10020
http://www.simonsays.com/
Division of Simon and Schuster that has published books by African-American erotica phenomenon Zane and others. A general trade publisher, their forays into erotica are few and far between.

Only accepts submissions by literary agents.
Erotic Titles: *Getting Buck Wild: Sex Chronicles II* by Zane

Atta Girl Press
Box 422458
San Francisco, CA 94142-2458
http://www.attagirlpress.com
Publisher: Gina Gatta
Editor-in-chief: Krandall Kraus
This independent publisher devoted to queer fiction is funded in part by Damron, the well-known gay travel guide publisher. Atta Girl published the Lambda Literary Award-winning erotica collection *See Dick Deconstruct* by Ian Philips. They have also taken over the anthology series

Men on Men now re-titled M2M. They are not currently seeking submissions, with the exception of literary short stories by and about the gay male experience for the M2M anthology series.
Erotic Titles: *See Dick Deconstruct* by Ian Philips

Aunt Lute Books
PO Box 410687
San Francisco, CA 94141
http://www.auntlute.com
Acquisitions Editor: Shahara Godfrey
Aunt Lute is a multicultural, feminist, women's press that focuses largely on social justice issues, but has published some erotica such as *Junglee Girl* by Gina Kumani.
"We seek to cultivate and build new bodies of thought and understanding about and between women. The priority of our culturally diverse staff is to publish work by women not traditionally served by mainstream publishers, particularly works by women of color. Our editing process is necessarily sensitive to the perspectives/voices/truths of the women with whom we work. We only accept poetry if it is submitted as part of a larger body of work or an edited anthology. If you wish to submit your manuscript, please send a cover letter, synopsis, a table of contents and two sample chapters of your work (or approximately 50 pages). Do not send queries or manuscripts by email. Please do not send manuscripts by certified mail or return receipt requested."
Erotic Titles: *Junglee Girl* by Gina Kumani

Baycrest Books
P.O. Box 2009
Monroe, MI 48161
submissions@baycrestbooks.com
http://www.baycrestbooks.com
CEO/Publisher: Nadine Meeker, CEO/publisher
Senior editor: Susan Carr
Baycrest Books publishes three titles per year on various topics, including erotica. Their focus is on trade paperback original works, the majority from first time authors. Submit a proposal package with a synopsis of your book.

Bearpaw Publishing
9120 Thorton Rd. #343
Stockton, CA 95209
(888)266-5704
Fax: (209)951-7284
stories@bearpawpublishing.com
http://www.bearpawpublishing.com

Owner: Jiana Behr

Bearpaw Publishing publishes fiction on various topics, including erotica, but the focus must be on gay, lesbian, and transgendered characters and issues.

Submit complete manuscript with SASE.

Erotic Titles: *Cost of Love* by Alexis Rogers

Beeline Books

Originally at http://www.beelinebooks.com, Beeline Books is no longer publishing. They were once the publisher of a line of pornographic books that included titles such as *Diary of a Divorced Slut* and *Sex Secrets*.

Bella Books
PO Box 10543
Tallahasse FL 32303
http://www.bellabooks.com
Editor: Linda Hill

Bella Books is the successor to popular lesbian fiction publisher Naiad Press, known for its line of lesbian romance novels. Since taking over, they have largely focused on publishing the same type of romances Naiad was famous for, which feature various kinds of lesbian love stories, usually of the vanilla variety, though *Back To Basics: A Butch/Femme Erotic Reader*, edited by Therese Szymanski, may buck that trend.

"We publish romance, mystery/thriller, sci-fi/fantasy, erotica, and general lesbian fiction. We are interested in novels with a solid plot and engaging, fully realized characters. The main characters must be lesbians and the story must be credible. The manuscript can be 50,000 to 80,000 words. Please send a cover letter, a précis, and a self-addressed, stamped envelope to the above address. The cover letter should very briefly describe your book, including the title and word count, and contain a biographical sketch of yourself. The précis should include a detailed outline of the plot and some information about all of the main characters." Bella will contact you if they are interested in reading the full manuscript.

Erotic Titles: *Back to Basics: A Butch-Femme Erotic Reader*

Bi Press
PO Box 10048
London SE15 4ZD
UNITED KINGDOM
diversity33@hotmail.com
http://kcl.bi.org/bipress.html

This extremely small British publisher specializes in bisexual titles.

Does not currently accept book proposals, but does accept submissions for current anthologies. See website for the most up-to-date submission details.
Erotic Titles: *Unlimited Desires*

Black Lace Books
Virgin Books Ltd
Thames Wharf Studios
London W6 9HA
UNITED KINGDOM
http://www.blacklace-books.co.uk
Editor: Kerri Sharp
Black Lace, the women's erotic imprint of Virgin Books, features some of the most detailed submission guidelines you'll find. They have created a very successful formula (the series has sold over 4 million books and counting) and prospective writers should consult carefully the details on house style, themes, etc. laid out in the complete guidelines, which are available on their website. We include a few pertinent highlights below. As with any series imprint like this, reading a few of the books is the best way to get a feel for tone and style. Black Lace primarily publishes erotic novels by and for the enjoyment of heterosexual women, leaning toward the kinkier side of the spectrum. They do also accept short stories for a series of anthologies (see entry for Wicked Words in the anthology series section).

Important note: Black Lace accepts submissions from female authors only, no exceptions.

"A Black Lace novel should be between 70,000 and 80,000 words long. What we want to see in the first instance is a paragraph explaining what the novel is about, a full synopsis of the story (about 1,000 words) and about 10,000 words (usually the first couple of chapters) of finished text. We do not accept proposals as emails.

"You cannot earn a living writing for Black Lace. However, your book should earn you approximately £2000 in total (including your advance, which will be in the region of £1000–£1500 (paid half on signature of contract, half on publication). Royalties are paid biannually. Any foreign rights sales will be in addition to these sums."

While the Black Lace backlist is almost 40% historical settings, they are moving away from this now. "We don't have a block on historical stories, but they should be startlingly original and/or exceptionally perverse. We are unlikely to commission more than two per year. The paranormal is a difficult area, too. When it comes to contemporary settings, please try to avoid the following: women's health clubs/hotels 'with a difference'; luxury yachts; fantasy islands; impossibly wealthy suitors (i.e. Arab princes); fetish nightclubs; masked balls; sex shops or the sex industry; and sex as therapy. Stories about 'swinging' or the 'mile-high club' are as passé as it gets. We like writing styles and characters that are full of attitude, and we prefer a narrative voice that has more in common with hardboiled or pulp fiction than 'sensual romance'. Black Lace books must keep pace with the developments in popular fiction. We want an upbeat, contemporary flavour to the writing, and central female characters who are culturally clued-up, streetwise, adventurous and don't suffer fools gladly. Black Lace girls should kick ass! The erotica-buying public is practically unshockable these days, and would rather a cock was called a cock than 'a pulsing rod of desire'. I would also like to put an end to descriptions of sex acts where the anatomical detail is so thorough that you can't see the wood for the trees. What's going on in the characters' heads is usually more arousing than prolonged close-up detail of every millimetre of their genitals. Pull back occasionally; remember that dirty dialogue and more basic and clear descriptions have a place, too. 'Sexually explicit' need not mean 'the minutiae of genital anatomy'. For instance, a common female fantasy is having sex with a stranger on a train. What's arousing about it is the situation, and not the exact length, color and consistency of the guy's cock. A hypothetical 'worst case' example would be something like:

'He moved his erection to her genital lips and then parted the inner folds of her labia to insert a finger in the core of her vulva. He then flexed the second finger of his left hand so as to produce sexual lubricant from her vaginal walls. He enjoyed the swell of his own shaft's engorgement while he stimulated her in the G-spot area'.

"See what I mean? It's explicit but it's so not sexy. We know how the plumbing works. Try to use words that are in common currency, too. People do not think about their 'glans' and 'labia' when they're horny. In fact, you'll have a job finding a guy who has ever said 'glans'. Also, when describing genitals, be sparing with the modifiers. Not every clit or cock has to be 'engorged' and 'pulsating'. Also, we want to take the 'YUK' factor out of Black Lace sex scenes. Our readers do not want endless references to 'sopping vaginas' and 'semen-filled cunts'. Please, a little more decorum!

"Our readers do like to read about experimental sex, about SM, bondage, spanking, fetishism, dressing up, and sex in unusual places. And this stuff should be fun for all concerned. If you do not understand the difference between consensual SM and sexual violence, please do not submit your story to Black Lace. We will not publish a novel that suggests women enjoy being subjugated to men outside of sexual role-play."

Erotic Titles: *Sweet Thing*, *Stormy Haven*, *Valentina's Rules*, *Strictly Confidential*, *In The Flesh*, *Cooking Up A Storm*, *Sticky Fingers*, *Odalisque*, *Shameless*, *Coming up Roses*, *Noble Vices*, *A Multitude of Sins*, *King's Pawn*

Blue Moon Books
Avalon Publishing Group
245 West 17th Street, 11th floor
New York, NY 10011-5300
(212) 981-9919
Fax: (646) 375-2571
http://www.avalonpub.com
Editor: Andrew Merz
Blue Moon, a division of Avalon Publishing Group, publishes a wide range of erotic fiction, including much fetish and BDSM work, in both mass-market and/or trade paperback editions. Their books are primarily heterosexual in nature, and include reprints of many classic erotica titles, as well as numerous books by "Anonymous." They primarily publish novels, although they have also published anthologies of short stories or erotic non-fiction. They do not want to receive unsolicited manuscripts but do not offer guidelines. We suggest you read some of their books to see whether they're right for your work, then query with a synopsis.
Erotic Titles: *Caning Able* by Stan Kent, *Incognito* by Lisabet Sarai, *Sacred Exchange* by Lisabet Sarai

Boheme Press
No longer publishing. Boheme Press was a small Canadian publisher, originally at http://www.bohemeonline.com.

Broadway Books
Division of Random House
1540 Broadway
New York, NY 10036
http://www.randomhouse.com/broadway/
This general trade publisher does publish the occasional erotic title and is best approached through an agent.
Erotic Titles: *Eat Me* by Linda Jaivin, *Nerve: Literate Smut* Anthology

Brown Skin Books
PO Box 46504
London N1 3YA
UNITED KINGDOM
(44) 020 7226 4789
info@brownskinbooks.co.uk
http://www.brownskinbooks.co.uk
Managing director: Vastiana Belfon
Length 75-90,000 words for novels, 6,000-10,000 words for short stories.
From the guidelines: "Brown Skin Books erotic fiction is written by

women of color, specifically for the modern woman of color. This means that the heroine is likely to be a strong dynamic, intelligent woman of color, probably based in the UK, Europe, the US, Canada, the Caribbean or Africa.

"Whether contemporary or historical, the plot, characters and settings should be based in a reality that will be recognizable to women of color. This does not rule out fantasy, which could form the basis of the novel/story, but that fantasy needs to have resonance with women of color.

"The novels/stories will be sensual, sexy and erotic, but not sleazy. They will need to be driven by plot and character—i.e. they need to have a 'good story' and strong, intriguing characters. Formulaic, repetitive sex will soon become a turn-off. The plots, across the series, will represent the broadest possible range of lifestyles and viewpoints. The books may well have serious, thought-provoking, innovative or controversial points to make about life, sex, sexuality, desire etc, but they do not all have to be too serious. Humor could well be an important element. The aim of the series is to explore various aspects of female sexuality in a way that our readers will find interesting, possibly informative, but, at the same time, entertaining.

"Authors need to write about what they know—whether sex, settings, fantasies—or else do extensive research.

"Erotic fiction really does need to be fiction. We (publisher and writers) do not wish to run the risk of being sued. Changing names or adding 'any resemblance to persons living or dead is purely coincidental' would be no protection in a court of law.

"While we would hope not to censor our authors, we are not publishing hard-core porn and would not wish to publish anything that would degrade women, be illegal, or offend our readership. Generally, that means that sexual acts will be consensual, will not involve minors, violence, force, brutality or any form of coercion, including drugs and alcohol.

"We are publishing erotic fiction that women of color will enjoy reading. So, we hope that our authors enjoy writing!

Send a synopsis (no more than one A4 sheet) of novel along with a sample chapter (around 10,000 words) or a few pages of your story (around 2,000 words).

"Email submissions accepted."

Pays an advance of £1,500 for novels, plus a share of royalties on all subsidiary rights sales. Short stories pay between £150 and £200 each.

"There are many reasons why our authors might choose to write anonymously and with Brown Skin Books, you may publish under a pseudonym. We will respect confidentiality."

Erotic Titles: *Scandalous* by Angela Campion, *Hot Chocolate*

Bullock Publications
jfb24@dana.ucc.nau.edu
Publisher: Judith F. Bullock
This new publisher of lesbian erotica has produced one anthology, *Delicate Friction*, and its future is unknown. Contact the publisher via email to find out the latest news and submission guidelines. Do not send attachments.

Carroll & Graf Publishers
Avalon Publishing Group
245 West 17th Street, 11th floor
New York, NY 10011-5300
(646) 375-2570
Fax: (646) 375-2571
http://www.carrollandgraf.com
Carroll & Graf, an imprint of the Avalon Publishing Group, was established in 1982 in New York City and publishes a combination of original and reprinted fiction and nonfiction. Their Mammoth Book series produced in co-edition with UK publisher Constable Robinson has included various erotica titles, many edited by Maxim Jakubowski, which have featured many popular erotic authors, including Anne Rice. Currently, the Mammoth series is doing a Mammoth Best Erotica of the Year volume (see: anthology series section). Carroll & Graf also publish occasional other erotic titles, including both novels and anthologies. They do not provide guidelines.
Erotic Titles: *Mammoth Book of Erotica* series edited by Maxim Jakubowski, *Mammoth Book of Illustrated Photography* edited by Maxim Jakubowski and Marilyn Jaye Lewis, *Mammoth Book of Gay Erotica* edited by Lawrence Schimel, *Tart Tales* by Carolyn Bank

Cellar Door Publishing, LLC
3439 NE Sandy Blvd. Suite 309
Portland, OR 97232-1959
info@cellardoorpublishing.com
http://www.cellardoorpublishing.com
Publisher: Jade Dodge
Cellar Door Publishing, LLC specializes in illustrated stories and graphic novels. They publish originals in hardcover, trade paperback, and electronic formats on a variety of topics, including erotica. Manuscript guidelines are on their website. Send queries with a SASE to the "Submissions Department." Per their website, your proposal package should include: "Cover letter introducing yourself, one page synopsis, brief character bios, two chapters of manuscript for literary submissions, 10-15 pages for graphic novel submissions, and artwork (if applicable). If your manuscript is not completed, include information

on the estimated time for completion in your cover letter. We attempt to respond to all submissions, but, due to the large amount of submissions we receive, we cannot guarantee you will receive a response. If it has been over a month since your submission and you have not received a response, you can email us at info@ cellardoorpublishing.com and ask about the status of your submission."

Chapultepec Press
4222 Chambers
Cincinatti, OH 45223
(513)681-1976
chapultepecpress@hotmail.com
http://www.tokyoroserecords.com
Acquisitions: David Garza
Chapultepec Press is a general purpose publisher that accepts erotic fiction with a majority of their titles coming from first time authors. Submissions should include a proposal package with a synopsis and two to three sample chapters, as well as artwork samples.

Chimera Publishing Ltd.
PO Box 152
Waterlooville
Hampshire PO8 9FS
UNITED KINGDOM
info@chimera-online.co.uk
http://www.chimerabooks.co.uk
Chimera is a British publisher which specializes in fetish and BDSM novels, especially spanking, caning, corporal punishment and bondage. Because of their specific interests, it is important to closely follow their detailed guidelines, available on their website. We include here some important excerpts: "Your novel should contain a plot built around males/some females dominating the central submissive female character(s). The story needs to contain S&M, bondage and CP [Corporal Punishment -ed] (all of a sexual and not violent and spiteful nature). For the CP we are looking for caning and spanking, but be careful, as a heroine stumbling from one beating to the next is physically unrealistic, and can become monotonous. These themes should be used as integral ingredients of the plot and to enhance imaginative and exciting sex using varied methods, clothing, toys/implements and settings.

"All sex must be consensual. Although the required theme is one of domination and submission, be careful not to step over the line into the realms of rape. This and the hatred of women are not acceptable whatsoever. No bestiality. No underage sex. No incest. No 'golden rain.' No branding. No sexual acts that can cause bloodshed, physical damage, or emotional anguish. We do not publish short stories, although we may consider a compilation of short stories. The finished novel should be 75,000 to 80,000 words in length, and in the first instance we require three chapters and a full synopsis."

Detailed guidelines on preparing manuscripts for submission are available online.

Erotic Titles: *Fantasies of a Young Submissive* by Rosaleen Young, *Under a Stern Reign* by Raymond Wilde, *Obliged to Bend* by B.A. Bradbury

Chippewa Publishing LLC
678 Dutchman Dr. #3
Chippewa Falls, WI 54729
submissions@chippewapublishing.com
http://www.chippewapublishing.com
Executive managing editor: Kimberly Burton

Nearly half of Chippewa Publishing's titles come from first time authors. This publisher covers many topics, but specializes in shocking their audience with dark romance, horror, science fiction, fantasy, and erotica. Chippewa Publishing's focus is increasingly on ePublishing, although they are still publishing in print as well.

Extremely detailed guidelines for submitting manuscripts and files are online. We suggest reading them in their entirety and following them closely. Submit complete manuscripts.

Erotic Titles: *Sexual Feeding* by Alyssa Brooks, *My Master's Chamber* by Emy Naso and JJ Giles

Chronicle Books
85 Second Street, Sixth Floor
San Francisco, CA 94105
http://www.chroniclebooks.com

Chronicle Books are known for their very stylish designs and highly-visual books and other paper products (notebooks, calendars, etc.), and are especially known for offbeat or whimsical subjects and presentations. They publish a diverse list that includes the bestselling *Worst Case Scenario* guidebook series, *The Bad Girl* guides by Cameron Tuttle, regional guidebooks, cookbooks, books for children, and many other types of titles. They have published a collection of Nerve.com photography amongst other sex-related books, such as *The Worst Case Scenario Guide to Love and Sex*. For submissions send: "a proposal, including outline, introduction, illustrations list, sample captions, and text/sample chapters (approximately 30 pages of text). A market analysis of the potential readership for the book, including title, publisher, and date of all similar books, with an explanation of how your book differs from each. Author/illustrator/photographer biography, including publishing credits and credentials in the field." Address the packet to "Chronicle Books - Adult Trade Division." They do not accept online submissions. See their guidelines on their website for more details on submission.

Erotic Titles: *Nerve: The New Nude*, *Going Down: Great Writing On Oral Sex*, *Hot & Steamy: Erotic Baths for Two*, *The Body: Photographs of the Human Form*

Citadel Press
850 Third Avenue
New York, NY 10022
(212) 407-1500
http://www.kensingtonbooks.com/

This imprint of larger publisher Kensington Press has published several books by Claudia Varrin about the fetish and BDSM arenas. Like Kensington, there are no specific guidelines.

Erotic Titles: *A Guide To New York's Fetish Underground* by Claudia Varrin, *The Art of Sensual Female Dominance: A Guide for Women* by Claudia Varrin, *Erotic Surrender: The Sensual Joys of Female Submission* by Claudia Varrin.

Cleis Press
P.O. Box 14684
San Francisco, CA 94114
(415) 575-4700 or (800) 780-2279
Fax: (415) 575-4705
http://www.cleispress.com
Editor: Frederique Delacoste

Cleis Press is a frequent publisher of erotica, primarily via several annual series such as *Best Women's Erotica*, *Best Lesbian Erotica*, and *Best Gay Erotica*. Having begun as a women's press with a strong lesbian focus, they have expanded to also include gay male titles and now are even branching into distinctive heterosexual erotica (usually with a strong fetish element) such as the reprint of *Carrie's Story* by Molly Weatherfield. They are especially known for ground-breaking transgender politics titles, such as the anthologies *Switch Hitters: Lesbians Write Gay Male Erotica and Gay Men Write Lesbian Erotica*, or *PoMoSexuals: Challenging Assumptions About Gender and Sexuality*, both co-edited by Carol Queen and Lawrence Schimel, *Body Alchemy* by Loren Cameron, *I Am My Own Woman* by Charlotte van Mahlsdorf, and various collections by Patrick Califia-Rice. Cleis also publishes sexual how-to books such as *The Good Vibrations Guide to Sex* or various titles in their the Ultimate Guide series (*The Ultimate Guide to Anal Sex for Women* by Tristan Taormino, *The Ultimate Guide to Strap-On Sex* by Karlyn Lotney, etc.).

"We publish 20 new books each year and receive over 400 manuscripts and query submissions annually. We also accept unsolicited manuscripts, as well as manuscripts not represented by agents. Please do not send poetry, resumes, or recommendation letters."

Cleis Press maintains an email announcement list to send out calls for submissions to erotic anthologies. See the website submissions page for more details.

Erotic Titles: *Best Lesbian Erotica* series edited by Tristan Taormino, *Best Gay Erotica* series edited by Richard Labonte, *Best Women's Erotica* series edited by Marcy Sheiner, *Best Fetish Erotica* edited by Cara Bruce, *Best Bondage Erotica* edited by Alison Tyler, *The Good Vibrations Guide to Sex* by Anne Semans and Cathy Winks

Collective Publishing
PO Box 474
Fareham PO15 6WZ
UNITED KINGDOM
http://www.collectivepublishing.co.uk/

"We are an independent publisher. We publish paperback books of erotic short stories and welcome submissions from authors. The market we are targeting is both men and women. The main subject matter is heterosexual sex and girl-girl sex. We only accept submissions in the form of typed hardcopy (no disks or email attachments please). The length of the stories should be between 2,000 and 10,000 words (approx). Please include an s.a.e. with your submissions. Within each book the themes and storylines are varied, including stories containing heterosexual sex, girl-girl sex, group sex, soft-core bondage, domination etc. However, all stories need to include sex and erotica (and plenty of it!). As it is for the adult market, they should be very explicit.

"We would prefer that they also be contemporary. The payment we offer is £20.00 per 1,000 accepted words. This is based on a fee of £1,000 for a whole book. We have no submission deadlines, as we always need a regular supply of stories. It will help you to get an idea of the style of story we are looking for if you take a look in one of our books. Our later books, Erotica 3 and 4 are a better guide for writers than Erotica 1 and 2, as they have gone in a slightly different direction."

Erotic Titles: *Erotica 1: Bettina's Tales*, *Erotica 2: Bettina and Candy*, *Erotica 3: Bettina's Playtime*, *Erotica 4: Bettina's Strip and Tease*, *Bettina's Bedtime Stories*

Companion Press
Publisher: Steve Stewart
An independent publisher specialized in gay porn-related non-fiction books and gay erotic fiction. No longer publishing.

Conari Press
Red Wheel/Weiser
368 Congress St.
Boston, MA 02210
http://www.conari.com
Editor: Ms. Pat Bryce
Conari Press, an imprint of Red Wheel/Weiser, LLC, "seeks to be a

catalyst for profound change by providing enlightening books on topics ranging from relationships, personal growth, and parenting to women's history and issues, social issues, and spirituality." They publish many topics of interest to women and have ventured into the sex education field with Isadora Alman's *Doing It: Real People Having Really Good Sex.* They are unlikely to publish erotic fiction, but would rather incorporate sexuality into their mission as educators. If you can work some social justice or meaning into your work, the better your chances.

Erotic Titles: *Soulful Sex, Doing It: Real People Having Really Good Sex* by Isadora Alman

Crescent Moon Publishing
P.O. Box 393
Maidstone Kent ME14 5XU
UNITED KINGDOM
jrobinson@crescentmoon.org.uk
cresmopub@yahoo.co.uk
http://www.crescentmoon.org.uk/
Director: Jeremy Robinson
Crescent Moon Publishing prefers agented, established writers, and while they do accept erotic fiction, it is not their focus. Only work of the highest quality will be considered.

Query with a SASE. Submission package should include an outline, synopsis, and two sample chapters.

Daedalus Publishing
2807 W. Sunset Blvd
Los Angeles, CA 90026
(213) 484-3882
Fax: (213) 484-8677
info@daedaluspublishing.com
http://www.daedaluspublishing.com
Publisher: Race Bannon
This small publisher of BDSM fiction and nonfiction does not seem to have formal guidelines, but only publishes work dedicated to the intricacies of BDSM, including fiction, nonfiction, and memoir. They do state that "Daedalus is dedicated to continuing to publish cutting edge books on the subject of leathersex and other alternative sexual practices."

Erotic Titles: *Urban Aboriginals: A Celebration of Leathersexuality* by Geoff Mains, *The Compleat Slave* by Jack Rinella, *Carried Away: An S/M Romance* by david stein, *Chainmale 3SM* by Don Bastian

Delectus Books
27 Old Gloucester Street

London WC1N 3XX
UNITED KINGDOM
mgdelectus@aol.com
http://www.delectusbooks.co.uk
Publisher: Michael R. Goss
Publisher and book dealer of erotica, sexology, and curiosa. "We don't really have guidelines—but it does help if the submitter can write. Generally we reissue a lot of classic erotica but we do occasionally issue contemporary works—we do prefer the darker side though—kind of sex, satanism and rock n' roll. Our specialties include Erotica, Sexology, Psychology, Criminology, Anthropology, Folklore, Latin America, Drugs & Alcoholism, Occult, Surrealism, Symbolism, Decadence, 1890s, Horror, Gothic, Fantasy, Vampires, Politics, Social History etc."
Erotic Titles: *Scream, My Darling, Scream* by Angela Pearson

Down There Press
938 Howard Street, Suite 101
San Francisco, CA 94103
(415) 974-8985, ext 205
Fax: (415) 974-8989
downtherepress@excite.com
http://www.goodvibes.com
Editor: Leigh Davidson
Down There Press is the publishing arm of sexuality store Good Vibrations, founded by Joani Blank. Their books are sex-positive, and include both sexual nonfiction and erotica, basically anything that helps break down taboos about sexuality (a recent title, Still Doing It, includes first person essays about sex from people over 60). Other notable titles include *Femalia, The Cunt Coloring Book, Anal Pleasure and Health, Exhibitionism for the Shy, Sex Toy Tales*, and the *Herotica* series (see Annual Series section below). They publish only a few books per year and are highly selective. They do not primarily publish fiction, with the exception of some anthologies (check the Writing Wanted section on their website for a list of anthologies currently accepting submissions).
"Down There Press publishes sexual health and self-awareness titles for children and adults, emphasizing non-judgmental books that are innovative, lively and practical in both form and content. We're always on the lookout for good manuscripts, although our publishing schedule is limited. We prefer to receive book proposals, rather than entire manuscripts. We do not open email attachments. Please send a cover letter pitching the book, a table of contents, with descriptions of what's in each chapter, and a couple of sample chapters, representative of your writing. We'll usually respond within two to three months."
Erotic Titles: *Sex Spoken Here, First Person Sexual, Still Doing It, Exhibitionism*

for the Shy, *The Big Book of Masturbation: From Angst to Zeal*

ECW Press
2120 Queen Street East, Suite 200
Toronto ON M4E 1E2
CANADA
(416) 694-3348
Fax: (416) 698-9906
info@ecwpress.com
http://www.ecwpress.com
Publisher: Jack David
Poetry and Fiction editor: Michael Holmes
Non-fiction and Pop Culture editor: Jen Hale
ECW is a Canadian publisher focusing on popular culture that has explored sex in various areas, such as Sex Carnival by Bill Brownstein and *Good Girls Do: Sex Chronicles of a Shameless Generation* by Simona Chiose, both personal accounts of sexual endeavors mixed with social commentary. A playful tone is useful but not necessary, and as their guidelines note, there is room for variety amongst works ECW chooses to publish.

"We do accept unsolicited manuscripts, but a familiarity with ECW literary titles published in the last five years never hurts—and sometimes saves postage. We receive close to 1,000 submissions per annum and publish between eight and twelve, poetry and fiction and literary non-fiction combined. We don't do greeting card or doggerel, and are idiosyncratically picky about what kind of fiction we can stomach. We publish only Canadian-authored poetry, and dabble almost exclusively in Canadian-authored fiction: unless you're Don DeLillo or Martin Amis.... Response time? Between two weeks and four months, usually. (We hope for the former and apologize for the latter.)"

Erotic Titles: *Sex Carnival, Good Girls Do: Sex Chronicles of a Shameless Generation*

Éditions Logiques/Logical Publishing
7 Chemin Bates
Outremont, QC H2V 1AG
CANADA
(514)490-2700
Fax: (514)270-3515
E-Mail: logique@logique.com
President and general manager: Louis-Philippe Herbert
This general purpose publisher will only publish works in or translated from French. For erotic fiction, submit the complete manuscript.

Ellora's Cave Publishing, Inc.
1337 Commerce Dr. #13

Stow OH 44224
submissions@ellorascave.com
http://www.ellorascave.com
Editor: Raelene Gorlinsky, managing editor
Elora's Cave Publishing specializes in romantic fiction with erotic content. Although the topics may vary from Gothic to Western, the focus is sex.

Submissions should include a synopsis and three sample chapters. Send via email in RTF or Word .doc format.

Erotic Titles: *Down and Dirty, And Lady Makes Three*

eXtasy Books
P.O. Box 2146
Garibaldi Highlands, BC V0N 1T0
CANADA
(604) 898-9703
submissions@extasybooks.com
ZumayaPublishing@aol.com
http://www.extasybooks.com/
eXtasy is the erotic imprint of Zumaya Publications. They publish novels of at least 75,000 words, and also novellas of 20,000-40,000 words (which may be combined with others in books). Submissions should include cover letter, synopsis, length of manuscript, and the first five chapters (in RTF format; they prefer electronic submissions). Submission guidelines are on their webpage. They are currently not accepting submissions. Check their website for updates.

"Aim of books: To cause sexual arousal in reader. Frequent, varied sexual acts required. Kinky sexual practices are acceptable. Take care with humor—can undermine eroticism. Efficient use of words required to convey sex and story. Narrate sex acts through characters' perceptions. Stay in character's POV. Contemp settings are good for all readers. Historical settings such as Roman, Britain/18th century, are done to death. Avoid bodice-rippers. We'd like to see time travel, science fiction and paranormal.

"Favorite obsessions: SM, power games, sex in unusual places, clothes, bondage etc. The limits: Anything goes, except children (i.e. under 18, or flashbacks to childhood experiments), lasting physical damage, parent/child incest, and no bestiality. Kinky and 'rough' sex is fine as long as it's with the character's consent and enjoyment. No bondage that involves restriction around the neck or suffocation. Hold the euphemisms! Please try to refrain from using expressions such as 'the center of her womanhood'. We want to dust off the traces of romantic writing and aim for streamlined economical prose, which is more upbeat in pace and less meandering in description. Not less explicit, just less flowery. The erotica buying public is practically unshockable these days and would rather a cock was called a cock, than 'a pulsing rod of desire.' Please, no anatomical detail that is so thorough that you can't see the wood for the trees. We don't need a prolonged close-up detail of every millimeter of their genitals. Remember that dirty dialogue and more basic and clear descriptions have a place, too. For instance, a common female fantasy is having sex with a stranger on a bus or train. What's arousing about it is the situation, and not the exact length, color and consistency of the guy's cock. Avoid clichés or over-used scenarios, like Italian lovers wearing an Armani suit. Arabs... Native tribes people... Spanish lovers with names like Ramon, Juan and Raoul... Female characters with impossibly glitzy names."

Erotic Titles: *Ravished Wings*, *Sea Orphan*, *Cupid's Wicked Arrows*

Fairview Press
2450 Riverside Avenue
South Minneapolis, MN 55454
press@fairview.org
http://www.fairviewpress.org
Editor: Stephanie Billecke
Fairview publishes books on "family issues" and they have published some sexual self-help titles. They do not publish any fiction.

Erotic Titles: *Sex Smart* by Susan Browning Pogany, *The Underground Guide to Teenage Sexuality: An Essential Handbook for Today's Teens and Parents* by Michael J. Basso

Feral House
PO Box 39910
Los Angeles, CA 90039
submissions@feralhouse.com
http://www.feralhouse.com
"Please do not ask us to read novels, short stories, plays, screenplays, or poetry. We do not publish fiction. But if a personal obsession has caused you to investigate a fascinating piece of history or cultural phenomenon, we'd be interested to hear about it. Email a profile of your project, its intended audience, a table of contents and sample chapter to submissions@feralhouse.com." Prefers text email. If you must send an a file attachment, make it a PDF file.

Erotic Titles: *The X-Rated Bible* by Ben Edward Akerly, *Sexuality, Magic and Perversion* by Francis King

Firebrand Books
2232 South Main Street #272
Ann Arbor, MI 48103
(248) 738-8202
Fax: 248-738-7786

http://www.firebrandbooks.com/
Publisher: Karen Oosterhous
Independent feminist publishing house focused on literary fiction by women, primarily novels. They have one overtly erotic title on their backlist, a collection of lesbian stories by Kitty Tsui.

Per the submission guidelines on their website, "Firebrand Books is an award-winning press dedicated to publishing high quality work. We have a very selective but open submissions policy. We are currently accepting submissions of fiction and non-fiction. We are not accepting poetry. Please send a one page query letter describing your work. Include a bio and information about the potential audience. Include a self-addressed stamped envelope and we will respond within 90 days."

Erotic titles: *Breathless* by Kitty Tsui

First Tribe Books
5632 Van Nuys Blvd. #337
Van Nuys, CA 91401
(818) 693-6757
editor@firsttribebooks.com
http://www.firsttribebooks.com
"Query letter first, please. Looking for erotic literature, short stories, novels, essays, poetry, illustrated fiction and comix. FTB stories are less about the mechanics of sex, more about the philosophies of sex. Think Emmanuelle Arsan, Robert Rimmer and Anais Nin and you'll be on the right track to getting your story published with us."

Flowers In Bloom Publishers
P.O. Box 473106
Brooklyn, NY 11247
nanceyflowers@msn.com
http://www.nanceyflowers.com
Editor: Nancey Flowers Wilson
This independent publisher of African-American erotic works has published novels written by and anthologies edited by owner Nancey Flowers. Not accepting submissions; query for future anthologies.

Erotic Titles: *Twilight Moods*

Gay Men's Press
Spectrum House
32-34 Gordon House Road
London NW5 1LP
UNITED KINGDOM
http://www.millivres.co.uk/gmp
Publisher: Kathleen Bryson
Part of the Millivres Group, primarily publishes fiction by and for

gay men. See Zipper Books and Prowler Books entries for erotic imprints in the Millivres Group.

GMP prefers hardcopy submissions, requesting a synopsis and sample chapters. "We need to see at least 10,000 words in order to judge fairly a proposal and, in the case of short stories, we need to see the collection in its entirety."

Gay Sunshine Press/Leyland Publications
PO Box 410690
San Francisco, CA 94141
(415) 626-1935
Fax: (415) 626-1802
castrodreams@eudoramail.com
http://www.gaysunshine.com
Publisher: Winston Leyland

One of the earliest gay presses in the US, founded in 1975, Gay Sunshine and Leyland Publications have published many gay erotic titles over the decades, especially thematic anthologies, often with military settings, as well as the occasional single-author collection or erotic novel. They published many of the Boyd Straight to Hell collections, and are also the publishers of the erotic gay comix anthologies, Meatmen.

Authors must query with a SASE. All unsolicited manuscripts will be returned unopened.

Erotic Titles: Meatmen
Website is currently NOT responding, 12/18/2005.

Genesis Press
1213 Hwy 45 N.
Columbus, MS 39705
(888) 463-4461
Fax: (662) 329-9399
books@genesis-press.com
http://www.genesis-press.com

African-American publisher which publishes upscale erotic romance under its Indigo After Dark imprint. Primarily interested in erotica by women, and all books must feature African-American or multi-cultural characters. "Do not use offensive language in your descriptions or dialogue. The occasional use of a cuss word is allowed when emphasizing a climactic point. It must be very tastefully done and its use limited. Do not submit any S&M, 'golden showers,' mutilation, bestiality, pedophilia, or homosexuality between men."

Query with synopsis and first three chapters. Make sure to indicate if it's a multiple submission (acceptable with notification). Detailed guidelines at their website.

Erotic Titles: *Indigo After Dark, volume 1*

Goofy Foot Press
PO Box 1719
Waldport OR 97394-1719
(310) 563-7550
Fax: (310) 563-7551
bigbang@pioneer.com
http://www.goofyfootpress.com
Not currently accepting submissions.
Erotic Titles: *The Guide to Getting It On* by Paul Joannides, *The Guide to Great Dates* by Paul Joannides

Green Candy Press
601 Van Ness Ave, E3-918
San Francisco, CA 94102
editorial@greencandypress.com
http://www.greencandypress.com
Green Candy Press is a small press that publishes gay fiction and non-fiction, often with strong sexual or erotic content, as well as fetish tales such as *I Was For Sale: Confessions of a Bondage Model* by Lisa B. Falour.
Complete guidelines are online. "Submissions may be sent via e-mail or regular mail (on a Zip disk). Please provide a self-addressed stamped envelope for regular mail submissions if you would like your work returned to you. Complete manuscripts will require a longer response time. We suggest that you submit a synopsis, table of contents, and sample of your work first."
Erotic Titles: *I Was For Sale*, *The Sperm Engine* by Stephen Greco, *Wild Animals I Have Known*, *Fetish Fashion: Undressing the Corset*

Greenery Press
4200 Park Blvd., PMB 240
Oakland, CA 94602
http://www.greenerypress.com
Editor: Janet Hardy
Greenery has published many BDSM how-to books, such as *The Bottoming Book* or *S/M 101*, and books on specific fetish topics such as flogging or spanking. Their motto: "reading for the sexually adventurous." They also have a fiction imprint, Grass Stain Press, though they aren't currently accepting submissions. Check their website for information about current titles and calls for submissions.
"Your best bet for selling a book to us is to develop a well-written and well-organized how-to book on some aspect of human sexuality, preferably an aspect that has not been extensively written about in the past. We prefer books between 30,000 and 80,000 words in length, although we have accepted books which are both longer and shorter. We like books with a distinct authorial voice and a touch of humor. We

insist on an extremely responsible stance on issues of consent and safety.

"Do not send us complete manuscripts. Do not send manuscripts, queries or samples by e-mail. Send us an outline or synopsis plus two sample chapters, along with a cover letter explaining who you think would read your book and why. Please understand that we are a very small company and that our editorial staff is pressed for time. It may take several months or more for us to get back to you."

Erotic Titles: *The Ethical Slut, S/M 101*

Grove/Atlantic Press
841 Broadway, 4th Floor
New York, NY 10003-4793
(212) 614-7850
Fax: (212) 614-7886
http://www.groveatlantic.com

Grove/Atlantic, Inc. only accepts manuscripts through literary agents. They are a mainstream literary house with a diverse publications list, including Charles Frazier's Pulitzer-prize-winning novel *Cold Mountain*. They are also known for edgy, contemporary novels and short story collections, which has included some upscale erotica, such as Elissa Wald's collection *Meeting the Master*. Grove has lately been publishing a number of translations of erotic novels by Spanish or Latino writers, such as Almudena Grandes' *The Ages of Lulu*.

Erotic Titles: *Spanking the Maid, Meeting the Master, The Ages of Lulu*

Guernica Editions
Box 117
Station P
Toronto ON M5S 2S6
CANADA
(416) 658-9888
Fax: (416) 657-8885
guernicaeditions@cs.com
http://www.guernicaeditions.com

Editors: Antionio D'Alfonso, editor/publisher (poetry, nonfiction, novels) and Ken Scambray, editor (US reprints)

Guernica Editions is a general purpose publisher whose subjects include nonfiction sex and erotic fiction.

Authors must query with a SASE. All unsolicited manuscripts will be returned unopened.

Gutter Press
56 The Esplanade, Suite 503
Toronto, ON M5E 1A7

CANADA
Gutter@gutterpress.com
http://www.gutterpress.com
Gutter Press seeks submissions of cutting-edge, high-quality novels, and is open to erotic literary work. They publish almost exclusively Canadian authors.
Erotic Titles: *Diana: a diary in the second person* by Diane Savage

Harlequin Blaze
Harlequin Books/MIRA Books
225 Duncan Mill Road
Don Mills ON M3B 3K9
CANADA
http://www.eharlequin.com
Senior Editor & Editorial Coordinator: Ms. Brigit Davis-Todd
Publishing four books per month, Harlequin Blaze features sexier, longer contemporary romances than other Harlequin category romance imprints. Books are 70,000-75,000 words in length.
"Blaze will feature sensuous, highly romantic, innovative plots that are sexy in premise and execution. The tone of the books can run from fun and flirtatious to dark and sensual. Submissions should have a very contemporary feel—what it's like to be young and single in the new millennium. We are looking for heroes and heroines in their early 20s and up. There should be an emphasis on the physical relationship developing between the couple: fully described love scenes along with a high level of fantasy and playfulness. The hero and heroine should make a commitment at the end. Your manuscript should be told in the third person, primarily from the heroine's point of view. However, the hero's perspective may be used to enhance tension, plot, or character development. Unless otherwise noted, we do not accept unsolicited complete or partial manuscripts, but ask instead that you submit a query letter. The query letter should include a word count and pertinent facts about yourself as a writer, including your familiarity with the romance genre. Also include a synopsis of your story that gives a clear idea of both your plot and characters and is no more than two single-spaced pages."
Multiple submissions not accepted. Does accept unagented submissions. Helpful and detailed website provides submission guidelines.
Erotic Titles: *Fire and Ice, The Sex Files, The Sweetest Taboo*

Harpercollins
10 East 53rd Street
New York, NY 10022
(212) 207-7000
http://www.harpercollins.com

HarperCollins is a large mainstream publisher, which has published a handful of literary erotic titles, such as Michelle Slung's anthologies of women's erotica, *Fever and Slow Hand* and the erotic science fiction/fantasy anthology *Sirens and Other Daemon Lovers* edited by Ellen Datlow and Terri Windling. They do not accept unsolicited manuscripts. Only accepts work from agents.

Erotic Titles: *Black Feathers* by Cecilia Tan, *Slow Hand* edited by Michelle Slung

Hatala Geroproducts
P.O. Box 42
Greentop, MO 63546
editor@geroproducts.com
http://www.geroproducts.com
President: Mark Hatala, Ph.D.

Hatala Geroproducts specializes in works interesting to adults sixty years and older. They are seeking both non-fiction sex-related manuscripts and erotic fiction.

Query with a SASE. Your proposal package should include an outline and three sample chapters. Submission guidelines are on their website.

The Haworth Press, Inc.
10 Alice Street
Binghamton, NY 13904-1580
http://www.haworthpress.com
Managing Editor: Bill Palmer

Haworth Press is largely an academic publisher that has recently been making inroads in the gay and lesbian fiction market as well, including erotica, under the imprints Southern Tier and Alice Street Editions. They are known for non-fiction titles exploring sexuality, especially Steven Seeland's books focusing on gay sex in various branches of the military. They have also published a number of erotic anthologies, often a mix of fiction and essay, such as *Love Under Foot: A Celebration of Feet*, edited by Greg Wharton and M. Christian.

Submissions should include the following: working title of the proposal, professional vita or resume for all authors/editors, sample chapters (1 to 3, if possible), description of the work, descriptions of any competing works and how this new work is to differ from the earlier works, information on a target audience, approximate date when the final manuscript is projected to be completed, approximate size of the work in manuscript pages, table of contents with as many subheads as possible, and any other information which the proposer feels might be pertinent to making a decision on the work. Does not accept simultaneous submissions, multiple submissions, or electronic submissions. Guidelines for submission are on their website.

Erotic Titles: *Strategic Sex: Why They Won't Keep It In The Bedroom* edited by D. Travers Scott, *Between the Palms: A Collection of Gay Travel Erotica* edited by Michael T. Luongo, *Love Under Foot: An Erotic Celebration of Feet* edited by Greg Wharton and M. Christian

Holloway House Press Publishing Co.
8060 Melrose Ave.
Los Angeles, CA 90046
(323) 653-8060
Fax: (323) 655-9452
http://www.hollowayhousebooks.com/
Holloway House Press Publishing Company is seeking erotic fiction. Query with a SASE. Your proposal package should include a synopsis, outline, and two sample chapters.

Hunter House
PO Box 2914
Alameda CA 94501
(510) 865-5282
editorial@hunterhouse.com
http://www.hunterhouse.com
Hunter House publishes self-improvement titles, and is open to sexuality books that would be of interest to women, such as *Sex Tips & Tales* and Deborah Sundahl's *Female Ejaculation and The G Spot*. They do not publish fiction or autobiography.

"Personal growth topics that we are currently interested in are sexuality; partner and family relationships; and changing, evolutionary lifestyles. Successful titles provide step-by-step aids or a program to help readers understand and approach new perspectives on family issues or dynamics, celebrate their sexuality, and establish healthy, fulfilling lives that incorporate a planetary perspective. Examples include: *Sexual Pleasure; The Pleasure Prescription; Pocket Book of Foreplay;* and *Intellectual Foreplay.*"

Book proposals should include an overview; a chapter-by-chapter outline; an about the author(s) section; and marketing considerations. "If we are interested in pursuing your project further, we will request sample chapters. Please send only two to three sample chapters-not the whole manuscript. Each chapter should have one concept, subject, skill, or technique. Use main headings and subheadings so a reader can know at a glance where the chapter is going. To effectively teach an individual step of a process or technique, follow this sequence: state the rule or instruction first. Be clear and to the point. Then give an example of how someone else did this step. Finally, provide an exercise for the reader to perform. This gives the reader three ways to learn the technique: intellectually by precept, emotionally by example, and experientially by

doing." Submission guidelines are on their webstie.
Erotic Titles: *Sex Tips & Tales, G Spot, Sexual Pleasure*

Idol Books
Virgin Books Ltd
Thames Wharf Studios
London W6 9HA
UNITED KINGDOM
Editor: Kerri Sharp
Virgin's imprint for gay erotica publishes novels only, with a diverse range of contemporary and historical settings and location.
"An exploration of all aspects of homoerotic desire, Idol stories continue to mix romance with steamy sex and strong plots. They're sexy not sleazy, hot but not crude and, above all, the classiest and most seductive homoerotic fiction in print."
Erotic Titles: *Booty Boys, Chains of Deceit, Hard Time, Code of Submission, The Fellowship of Iron, Street Life, More and Harder, The Pheromone Bomb, To Serve Two Masters*

Kensington
850 Third Avenue
New York, NY 10022
(212) 407-1500
Fax: (212) 935-0699
http://www.kensingtonbooks.com
Editorial Director: John Scognamiglio
This general interest press has various lines that may be of interest to erotic writers, and is well-known for its romance publishing, including the chick-lit line of romances, *Strapless*. While not specializing in erotica per se, Kensington has published numerous sex manuals including Marcy Sheiner's *Sex for the Clueless*. They do not have any official guidelines, and having a literary agent is advised when trying to get in contact with them.
Erotic Titles: *Sex for the Clueless* by Marcy Sheiner, *Asian Secrets for Sexual Ecstasy, Back to Great Sex, Love, Sex and Magick, Sexicon, The Price of Pleasure*

Denis Kitchen Publishing Co., LLC
P.O. Box 2250
Amherst, MA 01004-2250
(413)259-1627
Fax: (413)259-1812
publishing@deniskitchen.com
http://www.deniskitchen.com
The Denis Kitchen Publishing Co. is a general purpose graphic novel publisher. They are seeking erotic fiction by cartoonists or writer/illus-

trator teams. They are not interested in text-only works, instead focusing on text and pictures. Query with a SASE. Include sample illustrations or comic pages.

Currently not accepting book submissions.

Last Gasp
777 Florida Street
San Francisco, CA 94110
(415) 824-6636
Fax: (415) 824-1836
http://www.lastgasp.com
Publisher: Ron Turner

Last Gasp is a publisher and distributor of books, comics, graphic novels, etc. Submission details on their website. Not currently accepting erotic writing submissions. Publishes English-language translations of European adult graphic novels under its Priaprism Press imprint.

Erotic Titles: *I Was A Teenage Dominatrix* by Shawna Kenney, *The Troubles of Janice*

Limitless Dare 2 Dream Publishing
100 Pin Oak Court
Lexington, SC 29073
LimitlessD2D@aol.com
http://www.limitlessD2D.net
Publisher: Samantha E. Ruskin and Anne Clarkson

Limitless Dare 2 Dream Publishing is a lesbian publisher, open to erotica of varying lengths, with shorter pieces being considered for collections of short stories. Also open to collections of erotic lesbian-themed poems. Absolutely no work which degrades or demeans women in any way, even if by other women. Prefers to see completed manuscripts, can be sent via email as attachments only (preferably in .doc format) or regular mail. Pays in royalty only.

"Previous publication is not particularly important to us as long as the story is good. We do feel we should add that, in our minds, there is erotica and there is RAUNCHY erotica. We do erotica. We do NOT do raunchy erotica. Please submit that elsewhere." Their website is offline as of this writing.

Erotic Titles: *Passion's Phrases* by Charlise Todd, *Plot? What Plot?* by Mavis Applewater

Lonely Planet Publications
Locked Bag 1
Footscray, Victoria 3011
AUSTRALIA
http://www.lonelyplanet.com

Lonely Planet publishes travel guides, but has started publishing novels and ventured into the world of sex with the travel erotica anthology *Brief Encounters: Stories of Love, Sex, and Travel*. Detailed submission guidelines online.

Erotic Titles: *Brief Encounters: Stories of Love, Sex, and Travel* edited by Michelle de Kretser

Ludlow Press
Ludlowpress@ludlowpress.com
http://www.ludlowpress.com
Publisher: Jun Da

Small independent press based out of New York looking for cutting-edge non-mainstream books. "The novels we go for have been called 'urban' books—'dirty realist'—literary and polished, but somewhat darker in tone, with unconventional, sometimes transgressive themes. The books so far have been geared to a younger crowd (ages 18-40) and around 40,000 words total."

Submissions should include a short description of the book and the first 50 pages. Per the website, "Literary erotica is fine, but there must be a psychological subtext." Ludlow Press expects authors to be actively involved in promotion.

"It's very hard to find a sexy, erotic novel that is literary at the same time. We'd love to find a good, sexy novel to work with." Submission guidelines are available on their website.

Magic Carpet Books
P.O. Box 473
New Milford, CT 06776
mariaisabelmissa@hotmail.com
RKASAK@aol.com
http://www.magic-carpet-books.com/
Publisher: Richard Kasak

This small publisher run by Richard Kasak, former head of Masquerade Books, publishes only erotic romances in trade paperback formats. Their books are distributed solely through Barnes & Noble stores nationwide. Books are approximately 70,000 words, and must be explicitly erotic, but stay 100% within the heterosexual romance formula of strong female characters, admirable male characters, no superfluous scenes or extra characters, no degrading sex. Only publishes books by women. Email a writing sample in Word format, Rich Text Format, or PDF.

Erotic Titles: *The ESP Affair* by Alison Tyler, *That Certain Someone* by Shauna Silverton, *Blue Valentine, When Hearts Collide* by Marilyn Jaye Lewis, *The Engagement* by Lucy Niles

Manic D Press
P.O. Box 410804
San Francisco, CA 94141
info@manicdpress.com
http://www.manicdpress.com
Contact: Jennifer Joseph
Manic D is a San Francisco alternative press, focusing on the spoken-word and performance poetry scene. Often works with local writers, such as Michelle Tea or Tarin Towers. Read at least one Manic D title for an idea of the tone of the kinds of books they publish. Note: they read submissions during the months of January and July ONLY. Writing and proposals sent any time other than these months will sit in a pile until the next reading time rolls around. For submissions, send 5-10 poems, 3-5 short stories, a synopsis and first chapter only for novels (do not send entire manuscript), or a complete copy of a graphic novel/visual art book.
Erotic Titles: *Bite Hard* by Justin Chin, *Depending on the Light* by Thea Hillman

Melcher Media
124 West 13th Street
New York, NY 10011
(212) 727-2322
Fax (212) 627-1973
greatbooks@melcher.com
http://www.melcher.com
Melcher is a packaging company that specializes in translating name brands like Harley Davidson or National Enquirer into book products, as well as genre-defying titles like *The Pop-Up Book of Phobias*. They have produced a handful of erotic titles such as the photo book *Voyeur*, the *Aqua Erotica* series edited by Mary Anne Mohanraj (printed on special water-proof paper) and a series of erotic choose-your-own-adventure stories. Projects are developed in house, and then they look for writers to develop them.
Erotic Titles: *Aqua Erotica* edited by Mary Anne Mohanraj, *The Classics Professor* by Michael Hemingson

Mystic Ridge Books
Subsidiary of Mystic Ridge Productions, Inc.
P.O. Box 66930
Albuquerque, NM 87193-6930
(505) 899-2121
http://www.mysticridgebooks.com
President: Richard Brown
Mystic Ridge Books publishes a variety of topics, including nonfic-

tion sex books and erotic fiction. Detailed submission guidelines online specify that prospective authors should only send a query letter, a complete list of chapters, and two or three sample chapters. The query letter should include a short resume of your experience as a writer, including a list of any and all books you have had published, an explanation of why you feel your book is unique in its genre AND marketable and sellable, the potential readership (including: the book's target audience, and your best estimate of its sales potential, with a mention of two or three books that are comparable), the category under which your book falls, a list of media outlets who you think might be interested in the book, how proactive you plan on being regarding getting publicity for your book, on your own (be as detailed as possible about how you would go about this), and any special qualifications you have for writing the book.

Do not submit unless your manuscript is already complete. Deviations from their guidelines will automatically disqualify you for consideration. Do not bother to submit unless you have read the guidelines and followed them to the letter.

Erotic Titles: *Baring It All*, edited by Layla Shilkret (nonfiction, women's erotica)

Mystic Rose Books
P.O. Box 1036/SMS
Fairfield, CT 06432
(203) 374-5057
Fax: (203) 371-4843
Writermol@aol.com
http://www.mysticrose.com
Contact: Molly Devon
Mystic Rose is a small publisher of BDSM fiction and nonfiction books, probably best known for Laura Antoniou's *The Marketplace Series* and Molly Devon and Phil Miller's *Screw the Roses, Send Me The Thorns, a BDSM primer.*

Erotic Titles: *Screw the Roses, Send Me the Thorns* by Molly Devon and Phil Miller, *To Love, To Obey, To Serve* by Vi Johnson, *The Marketplace* by Laura Antoniou, *The Academy* by Laura Antoniou

New Age Dimensions, Inc.
P.O. Box 772097
Coral Springs, FL 33077
(954) 345-5867
Fax: (574) 975-8112
query@newagedimensionspublishing.com
http://www.newagedimensionspublishing.com
Publisher/CEO: Melissa Alvarez

Senior Editor: Mimi Riser

New Age Dimensions is a general purpose publisher seeking non-fiction sex titles and erotic fiction. They publish electronic versions of their books first. Popular titles may be considered for print. Occasionally, books come out in both formats.

Their website contains detailed submission guidelines on topics such as: email queries, how to query, manuscript formatting instructions, manuscript considerations, word count guidelines, and cover art. Read the guidelines before considering submitting. For nonfiction, your proposal package should include an outline and three sample chapters. Electronic submissions in RTF or Word .doc format are accepted. For fiction, your proposal package should include a synopsis (or chapter-by-chapter outline) and three sample chapters. Include the book's ending in the synopsis. Query with a SASE on both topics.

Erotic Titles: *Ecstasy* by Chevon Gael, *Soulful Sex: Erotic Tales of Fantasy and Romance, volumes I and II* by Diana Laurence

New American Library
Penguin Putnam, Inc.
375 Hudson St.
New York, NY 10014
(212) 366-2000
Fax: (212) 366-2889
http://www.penguinputnam.com

New American Library is seeking erotic fiction but accepting agented submissions only. Occasionally, an imprint within the Penguin Group (USA) Inc. may consider unsolicited manuscripts. Check the website to determine whether the imprint you are pursuing is accepting unagented submissions.

Query with a SASE.

Erotic Titles: *Make Over Your Sex Life Tonight* by Susan Crain Bakos

New Concepts Publishing
4729 Humphreys Rd.
Lake Park, GA 31636,
http://www.newconceptspublishing.com
Editor-in-Chief: Madris Gutierrez
Senior Editor: Andrea DePasture
Associate Editor: Tiffany Ayers

New Concepts was one of the first electronic romance publishers, and continues to publish romances in a wide variety of genres, lengths, and levels of sexual explicitness, which they define as follows:

SWEET: behind-closed-doors sex and/or very mild love scenes and sexual encounters

SENSUAL: love scenes comparative to most romance novels published today

SPICY: heavy sexual tension; graphic details and more sexual encounters

CARNAL: graphic sex and language; may be offensive to delicate readers; contains many sexual encounters and can include unconventional sex not normally found in romance; may or may not be romance; typically known as erotica.

They only publish work that is heterosexual in nature and publish two erotic romance series:

"In a Dark Desire, the hero and/or heroine is someone who struggles with the dark, baser side of themselves. Their sexual appetites may run to the more extreme. There is an element of danger to these books. Their lives or their very souls are in danger of being consumed by their passions and obsessions. Tortured heroes are typical fare here but not a necessity to become a Dark Desire. Dominant heroes and/or heroines would definitely find their place here as would bondage, forced seduction, etc.

"A Carnal Pleasures book is the lighter side of the erotica coin. These books could contain humor and should have strong, believable heroes and heroines. The hero and/or heroine may or may not have a domineering type personality, however, their mate is always more than a match for them. A Carnal Pleasures book is most typically a normal romance, expanded into erotica."

Books should be a minimum of 60,000 words in length. Accepts email queries; present manuscripts in hardcopy.

They also publish erotic romances at novella lengths (20,000-39,000 words) in thematic anthologies (see website for current themes) and short stories (10,000-15,000 words) for their Love Bites series. Examples of some of their themes would include Dark and Dangerous featuring erotic romances mixed with the paranormal (vampires, werewolves, etc.) or Captured featuring erotic romances with settings such as Viking Raiders or Stolen Brides. For erotic romance anthologies, query with publishing history, detailed synopsis, and first ten pages to Andrea De Pasture.

Each editor is looking for particular types of work; below are excerpts from their comments to better help you address your work appropriately.

Madris Gutierrez, Editor-in-Chief

"I like romances that are filled with sexual tension that culminate, finally, in one or two really hot love scenes. For the most part, raw, raunchy sex does not appeal to me. As in real life, waiting is the essence of sexual tension and makes the culmination all the more explosive. We should see the two main characters coming closer, feeling a growing attraction both mentally and physically, in situations that provoke an intense physical response but won't allow for culmination, until finally the time and circumstances are right and the hero and heroine (and reader) share a soul shattering experience.

"At the moment I'm most particularly interested in acquiring Historical Romance. Storylines and/or situations that have high sensuality built into them would be of special interest as readers are also clamoring for hot/sexy novels. Bondage type stories, where the heroine is allowed to exploit sexual fantasies while still being 'innocent' seem to be the most highly desirable; i.e. Indian/Viking/Enemy captive; the secret lover; mistaken identity; arranged marriage, mail order bride and so forth."

Andrea DePasture, Senior Editor
"I am currently acquiring all genres to round out my list:

"HISTORICAL EROTIC ROMANCE: I have a love of history and would like to publish books that vibrantly bring the past to life for readers. I am interested in all time periods, including the shorter Regency romances (Regency period is a long time favorite for me) and Decades (1900-1970). I always enjoy a good medieval and am particularly interested in books set during time periods not frequently written about or set in unusual locales such as Russia, Germany, France, Caribbean, etc.

"PARANORMAL EROTICA: I love all things supernatural, having cut my teeth on horror when I first began reading as a child. Time travel, ghosts, reincarnation, vampires, shapeshifters, fairies, anything otherwordly—it's all vastly fascinating for me and for many a person, hence the rise of paranormal television shows, movies, and more. Erotic and sexually charged books in the vein of Laurell K. Hamilton are something I am on the particular lookout for."

Also open to Romantic Comedy, and Fantasy, and Science Fiction romances. "I have no interest in religious/inspiration/new age, politics or espionage, organized crime, or the drug trade. PEEVES: Excessive crudity—sexual or otherwise, overuse of semicolons (really, they don't need to be there at all), incorrect grammar and spelling, wimpy heroines, telling instead of showing, not following submission instructions."

Tiffany Ayers, Associate Editor
Is interested in, but not limited to, "romance, horror, paranormals, fantasy, and sci-fi. I enjoy different time periods and unusual settings. I pay little attention to what is politically correct. Real life is seldom so. Therefore, I would enjoy seeing a good old-fashioned civil war novel, if anyone out there has one."

Erotic Titles: *Cyborg* by Kaitlyn O'Connor, *Thief of Hearts* by Kimberly Zant

New Mouth From The Dirty South
828 Royal St. #248
New Orleans, LA 70116
(504) 598-4685
books@newmouthfromthedirtysouth.com
http://www.newmouthfromthedirtysouth.com
New Mouth From The Dirty South is an extremely small publisher who published the groundbreaking anthology *Gynomite: Fearless, Feminist Porn*, which featured unusual kinds of women's erotic writing. They are currently only accepting zines for their zine subscription service.
Erotic Titles: *Gynomite: Fearless, Feminist Porn* edited by Liz Belile

New Victoria
P.O. Box 27
Norwich, VT 05055-0027
(802) 649-5297
Fax: (802) 649-5297
queries@newvictoria.com
http://www.newvictoria.com
Editors: ReBecca Beguin and Claudia Lamperti
New Victoria publishes a small selection of lesbian nonfiction as well as lesbian fiction in a variety of genres, including erotica.
Send a SASE for manuscript guidelines. Submissions should include an outline, a synopsis, and sample chapters.

Nexus
Virgin Publishing Ltd.
Thames Wharf Studios
Rainville Road
London W6 9HA
UNITED KINGDOM
http://www.virginbooks.com
Nexus was the first British book imprint devoted exclusively to erotica, and publishes two new titles each month. Novels are 70,000-80,000 words. They do not, as a rule, publish 'vanilla' erotica—rather, they favor proposals dealing with bondage, fetishism, SM, CP, fem-dom or anything experimental—"our favorite books are written (and read) by enthusiastic perverts." Nexus books are read by both men and women, but are targeted primarily to appeal to heterosexual men. Dislikes science fiction or supernatural settings. "Historical settings have been traditionally popular, because they maintain an intrinsic balance between believability and fantasy, but they are not as well liked as contemporary settings." Likes multiple viewpoint characters, which allows for more variety and less limitation in the number and variation of sexual scenes. Quite open to lesbian sex or scenes, but try and keep gay

male sex to a minimum.

"A Nexus novel should be an arousing, escapist fantasy. Men and women tend to differ in the aspects of sex they put most emphasis on: men like anatomy, women like environment. Readers tend to enjoy a balance between believable escapist fantasy and realistic, down-to-earth storylines, so we try to publish novels with a variety of settings and themes. Published collections of sexual fantasies, such as those compiled by Nancy Friday, support the theory of gender differentiation, and also the idea that men like to invent unreal (but just about believable) worlds in which their sexual fantasies can unfold. You should strive for credibility, but avoid mundanity. Readers don't like to be reminded of domesticity, gas bills, car maintenance, rising damp, illness, and, above all, they don't particularly want to read about wives, families, difficult relationships, or sexual inadequacies. We overwhelmingly prefer to publish novels heavily slanted towards SM and/or bondage or other forms of marginal or experimental sexual activity, either with men dominant, women dominant, or both. Use jokes judiciously; your characters can have a sense of humor, but not your narrator.

"Take care with anatomical descriptions – it is quite astounding how many men are confused about the relative positions of the female genitalia. Female orgasm is triggered in most instances by clitoral stimulation. The clitoris is not situated inside or adjacent to the vagina. If a penis (or anything else, for that matter) has penetrated the cervix, something very unusual is going on.

"No sex with children (i.e. people under 16) or flashbacks to childhood 'experiments'; in fact, we'd rather all participants in sex acts were 18 or over. No sexual acts that cause bloodshed or other permanent physical damage; no sex acts that would cause genuine tragedy or anguish; no incest from parent to child, or with close family if one of the participants is much younger; no bondage that involves constriction around the neck; no sex against anyone's will; and no sex with animals or corpses. Watersports are fine. It's often the tone of a piece rather than the actual content which is offensive—we don't publish misogynistic prose."

To submit, send: capsule summary, full-synopsis of story (1,500 words) and first couple of chapters (around 15,000 words) of finished text.

Erotic Titles: *Saturnalia* by Paul Scott, *New Erotica 5* (anthology), anything by Penny Birch

North Atlantic/Frog Limited
Brooke Warner, Editorial Assistant
North Atlantic Books
1435A Fourth Street
Berkeley, CA 94710

http://www.northatlanticbooks.com

North Atlantic/Frog is an eclectic independent publisher whose list covers everything from children's books to spirituality. Particularly known for their alternative health and martial arts titles, they are looking to expand their offerings of sex-related nonfiction titles, such as the anthology of first person essays about sex and culture, *2SexE: Tales of Life, Liberty, and the Pursuit of Getting it On*. They are not currently accepting fiction or poetry.

"Decide if North Atlantic or Frog, Ltd. is the kind of publisher you want. We are not a typical New York house which focuses on producing highly commercial or mass-market books. If you desire those characteristics, you should try all the large publishing solutions you want before you think of us. We are small. We are independent thinkers. We work carefully with our authors on writing and concept in an old-fashioned way. We are not a service bureau, and we are not a self-publishing solution."

Submit with query, describing project, author background, comparable titles, and why North Atlantic is an appropriate publisher for the book, along with two sample chapters. Responds in one to three months. Does not accept electronic submissions. Submission guidelines are available on their website.

Erotic Titles: *2SexE: Tales on Love, Liberty, and the Pursuit of Getting It On* edited by Antonio Cuevas and Jennifer Lee, *His Tongue* by Lawrence Schimel

Odd Girls Press
No longer publishing.

Olympia Publications
36 Union Street
Ryde IOW PO33 2LE
UNITED KINGDOM
(44) 01983 811783
Fax: (44) 01983 811785
olympia@bound.demon.co.uk
http://www.olympia-press.co.uk
Editor: Josephine Scott

Olympia is a British publisher with a very strict focus on BDSM, specifically bondage and S&M from a heterosexual, male dominant/female submissive perspective. They publish several new erotic novels of 30,000-35,000 words every month, and sell primarily through mail order, although their titles are also available at select sex shops in Europe and the U.S. They do not publish short stories. Payment is by royalty only, at a rate of £1 per book sold through the mail order outlet and £1 per copy sold electronically. No advance, but royalties are paid monthly, beginning when the first month titles are on sale.

Erotic Titles: *Slaveship* by Mark Andrews, *Punished in Servitude* by Cliff Hardy, *Strapwell School for Girls* by Steven Drukker

One World Books
Ballantine Publishing Group, Inc.
1745 Broadway, 18th Floor
New York, NY 10019
(212) 782-9000
Fax: (212) 572-4949
http://www.randomhouse.com
One World Books is a division of the Random House Publishing Group, a general purpose publisher seeking erotic fiction via agented submissions only.

On Your Own Publications
Brooklyn Navy Yard
Building 120, Suite 207
Brooklyn, NY 11205
(718) 875-9455
oyobooks@oyobooks.com
http://www.oyobooks.com
Editor: Jeff Brauer
On Your Own Publications publishes the Sexy series of guides, such as *Sexy New York* and *Sexy Miami*, which offer detailed accounts of erotic hotspots in various locations. Contact them to find out more about writing for future editions of these guidebooks, or to propose new city locales.
Erotic Titles: *Sexy Miami: The Annual Guide to Miami Erotica, Sexy New York*
MAY NO LONGER BE IN BUSINESS – webpage parked on 20 September 2005

Painted Leaf Press
No longer publishing.

Palm Drive Publishing
P.O. Box 191021
San Francisco, CA 94119
(707) 829-1930
Fax: (707) 829-1568
mark@PalmDrivepublishing.com
http://www.palmdrivepublishing.com
Editor: Mark Hemry
Established in 1997, Palm Drive Publishing is a one-man operation focusing primarily on gay male erotica, although they have published other titles—fiction and non-fiction—with gay themes. Palm Drive

publishes anthologies, novels, and short story collections. Authors may be of any gender, but their preference is for work about the (erotic) lives of gay men.

"Gay writing is not a cul de sac. Gay writing—minus political rhetoric—is an important tributary into the mainstream of American culture. Ideally, writing submitted should reflect something of the universal human experience through its use of the gay sensibility."

Averages 4-8 titles/year. Pays royalty or makes outright purchase. Reports in 6 weeks on queries with 1) a one-sentence TV Guide thumbnail synopsis with the hook that will grab the reader; 2) 1-page double-spaced treatment (250 words) of what the book is about; and 3) the complete first page as it appears in the book. Note: Queries may be faxed, but faxes of more than 5 pages will not be read. Submission guidelines are available on their website.

Erotic Titles: *Chasing Danny Boy: Tales of Celtic Eros*, *Tales from the Bear Cult*, *Some Dance To Remember*

Park Street Press
Division of Inner Traditions International
PO Box 388
Rochester, VT 05767-0388
(802) 767-3174
Submissions@innertraditions.com
http://www.parkstpress.com

Park Street Press focuses on holistic, metaphysical, occult, eastern philosophies and similar subjects and issues, including books on sacred sex or treatments of sex and sexuality from these backgrounds. In general, looks for "subjects that enhance our understanding of the world in which we live and that improve our quality of life." Rather than unsolicited manuscripts, they prefer proposals with one page précis of book, a summary of intended market, and biographical details. Also include a table of contents, the introduction, and sample chapter(s). Submission guidelines are available on their website.

Erotic Titles: *Celtic Sex Magic*, *The Complete Kama Sutra*, *The Encyclopedia of Sacred Sexuality*, *Sexual Secrets*, *Tantric Quest*

Passion Press
Part of the Open Enterprises Cooperative, Inc.
938 Howard Street, Suite 101
San Francisco, CA 94103
(415) 974-8985, ext 295
Fax: (415) 974-8989
passionpress@excite.com
http://www.passionpress.com/

This audio publisher of erotica is best known for the audio editions of the Herotica series and for their Orgasmatronic audio-originals. They are now part of Down There Press. "We're always looking for good material, although our publishing schedule is limited. Passion Press publishes erotic audio tapes and CDs, and audio books that promote sexual health and self-awareness. We also need talented readers!" Material submitted must be on an audio cassette, CD, or CD-ROM in MP3 format.

Erotic Titles: Cyborgasm, Herotica 6

Pedlar Press
P.O. Box 26, Station P
Toronto, ON M5S 2S6
CANADA
(416)534-2011
Fax: (416)535-9677
feralgrl@interlog.com
Editor: Beth Follett

Pedlar Press focuses on outsider voices. They may or may not be accepting work from US-based writers at this time. They are a general purpose press, seeking non-fiction illustrated books on sex and erotic fiction.

Query with a SASE. For nonfiction, your proposal package should include an outline, five sample chapters, and artwork or photos. For fiction, your proposal package should include a synopsis and five sample chapters.

Persea Books
853 Broadway
Suite 604
New York, NY 1000
Fax: (212) 260-1902
http://www.perseabooks.com
Editor: Karen Brazillier

Persea Books is a small, independent literary publisher of fiction and non-fiction, primarily novels, short story collections, multi-cultural anthologies, and literary criticism. They have only one book of literary erotica on their list. Query with cover letter, author background and publication history, a detailed synopsis of the proposed work, and a sample chapter. Indicate if submission is simultaneous.

Erotic Titles: Too Darn Hot: Writing on Sex Since Kinsey

Plume
375 Hudson Street
New York, NY 10014
(212) 366-2000
Fax: (212) 366-2666

http://www.penguinputnam.com/
This mainstream paperback imprint is part of the Penguin Putnam Group, and has published the occasional erotic collection, either single-author collections of literary erotic, such as *Quiver* by Tobsha Learner, or anthologies such as the *Flesh and the World* series edited by the late John Preston.
Erotic Titles: *Quiver, Flesh and the World, After Hours: A Collection of Erotic Writing by Black Men*

Pretty Things Press
P.O. Box 55
Point Reyes Station, CA 94956
prettythingsinc@aol.com
http://www.prettythingspress.com
Publisher: Alison Tyler
Run by erotic author Alison Tyler, Pretty Things Press publishes anthologies and single author collections of erotic writing. Regularly posts calls for submission on their website for anthologies open to new writers. They are not currently accepting unsolicited manuscripts.
Erotic Titles: *Naughty Stories from A to Z, Bondage on a Budget, Bad Girl*

Prometheus Books
59 John Glenn Dr
Amherst NY 14228
(716) 691-0133
editorial@prometheusbooks.com
SLMitchell@Prometheusbooks.com
http://www.prometheusbooks.com
Editor in Chief: Steven L. Mitchell
Prometheus Books is a general purpose publisher. Their scope includes a wide variety of topics, including erotica. They do not accept telephone or email inquiries, only written proposals addressed to Steven L. Mitchell, Editor-in-Chief. Detailed guidelines are available online.
"Before sending any materials, it is always best to submit a letter of inquiry that introduces the topic; briefly outlines the author's project; and discusses relevant competing works, the potential market, the availability of the complete manuscript (or its likely completion date), and the manuscript's (tentative) length. A copy of the author's vita/resume with publishing history should accompany your inquiry." Submissions are accepted from both authors and literary agents.
Erotic Titles: *Dancing Naked in the Material World, Dirty Talk, Half Straight, Raw Talent, The Horseman, Whips and Kisses, X-Rated Video Guide*

Prowler – see Zipper Books

Pulplit Publishing
411A Highland Ave.
#376
Somerville, MA 02144-2516
submissions@pulplit.com
http://www.pulplit.com
Editor-in-Chief: John O'Brien
Pulplit Publishing is a general purpose publisher that is seeking erotic fiction. They primarily publish a magazine, but also periodically put out books. Submissions guidelines are on their website. Submit complete manuscripts online (they do not accept hard copy).
Pulplit describes themselves thus: 1. a body of written work concerning pulp fiction or media; 2. publication exploring the interaction between high and low culture; 3. a publisher interested in new, quality fiction to be published in limited quantities and sold over the internet; 4. an online book store featuring self-published and small press books and zines exclusively.

Random House
1540 Broadway
New York, NY 10036
http://www.randomhouse.com
The Random House Publishing Group has many imprints and publishes on a wide variety of topics, including erotica. They only accept submissions through literary agents.

Really Great Books, Inc.
P.O. Box 86121
Los Angeles CA 90086
info@reallygreatbooks.com
http://www.reallygreatbooks.com
Mari Florence, Founder/Editor
Currently accepting submissions only from literary agents. This small publisher publishes various series titles, including food and drink guides Hungry? and Thirsty? as well as the Horny? series of sex guidebooks for various cities within the United States.
Erotic Titles: Horny? Los Angeles, Horny? San Francisco

Red Hot Diva (DIVA Books)
Millivres Prowler Limited
Spectrum House
32-34 Gordon House Road
London NW5 1 LP
UNITED KINGDOM
(44) 20 7424 7464

http://www.divadirect.co.uk
Editor: Kathleen Bryson
Red Hot Diva is an erotic imprint by and for lesbian and bisexual women. They publish novels ranging from 65,000 to 75,000 words. Submit one or two page synopsis plus first three chapters (10,000-15,000 words). For short story collections, submit the entire manuscript. No submissions via email.

"Try to pick a plot and setting that will make it easy for the characters to have a lot of sex and to have sex with different people. We choose books using the following criteria: lots of sex, absorbing plot and interesting characters, well written and a 'good read,' right length, not too similar to anything else we're publishing around the same time. The words and images we put into the community may affect people's sexual behavior and we want to help reduce the spread of HIV. So we ask authors to write safer sex, according to the current UK understanding of the term. Everyone involved should be fully conscious (not asleep or knocked out) and fully sober (not drugged or drunk)."

Erotic Titles: *Cherry* by Charlotte Cooper, *The Fox Tales* by Astrid Fox, *The Escort* by Ruby Vale

Red Sage Publishing
PO Box 4844
Seminole, FL 33775
AleKendall@aol.com
http://www.redsagepub.com
Publisher, Acquisitions Editor: Alexandria Kendall

Red Sage is part of the burgeoning erotic romance field, and publishes the Secrets series of erotic novellas that push the boundaries of romance by incorporating explicit sexuality into the plots. Looking for novellas of 20,000-35,000 words. Query with one-page synopsis (clear emotional and physical conflict defined) and the first ten pages of the story. Open to many different genres: contemporary, mainstream, mystery, historical, science fiction/fantasy, etc. Guidelines are online.

"We believe secret intimate stories told by women to women have forever been at the heart of civilization. We offer less restrictions for women writers to tell their Secret stories. We are searching for romance authors who dare to go where today's romance authors are forbidden to go. Highly intense love relationships involve an equally intense sexual relationship that are sometimes politically incorrect. We are looking for a high level of sexual tension throughout the story to maintain the necessary edge and arousing feel. These love scenes must be sophisticated, erotic, and emotional. We want to push the envelope beyond the normal romance novel. Be kinky, be wild, go far beyond spicy, but always write romance. If you're not sure, query. Any sexual position okay between a man and a woman. Tension and conflict can make love

scenes excruciatingly effective. Always a happy ending. These character driven stories always concentrate on the love and sexual relationship between the hero and the heroine."
Erotic Titles: *Secrets 1-15*

Regan Books
10 East 53rd Street
New York, NY 10022
(212) 207-7400
Fax: (212) 207-6951
http://www.reganbooks.com
Publisher: Judith Regan
Division of Harper Collins, known for their celebrity and popular culture titles. Seeking nonfiction sex and erotic fiction. No unsolicited manuscripts. Only accepts submissions by literary agents.
Erotic Titles: *Pucker Up* by Tristan Taormino

Retro-Systems.
No longer publishing printed books.

Rising Tide
No longer publishing.

Roam Publishing
Wade Wilson, Editor
Roam Publishing
2447 Santa Clara Ave., Suite 304
Alameda, CA 94501
submissions@roampublishing.com
http://www.roampublishing.com
Roam Publishing is looking for "sexually explicit, action-packed travel adventures about real men in exotic locations entwined in steamy intercultural relationships with beautiful women." Novels of 50,000 to 80,000 words. Also publishes travel-related how-to non-fiction on relationships, sex, lifestyles, technology, nomads, overseas living and business. Minimum of 30,000 words.
Erotic Titles: *Fantasy Islands: A Man's Guide to Exotic Women and International Travel*

Running Press
125 S. 22nd St.
Philadelphia, PA 19103-4399
http://www.runningpress.com
Running Press is a mainstream publisher, best-known for its illustrated gift book titles and its Miniature Editions. They are just beginning

to branch out into erotic fiction with the anthology *Five Minute Erotica* edited by Carol Queen. They also have several nonfiction how-to and gift titles about sexuality such as *The 10 Secrets to Great Sex* and *10 Minutes of Passion*.

"Running Press specializes in publishing illustrated nonfiction for adults and children. We very rarely publish any new fiction or poetry and are not seeking submissions in those categories at this time. We also do not accept proposals for Miniature EditionsAA of any kind." Guidelines are online.

Erotic Titles: *The 10 Secrets to Great Sex*, *Erotica: Three Tales of Lust and Passion* (Miniature Edition), *Sex for Dummies* (Miniature Edition), *10 Nights of Passion*, *5 Minute Erotica* edited by Carol Queen

Sable Publishing
P.O. Box 4496
Palm Springs, CA 92263
(760) 408-1881
sablepublishing@aol.com
http://www.sablepublishing.com
CEO: Ed Baron
Submissions editor: Glory Harley
Sable Publishing is a general purpose publisher seeking nonfiction sex titles. They also list erotic fiction among the genres they seek.

Query with a SASE. Nonfiction proposal packages should include an outline, an author bio, and three sample chapters. Fiction proposal packages should include a synopsis, an author bio, and three sample chapters. Guidelines are online.

St. Martin's Press
175 Fifth Avenue
New York, NY 10010
http://www.stmartins.com
"St. Martin's Press, Picador, and Minotaur Books do not accept unsolicited manuscripts." Only accepts submissions from literary agents.
Erotic Titles: *Topping from Below* by Laura Reese

Sapphire
http://www.virginbooks.com
This UK lesbian erotica imprint of Virgin Books is no longer publishing.
Erotic Titles: *Rika's Jewel*, *All that Glitters*, *Getaway*

Seal Press
Avalon Publishing Group
1400 65th Street, Suite 250

Emeryville, CA 94608
http://www.sealpress.com
Feminist publisher Seal Press is part of the Avalon Publishing Group, though retains its Seattle roots. Known for such feminist works as the young women's anthology *Listen Up* and Inga Muscio's groundbreaking *Cunt*, Seal has been moving towards publishing more erotic and sexual nonfiction with works such as Hanne Blank's solo collection *Unruly Appetites*, Blank's anthology *Shameless: Women's Intimate Erotica*, and Lee Damsky's *Sex and Single Girls*.

Seal's website states, "Before submitting a query regarding your own work, please review our website carefully in order to determine whether or not your project seems like a good fit. Do not send your full manuscript for consideration. Please send either a query letter or a proposal, with SASE to" the Acquisitions Editor. Telephone and email submissions are not accepted. Full guidelines are on their website.

Erotic Titles: *Shameless, Sex and Single Girls, Valencia*

Sheckys
Hangover Media, Inc
678 Broadway, 4th Floor
New York, NY 10012
(212) 242-2566
Fax: (212) 242-3704
info@sheckys.com
publishing@sheckys.com
http://www.sheckys.com
Shecky's, launched in 1997, is one of the largest publishers of New York City lifestyle guides. They are currently in the process of expanding their reach to Los Angeles, CA. The site's focus is on reviewing the "best" of NYC – everything from nightclubs to apartment hunting. No guidelines are available online.

Erotic Titles: *Erotic New York*

Simon and Schuster
1230 Avenue of the Americas
New York, NY 10010
(212) 698-7000
Fax: (212) 698-7007
http://www.simonsays.com
This mainstream publisher has published the *Best American Erotica* series, as well as other erotic titles by Susie Bright. They do not accept unsolicited manuscripts and are best approached through an agent.

Erotic Titles: *Best American Erotica, Tie Me Up, Tie Me Down*

Soft Skull Press
55 Washington Street, Suite 804
Brooklyn, NY 11201
(718) 643-1599
Fax: (866) 881-4997
http://www.softskull.com
Publisher: Sander Hicks
Soft Skull Press is a small, independent publisher known for its left-ist political slant on current topics. Where it has ventured into erotic publishing, it's always specifically looking for outside the mainstream work that defies convention and is not so easily classifiable as "erotica."

"For fiction and nonfiction submissions, send a cover letter and sample chapter no more than 30 pages, and an outline of the rest of the book. For poetry, send a cover letter and no more than 10 pages. For graphic novels, send a minimum of five fully inked pages of art, along with a synopsis of your storyline." Direct your proposal to the attention of: Poetry, Fiction, Nonfiction, or Graphic Novel Editor (whichever is appropriate). Guidelines are online.

Erotic Titles: *What the Fuck* edited by Michael Hemingson, *Bottoms Up: a collection of punk-ass porn* edited by Diana Cage

Stonewall Inn Editions
http://www.stonewallinn.com
No longer publishing.

Suspect Thoughts Press
2215-R Market Street, PMB #544
San Francisco, CA 94114-1612
(415) 713-7159
gregw@suspectthoughts.com
http://www.suspectthoughts.com
Publisher: Greg Wharton
Online magazine Suspect Thoughts began publishing a handful of titles in print, many by authors who have previously contributed to the magazine. They are receptive to new authors for the magazine, and are also the primary sponsors of the QueerLit competition for a first novel with queer and alternative themes.

"Suspect Thoughts Press is a terrible infant hell-bent to publish challenging, provocative, stimulating, and dangerous books by contemporary authors and poets exploring social, political, queer, and sexual themes. Send a query letter via email detailing your project. Give a short summary of the book, a chapter outline if you have it, approximate word count, what qualifies you to write this particular book, and contact information. We do not want to see sample chapters at this stage." Guidelines are online.

Erotic Titles: *Of The Flesh* edited by Greg Wharton, *Best of the Best Meat Erotica* edited by Greg Wharton

Ten Speed Press & Celestial Arts
P.O. Box 7123-S
Berkeley, CA 94707
http://www.tenspeedpress.com
A general independent publisher best known for its nonfiction titles, they brought out the groundbreaking collection, *Look Homeward Erotica.*

"To submit a book proposal, please include: a cover letter with an overview of the project and its target audience, a chapter-by chapter outline of the entire work, one or two sample chapters, a bio describing who you are and why you are the right person to write this book, and a rationale for why we are the best publishing house for our list." Guidelines are online.

Erotic titles: *Look Homeword Erotica, When the Earth Moves:Women and Orgasm*

Text Publishing
Swann House
22 William Street
Melbourne VIC 3000
AUSTRALIA
(03) 861-04500
Fax: (03) 962-98621
books@textpublishing.com.au
http://www.textpublishing.com.au
An Australian house that publishes just about every genre, fiction and non-fiction, from cook-books to biography to erotica. Recent titles include Susan Maushart's self-help manual, *What Women Want Next.*

To submit, send a copy of your manuscript, single-sided, double-spaced, with pages numbered. Guidelines are online.

Erotic Titles: *The Stranger Inside: An Erotic Adventure* by Red Symons, *Geography* by Sophie Cunningham

Thunder's Mouth Press
245 West 17th Street, 11th floor
New York, NY 10011-5300
(646) 375-2570
Fax: (646) 375-2571
http://www.thundersmouth.com
Publisher: John Oakes
Thunder's Mouth, an imprint of the Avalon Publishing Group, publishes mainly books about popular culture, current affairs, film, and political books. They ventured into the erotic publishing field with

Aroused, edited by Karen Finley, which featured very unusual tales such as art star Reverend Jen's reflections on getting the wax in her ears removed. Not considering fiction or poetry submissions. Does not consider unsolicited manuscripts, queries only.

Erotic Titles: *Aroused: A Collection of Erotic Writing* edited by Karen Finley, *The Delicious Grace of Moving One's Hand* by Timothy Leary

Trans Nation
2715 Buford Hwy. NE
Atlanta, GA 30324
Fax: (404) 634-3739
info@transnation.us
http://www.transnation.us
Editor: Ronald Ashley

A Spanish/English press that has just recently begun publishing fiction (2004). The editors are specifically interested in erotica writers, but will not publish anything related to science fiction. Well over half of authors published by Trans Nation are previously unpublished; those looking to gain this distinction have a better chance of selling if their manuscript is "geared towards a multicultural audience."

To submit a work of fiction, send a proposal package, synopsis, and one sample chapter. Non-fiction authors will have to provide a complete manuscript, cover letter, and outline. Response time can range from one to three months.

As of this writing, their website has been offline for several months (12/18/2005).

Twisted Shift
3300 Fresno Place
Schertz, TX 78154
submissions@twistedshift.com
http://www.twistedshift.com
Editor: S. "Rick" Richardson

Twisted Shift is a brand new (est. 2005) electronic publisher that specializes in "well-written fiction featuring human transformation" of the physical variety (i.e. vampires, werewolves, shrinking, etc.). The editors are specifically interested in erotica ranging in length from 1,000 to 130,000 words, and will respond to manuscript submissions in about six-eight weeks.

To submit stories over 10,000 words, send an email to the editors containing a synopsis and the first three chapters. For shorter stories, go ahead and send the complete manuscript. Although unsolicited manuscripts are the norm for Twisted Shift, be sure you read and follow the guidelines online before you submit your (non-simultaneous) work. Twisted Shift has also started offering writing contests.

Unbound Books
6366 Commerce Blvd.
PMB#155
Rohnert Park, CA 94928
unbndbks@sonic.net
unbndbks@yahoo.com
http://www.unbound-books.com/
Acquisitions Editor: Angela Bradford
Unbound Books is an independent publisher located in Northern California, publishing in hardcover, paperback, and sometimes novelty formats. "We welcome kinky, gay and lesbian writers in all categories!" Detailed guidelines are online. Please send a cover letter, synopsis and the first three consecutive chapters or approximately the first 50 pages of your manuscript. Novels should be complete prior to submission.

Unbound Books are also seeking writers for specific topics, including several erotic subjects, but query first to make sure that the status of the online story requests is up-to-date and any given story request hasn't already been assigned.

Erotic Titles: *The Erotic Adventures of Miss Taylor #1* by Desiree Thorn, *Gornoston* by F.R.R. Mallory and W.Z. Mallory

The Underground Who Chapbook Press
P.O. Box 13486
St. Petersburg, FL 33733
submissions@undergroundwho.com
http://www.undergroundwho.com/
Editor: BenjaminM. Scarlato
A subdivision of Rembrandt and Company Publishers International, The Underground Who ChapbookPress specializes in trade and mass market paperback originals. Half of books published by Underground Who have been by first time authors, and the editor notes that there is "[n]o need for an agent, just be creative in your work." Recent titles include *Love Orbits Venus*, by John Ramos, and *Resolution 258*, by Peter Ebsworth.

To submit, send either a query with self addressed stamped envelope (SASE) and a proposal package complete with synopsis, or send your entire manuscript. Fiction manuscripts should be no longer than 10,000 words, and authors should expect a reply within six months of submission. Submission guidelines are on their website.

Erotic Titles: *Love Orbits Venus* by John Ramos, *Resolution 258* by Peter Ebsworth

University Publishing Co.
1134-A 28th Street
Richmond, CA 94804

(510) 262-9333
unipub@earthlink.net
http://home.earthlink.net/~unipub/index.html
Editors: Elizabeth Kay and Robert Allred
A small, paperback press that describes itself as "open to almost any good writing." The editors are looking for good erotica, and will respond to your submission in about a month.

To submit, send a proposal package, outline, synopsis, the first 50 pages of your manuscript, a cover letter, and a self addressed stamped envelope (SASE).

Venus Book Club
Jeannine Laddomada
Venus Editor, c/o Bookspan
1271 Avenue of the Americas - 3rd floor
New York, NY 10020
http://www.venusbookclub.com
Bookspan's Venus Book Club, specializing in erotica titles from a diverse array of publishers, occasionally publishes an original title themselves. They accept outside submissions of original erotic novels and anthologies, as well as reprints of out of print erotic titles.

Erotic Titles: *Desires* edited by Adrienne Benedicks, *Bad Girl* by Alison Tyler, *Venus Book of Hot Women's Erotica* edited by Marilyn Jaye Lewis

Venus or Vixen? Press
http://www.venusorvixen.com
Venus or Vixen? Press was the publishing arm of the webzine Venus or Vixen? run by erotica author and editor Cara Bruce. They appear to be defunct or on hiatus at this time.

Erotic Titles: *Viscera* edited by Cara Bruce, *Dark Embraces* edited by Paula Guran

Villard
299 Park Avenue
New York, NY 10171
(212) 572-2211
Fax: (212) 572-6026
http://www.randomhouse.com/rhpg/villard/
Director: Bruce Tracy
This division of Random House has published a number of sexuality-related titles, such as the anthology *Dick for a Day*. Only accepts manuscripts submitted by an agent—"the volume of materials we receive is just too large to accept unsolicited submissions."

Erotic Titles: *Boyfriend 101*, *Different Loving*, *The Vagina Monologues*, *Miss Vera's Cross Dress for Success*

Vision Paperbacks/Fusion Press
101 Southwark Street
London SE1 0JF
UNITED KINGDOM
editorial@visionpaperbacks.co.uk
http://www.visionpaperbacks.co.uk
Editor: Stella Wood

This UK paperback publisher is very open to fresh voices and new ideas and publishes erotica through its Fusion Press line. "Vision is proud of its independent line and its ability to present balanced research into issues that the public needs to know about. We are not afraid to provoke controversy or debate through our titles." Publishes non-fiction titles on current affairs, society and media, investigative journalism, general science, and sexuality, alternative lifestyles and drug culture. "It's all popular culture and that's what want. We seek authoritative, reliable and safety-aware writing on sex, sexuality and drug culture that breaks new ground in an original and, where possible, controversial way. While we are not slaves to political correctness, please note that we will not publish books that encourage non-consensual activities or that encourage prejudice or discrimination."

They do not publish fiction or poetry. Submit comprehensive outline, working chapter title breakdown, 1-3 sample chapters giving an indication of style and direction of the project, estimated completion date, and a list of similar titles already published in the US or UK and how your project differs. Guidelines are online. They accept proposals through email but do not sent complete manuscripts.

Erotic Titles: In or Out: Stars on Sexuality by Boze Hadleigh, The Erotic Cookbook

Warner Books
1271 Avenue of the Americas
New York, NY 10020
http://www.twbookmark.com

Warner Books does not consider unsolicited manuscript submissions and unsolicited queries. They recommend that you submit through an agent.

"Unfamiliar packages and letters mailed to our offices will be returned to sender unopened."

Erotic Titles: Letters to Penthouse

Washington Square Press
1230 Avenue of the Americas
New York, NY 10010
(212) 698-7000

Fax: (212) 698-7007

http://www.washingtonsquarepress.com

This imprint of Simon & Schuster has published much erotica by authors of color, with the Brown Sugar series going into a fourth volume.

Due to the volume of submissions they receive, they do not accept unsolicited manuscripts and recommend that you submit through an agent.

Erotic Titles: Brown Sugar edited by Carol Taylor, Under the Pomegranate Tree: The Best New Latino Erotica

West Beach Books
PO Box 1726
Port Hueneme, CA 93044
Submissions@westbeachbooks.com
http://www.westbeachbooks.com
Editor: Jim Ericsson

West Beach Books publishes gay male erotica, and is best known for the Buttmen series focusing on men and their asses. Check their website frequently for updated information on anthologies currently open to submissions. Accepts email submissions as Word files attached to email.

Some things they like in submissions: "Stories that have a catchy title that is either hot, sexy, sexual, teasing, intriguing, daring, fun or funny (something that will make people browsing the table of contents want to buy this book). Stories that come from honest point of view and not one of 'I'm here to try to entertain you and make you hot with a sex story.' Stories that reveal something about the author, the characters or the subject matter through honesty. Stories that are daring in nature, especially by taking the reader somewhere new or giving a fresh, new spin on an old theme. Stories where the author tells us something he may not share with others...secret passions not readily shared can be very revealing about you and the reader."

Erotic Titles: Buttmen series, Uprising, Bridge Across the Ocean, and The Devil Inside, all by Randy Boyd

Windstorm Creative
PO Box 28
Port Orchard, WA 98366
submissions@windstormcreative.com
http://www.windstormcreative.com
Editor: (Ms.) Cris DiMarco

This independent house publishes in a number of different genres, including fantasy, science fiction, historical fiction, lesbian and gay fiction, erotica, poetry, and mixes of the above. Check their website to make sure they are currently accepting in the genre(s) you wish to submit.

"If you're writing erotica, please read the following books before submitting: 1001 *Nights Exotica* 1 by Cris Newport (published by Windstorm) and 1002 *Nights Exotica* 2 by Cris Newport (published by Windstorm). Note: The erotica we're looking for needs to be sexy but also smart. We aren't interested in stories containing incest; stories which contain misogyny, sexism or homophobia as a character traits that remain unexamined; sexual violence of any kind; obvious or 'preachy' lessons."

For submissions, "you need to first send a typed, one-page synopsis, a #10 business-sized, self-addressed stamped envelope and a completed Submission Form. You must also use a Submission Label. Do not send a manuscript until an editor requests it. Make very sure to include everything listed here just as it's listed. Because we receive such a vast number of submissions, if your submission doesn't follow these guidelines exactly it cannot be reviewed. We promise not to waste your valuable time if you do the same."

Do not even think of submitting to this publisher without reading the guidelines in detail (available online) and following their process.

Erotic Titles: 1001 *Nights Exotica* by Cris Newport

Zipper Books and Prowler Books
Millivres Prowler Limited
Spectrum House
32-34 Gordon House Road
London NW5 1 LP
UNITED KINGDOM
(44) 20 7424 7464
http://www.zipper.co.uk/zipper/
Zipper Brooks and Prowler Books are imprints of Millivres Prowler Limited, and they focus on gay male erotic novels. They publish novels ranging from 75,000 to 85,000 words. Submit a one or two page synopsis plus the first three chapters (10,000-15,000 words). For short story collections, submit your entire manuscript. No submissions via email.

"Try to pick a plot and setting that will make it easy for the characters to have a lot of sex and to have sex with different people. One of our popular authors sets all his books in the navy, for instance, where there is a limitless supply of horny young men. (But please don't set your book in the navy, he's got that covered.) We choose books using the following criteria: lots of sex, absorbing plot and interesting characters, well written and a 'good read,' right length, not too similar to anything else we're publishing around the same time. The words and images we put in to the community may affect people's sexual behavior and we want to help reduce the spread of HIV. So we ask authors to write safer sex, according to the current UK understanding of the term.

Everyone involved should be fully conscious (not asleep or knocked out) and fully sober (not drugged or drunk). It can, unfortunately, take up to six months for us to get back to authors because of the volume of submissions we receive. If you want to be sure your manuscript has been received, enclose a stamped postcard for us to return."

Erotic Titles: *Hard at Work, Rough and Ready*

Zumaya Publications
See eXstasy Books

Magazines & Periodicals

A few notes about periodical markets. This section includes not only traditional magazine markets like Hustler, but also web-based magazines, some alternative newspapers, newsletters/catalogs, and a small handful of non-paying but significant print markets like Prometheus. For clarity's sake we also list some well-known publications that are no longer publishing so you won't waste your time trying to hunt them down.

These guidelines are only a fraction of each market's full guidelines, which you should read in full before submitting. Look them up on the individual web sites or write to the publisher (with SASE) to receive a printed copy. Each has differing requirements as far as format of submissions, whether they prefer hardcopy or email submissions, plain text versus attachments in email, etc. And they often reject submissions that don't conform. Note that these markets will NOT accept any stories featuring bestiality, incest, or underage characters. These subjects are illegal to print in the United States and Canada so are universally avoided—don't even try it.

Almost every print periodical these days has a web site. Some publish the contents of their print versions online, while others differ in their content. Make sure when you are selling your work that you know which rights you are selling (print, online, or both). Some, like Playboy Online, have separate editors and separate needs from their print versions. Know whether you are submitting to the print version or online version of a magazine, if a market has both.

New magazines are popping up all the time, even as old titles fold up or go out of business. Before submitting to any of the markets listed here, check to see that they are still publishing. And if you don't see a market for the type of work you write, take a look at the Resources listing for other places you can look for news about new markets opening.

Not listed here are most of the "alternative newsweeklies" like *The Boston Phoenix* and *LA Weekly*. These types of newspapers exist in most cities in the USA and Canada, and tend to specialize in arts and entertainment news, restaurant reviews, and the like. Many cities have a number of competing publications in this category. Some of them have "adult" sections that feature classified ads and sexually-explicit advertising (strip clubs, massage parlors, etc.). From time to time these sections may need content and you may be able to pitch short articles, fiction pieces, or poetry to them. Because these markets open and close depending on the whims of the industry and their available page space, we have not listed them, but you can make contact with your local publications to see if you can work with them. They tend to work with local writers.

Likewise, weekly gay and lesbian newspapers, like the *Washington Blade* or Boston's *Bay Windows*, may buy from freelancers and prefer to work with local writers. These are generally nonfiction markets, but pick up your local editions to see what type of pieces they run and whether you might have something appropriate for them.

100% Beef Magazine
PO Box 1344
Palm Springs, CA 92263
(800) 672-3287
Fax: (760) 202-0328
http://www.beefmag.com
Editor: Scott McGillivray

100% Beef is a gay male magazine, who describes itself as: "an adult men's magazine by, for, and about regular, masculine gay men. The men in 100% Beef are solid, husky, and usually hairy. Beards and mustaches fit in well here, too. More than anything else, though, 100% Beef is about masculine men enjoying themselves and each other." They are "always looking for new and established talent in the areas of photography, writing, and illustration." As their guidelines state, "100% Beef buys first North American serial rights to dozens of pieces of fiction and nonfiction, illustrations, and free-lance photo shoots each year." Their full guidelines and Publication Authorization Form are on their web site, which you must read before submitting. Pays on a rising scale, $100 for your first fiction story, $125 for the next you sell, and so on. Nonfiction pays between $35-$100 to start and also rises with additional contributions. Pays 30 days after publication.

[2]
Specialty Publications
7060 Hollywood Boulevard, Suite 1010
Los Angeles, CA 90028
(323) 960-5400
Fax: (323) 960-1163
http://www.2mag.net
Specialty Publications publishes four erotic magazines that cater to a gay male audience: Men, Freshmen, [2], and Unzipped Monthly. [2] does not take freelance submissions, but see the listings for Men, Freshmen, and Unzipped for the details on those markets.

AVN (Adult Video News)
heidi@avn.com
http://www.avn.com
Monthly magazine covering the adult entertainment business, also posts updates on website. Publishes nonfiction news stories covering the adult industry as well as porn video, DVD, book, and toy reviews, covering all sexualities and fetishes. Relevant queries can be sent to Managing Editor Heidi Pike-Johnson at heidi@avn.com.

AVN Online
http://www.avnonline.com
Editor: Tom Hynes
A spin-off publication from AVN. Monthly print magazine covering online adult industry, information for adult webmasters, affiliate programs, legal decisions affecting adult websites, etc.

American Bear/American Grizzly
Amabear Publishing
P.O. Box 7083
Louisville, KY 40257-7083
(502) 894-8573
amabearinc@earthlink.net
http://www.amabear.com
Editor: Tim Martin

American Bear and American Grizzly share the same publisher and writer's guidelines (which are online). "If you would like to submit some fiction, just send it along to us. Send it in hard copy or email it to us using one of the formats mentioned below. We will let you know if we are interested. If so, we will send you a contract for your work and require you to either send us the story as a WORD document (for Mac or PC) or any compatible Macintosh format-Quark Xpress, Appleworks, Simple Text. Stories should be 3,000 to 3,500 words in length and deal with what a bear readership would like to read or fantasize about. And, yes, we do pay for fiction that we publish. Be sure to include your name and address."

Anything That Moves
http://www.anythingthatmoves.com
No longer publishing. This was a national bisexuality magazine, but according to their web site, as of April 2004: "We regret to declare that Anything That Moves magazine is officially ended. No further print issues will be produced; no further updates should be expected on this web site."

Bad Attitude
No longer publishing. Once this was one of the only lesbian SM magazines in the country, but it has disappeared from sight.

Barely Legal
Barely Legal, LFP, Inc.
8484 Wilshire Blvd., Suite 900
Beverly Hills, CA 90211
(323) 651-5400
Fax: (323) 651-2741
http://www.barelylegal.com
Hustler Barely Legal's fiction pieces focus on the blossoming sexuality of young women. Writing should be clever, amusing and arousing. All stories should celebrate a young woman's sexual coming-of-age without degradation or hackneyed descriptions. Length: 2,500-2,800 words. Pay: $500. The guidelines advise "Always tell the story from the perspective of an 18-year-old girl. Mention her age at the beginning of the story. Do not make reference to any sex she had before she became legal, including masturbation. Hustler Barely Legal wants new and refreshing erotic stories while maintaining a level of wit and intelligence not found in other adult publications." They accept both unsolicited manuscripts (which they do not return) and queries with SASE.

Bear Magazine
bcmsales@brushcreek.com
See Brush Creek Media listing for submission and contact information.

One of the seminal (no pun intended) gay men's magazines, Bear began in the late eighties as a local San Francisco 'zine, and grew quickly to national prominence. Their guidelines state: "Bear uses erotic fiction, media reviews, features, event reports, columns, illustrative erotic art, and photo spreads. All illustrations and nonfiction pieces are produced on assignment; most fiction is unsolicited." Fiction can be emailed to bcmsales@brushcreek.com. Expect a 3-6 month wait for a reply. Pay starts at $100 per story and rises with successive sales. Brush Creek also publishes Bunkhouse, Foreskin Quarterly, and International Leatherman, listed separately.

Beau
See Sportomatic, Ltd. listing for submission and contact informaton.

Their guidelines state: "Beau is a general-interest gayporn mag, not restricted to any one theme, though of course it must depict 'vanilla' sex such as is acceptable in Canada. Please note that we no longer publish 'Gay Style' nonfiction pieces in Beau."

Behind The Scene
Brooks Applications
PO Box 675750
Rancho Santa Fe, CA 92067-5750
(858) 759 8706
Fax: (858) 759 2226
jennifer@hotspankings.com
http://www.hotspankings.com
Editor: Jennifer Brooks

This magazine is published by Brooks as part of her "over the knee" empire of videos, DVDs, online streaming, and the like for spanking enthusiasts. She has published close to thirty issues as of press time, and the magazine features personal ads as well as erotic content.

Bitch
1611 Telegraph Avenue, Suite 515
Oakland, CA 94612
bitch@bitchmagazine.com
http://www.bitchmagazine.com
Bitch is subtitled the "Feminist Response to Pop Culture."

National feminist magazine, sometimes runs articles about erotica or sex as related to feminism. No fiction. See website for themes of upcoming issues. They state: "Our definition of pop culture is broad, encompassing cultural attitudes and myths, phenomena of the popular imagination, and social trends as well as movies, TV, magazines, books, advertising, and the like. Profiles of and interviews with feminist culture-makers and business owners are welcome, as are book and music reviews and nuanced analyses of particularly horrifying and/or inspiring examples of pop culture. Nonfiction essays only. We do not publish fiction or poetry. Ever. Finished work and query letters are both welcome. If sending only a query, please include clips and/or writing samples. And hey-everyone likes a nice cover letter. Don't forget to include a self-addressed, stamped envelope." Pays $100 for feature pieces, $50 for shorter, $10-$20 for "Love/Shove" submissions.

Bizarre
Dennis Interactive
30 Cleveland Street
London W1T 4JD
UNITED KINGDOM
(44) 020 7907 6000
Fax: (44) 020 7907 6020
Editorial Email (print version): bizarre@dennis.co.uk
Email: alistair_strachan@dennis.co.uk
http://www.bizarremag.com
Online Editor: Alistair Strachan
    Motto: "It's About Life In The Extreme." This magazine from England seems determined to tackle all the bizarre and disturbing subjects that formula erotica magazines would never touch with a ten foot pole. Whether the material is genuinely erotic or not is a matter of taste, especially since they seem to prefer nonfiction to fiction. True crime, real people, weird and perverse subjects. Some recent pieces have featured a man with a fetish for anorexics, a foot fetishist serial killer who severs the feet of his victims, and a piece on how to "fart your way to fame."

Blackfire
PO Box 83912
Los Angeles, CA 90083-0912
(310) 410-080
Fax: (310) 410-9250
Submit to: newsroom@blk.com
http://www.blackfire.org

Editor: Alan Bell

This magazine describes itself thus: "Blackfire features the erotic images, experiences and fantasies of black men in the life. Without compromising the sensual spell, it also includes provocative articles, useful information, delicious interviews, and fresh poetry." By "in the life" the editors refer to gay or MSM (men sexually attracted to men) life. Fiction 2,000-4,000 words. Also nostalgia, humor, first-person accounts, "where to" articles, and reviews, and 400-700 word shorts. Fiction can range from the romantic to the extremely sexual. The guidelines on their website make no mention of payment terms.

The Blacklisted Journalist
Box 964
Elizabeth, NJ 07208-0964
black@bigmagic.com
http://www.bigmagic.com/pages/blackj

This curious online magazine is the repository of legendary New York Post rock journalist Al Aronowitz, but also has columns and pieces by an impressive list of other writers on the canonical topics of sex, drugs, and rock-n-roll. Up and coming hip erotica poet and writer Tsaurah Litsky (Three the Hard Way) does a regular gig here. Although it looks like the website hasn't been updated since 2001, click through the indexes for more recent articles.

Black Lace
PO Box 83912
Los Angeles, CA 90083-0912
(310) 410-080
Fax: (310) 410-9250
http://www.blacklace.org

Not to be confused with Black Lace, the UK erotica book imprint, Black Lace Magazine (US) is the sister publication to Blackfire, this time aimed at black lesbians "in the life." Same terms as Blackfire. The guidelines on their website state "Erotic fiction can range from descriptions of idealized women having idealized sex ('she spurted a cupful of love juice'), to depictions of typical women in plausible encounters ('homegirl didn't have no titties, but I didn't care; I wanted that snatch'), to unconsummated hints at sex ('lingerie ads are the politically correct way for women to stare at other women's breasts in public'). We are partial to the latter two categories."

Black Male for Men

Go West Media Group, LLC
3230 E. Flamingo Rd. #8-171
Las Vegas, NV 89121
(877) 446-8682
(702) 974-0585
wes@gowestmediagroup.com
Contact: Wes Miller or Raul Mangubat
Looking for "clear, solid stor[ies] that can be sent on disc, uploaded on the website, or sent via e-mail." Black Male buys almost forty manuscripts a year, all ranging from 3,000-3,500 words in length and "focusing on the positive aspects of gay lifestyle, with an emphasis on humor and fitness." Simultaneous submissions are accepted, and writers should expect a response within two months. Submission guidelines are available online.

Black Sheets
No longer publishing. This was the magazine publication of Black Books, and for years it was an irreverent mélange of bisexuality, leathersex, humor, erotica, reviews, and the like. We miss it.

Blithe House Quarterly
adalvarez@aol.com
http://www.blithe.com
Fiction Editors: Tisa Bryant and Jarrett Walker
Publisher and Executive Editor: Aldo Alvarez
This online literary magazine specializes in gay, lesbian, bisexual, and transgendered fiction. BHQ has been publishing since 1997 and has featured fiction by many noted GLBT writers. Publishes quarterly with 6-10 stories per issue, ranging from 1,500-7,500 words. Does not pay at this time. Sometimes does special theme issues. Guidelines are on their website.

Blood Fetish
vampire@bloodfetish.com
http://www.bloodfetish.com
This online magazine specializes in stories that creatively use vampirism or blood fetish. The editor writes "I am tired of reading moody pieces about Dracula wannabes. Stop sending them." Wants sex-positive erotic stories "natural, fantasy or science fiction — that typically could not be published elsewhere. While all stories must have a blood element, they need not be about vampirism." Word limit: 4,000. No poetry or novels. Pays $50 per story. "No snuff stuff. Vampirism by its nature, is often non-consensual, but we do not publish rape stories. This is a fine line. Don't cross it." Submissions by email only.

Blue Food
http://www.bluefood.cc [note URL suffix]
This quirky online erotica magazine had a brief tenure as a print journal before becoming completely a web market. Does not pay at this time. Their guidelines state: "We want to discover the next Xaviera Hollander, Anonymous, or Marquis de Sade. We'll take fiction, poetry, or creative nonfiction of any length or non-excessive verbosity into consideration. What we like to see are erotic stories filled with eloquence, irony, humor, maybe a dash of suspense or intrigue, a little comic tragedy, an implied musical interlude or two and a shock is occasionally nice. Most of all, what we want to see are large doses of sticky, sweaty, moan-inducing, honey-pot-in-spasms alternative carnality. Every lifestyle is acceptable and every kink will be considered, based on the story or article's merits." Their contributors list reads like a Who's Who In American Erotica: Sage Vivant, Jamie Joy Gatto, M. Christian, Greg Wharton, James Williams, Helena Settimana, Debra Hyde, and many more.

Bound & Gagged
The Outbound Press, Inc.
http://www.boundandgagged.com/
Bound & Gagged discontinued operations on June 22, 2005.

Boy Next Door
See Sportomatic, Ltd. listing for submission details. Their guidelines state: "The 'boy' must be of age though young, must be a 'boy-next-door' type, and must be in some physical proximity that could qualify in the large sense as 'next door'-e.g. occupant of the next office, next campsite, etc., or of course literally the next-door neighbor."

Brush Creek Media
2215-R Market Street, PMB #148
San Francisco, CA 94114
(800) 234-3877, extension 112
bcmsales@brushcreek.com
http://www.brushcreek.com/
Publishers of magazines for gay men including Bear, Foreskin Quarterly, Bunkhouse, and International Leatherman.

Bump & Grind
P.O. Box 1319
Hudson, QU J0P 1H0
CANADA

(450) 458-1934
Fax: (450) 458-2977
Editor: Gaetan Gavin Dumont
This monthly magazine for heterosexual men says that it wants "hard-core, anything goes (not an anal title), very dirty and lusty." However all sex must be consensual and enjoyable for all participants. Accepts queries by mail, email, fax, and phone. Accepts simultaneous submissions, looking for stories 1,300-2,000 words and pays $10-15/1,000 words.

Bunkhouse
See Brush Creek Media for contact info
Their guidelines state: "Bunkhouse is the quarterly magazine that explores the authentic fetish value of Western Americana, historic and modern. Bunkhouse uses unsolicited fiction, assigned art, professional photography, and features on the erotic history of The West."

Busty Beauties
8484 Wilshire Blvd., Suite 900
Beverly Hills, CA 90211
(213) 651-5400 ext. 7354
Fax: (213) 651-2741
Busty Beauties is a magazine for heterosexual men with the theme of big-breasted women. Length: 1,500-2,000 words. "Story should have well-developed characters and a plausible plot, as well as sex scenes that are pivotal to the story itself. Humorous pieces are preferred. (Of course, the major female characters should be buxom.)" Pays $250-500 upon publication. Also buys "LewDDD Letters": 400-800 words "recounting sexual yarns with a large-breasted woman or women, or from the point of view of such a well-endowed lady." Pays $50-75 per letter. Boob Jokes: 25-200 word jokes involving bosomy women or situations, items, etc. of interest to devotees of large breasts. Price: $25 per joke.

Buttman Magazine
Queries to: elliebatt@hotmail.com
http://www.buttmanmagazine.com
Editrix: Ellen Thompson
This is the print magazine arm of John "Buttman" Stagliano's Evil Angel Video series of porn videos. The magazine, which appears every two months, features photos from the movies as well as interviews, erotic "nasty" stories, contests, and more. Naturally, everything in it is butt-based or anal in theme. Past contributors have

included Tristan Taormino (The Ultimate Guide to Anal Sex for Women, Pucker Up) and Darklady (former editor of Exotic magazine).

CF Publications
P.O. Box 706L
E. Setauket, NY 11733
cfpub@ix.netcom.com
http://www.cfpub.com
CF Publications calls itself "the oldest and largest publisher of spanking stories in the world." They sell print publications as well as stories online for download. They seek spanking-themed stories with "all combinations of the sexes." Pays 1.5 cents per word if in readable electronic format, 1.25 cents if not. "Stories should probably not be shorter than three single spaced pages or longer than about twenty. Lengthier pieces may be published in parts." The editors also urge you to "write what turns you on, it probably will have the same effect on other readers."

Cherry Boys
See Coming Out.

Cleansheets
Fiction submissions: exotica@cleansheets.com
Poetry submissions: poetry@cleansheets.com
Questions: articles@cleansheets.com
Fiction editors: Bill Noble and Julia Peters
Poetry Editor: Devan Macduff
http://www.cleansheets.com
This updated-weekly webzine was founded by erotica writer/editor Mary Anne Mohanraj in 1998, though she is no longer actively involved with it. They publish poetry, fiction, "exotica" ("things excitingly different or unusual that don't fit our normal sections"), and articles (how-tos, personal essays, interviews with prominent sexual community activists, writers, etc.). Fiction: 1,500-3,500. Articles: 1,500-2,000 words. Poems, 100 lines or shorter. Does not pay at this time. Submission guidelines are available on their website.

Coming Out
See Sportomatic, Ltd. listing for submission details. Their guidelines state: "Coming Out and Cherry Boys are about a man's first man-to-man sexual experience. Stories in Coming Out are told from the point of view of the first-timer. Stories in Cherry Boys are told

from the point of view of the guy who gets the cherry. In all our magazines, a character portrayed as 'cherry' should demonstrate some emotional reaction (e.g. fear, excitement) to the step he contemplates taking."

Cthulhu Sex Magazine
PO Box 3678
Grand Central Station
New York, NY 10163
submissions@cthulhusex.com
http://www.cthulhusex.com
Editor: St. Michael Amorel
"CSM: For Connoisseurs of Sensual Horror." Their guidelines state: "All submissions to Cthulhu Sex must contain at least one of the three themes in the subtitle 'Blood, Sex and Tentacles.' We look for horror, erotica, humor, combinations of such and/or crossover works that touch on such. We don't publish stories that are based in glamorizing rape, hatred, racism, homophobia, child abuse, or other degrading acts." Fiction up to 5,000 words, prefers 2,500-3,500, poetry to 120 lines. Does not pay but provides 3 comp copies. Submission guidelines are on their website.

Cybersocket
editor@cybersocket.com
http://www.cybersocket.com
Bi-monthly magazine about the online community of gay, lesbian, bisexual, and transgendered people. Cybersocket also publishes an annual book. Accepts nonfiction queries from freelancers: please read the magazine to see what type of pieces they prefer. Typically pays 10 cents per word. Megabytes: smaller items ranging from mere lists of, say, 10 favorite sites, to small stories of 60 to 80 words, and also medium stories of 150 to 300 words in length. Feature stories: 1,500 words plus sidebar of 50-100 words. Department pieces: 700-800 words, reviews of websites and media—see online magazine for the departments.

Dare Magazine
P.O. Box 99
Quantico, VA 22134
DareMag@aol.com
http://www.daremag.com
This online magazine appears to have ceased operations.

Desire
Moondance Media Limited
1a Fentiman Road
London SWB 1LD
UNITED KINGDOM
(44) 020 7820 8844
Fax: (44) 020 7820 9944
desire@easynet.co.uk
http://www.desire.co.uk
Editors: Ian Lowey or Ian Jackson
"Uniquely, Desire is aimed equally at male and female readers and all material should reflect this, so we'd strongly recommend you have a look at a copy of the magazine first, before submitting any work." No fiction. Pitch feature ideas with queries, allow 4-6 weeks for reply. Features cover topics of sexual diversity (body piercing, aphrodisiacs, female ejaculation, Tantric sex, swinging, etc...), run 1,600-3,000 words. Columns run 800-900 words. Pays £165 per 1,000 words. "Fantasy scenarios for 'Decadent Dreams & Desires' are first person descriptions of a fantasy, experience, or sexual desire." These shorter items need to be fairly intense, raunchy, unashamedly explicit and graphic, imaginatively written with originality rather than merely conventional, vanilla 'confession' fare." 1,000-2,000 words, pays £40 each. Poetry 12-24 lines, £15.

Dr. Susan Block's Journal of Sex, Art, Politics & Culture (was Sex in Review)
http://www.drsusanblock.com/
This online site is run by popular radio sexpert Dr. Susan Block. She writes: "It is easy, and common, to write about sexual topics in a snide or negative fashion. That type of writing has no place here. In fact, to counteract the typically negative tone in media coverage of sexuality, it is our policy to present sexual topics in a positive, educational light."
Articles 500 to 2,000 words. Assigned reviews range between 300-1,000 words. "Eventually, we hope to be able to pay writers, but for now, we do not pay for articles." May offer trade advertising or promotional partnership.

E.L. Publications
315 Nassau Road, PMB 138
Roosevelt, NY 11575
trowelfraz@lycos.com
http://www.elpub.com
E.L. Publications specializes in "growth" erotica, described as

"primarily, women growing into giantesses. Some of our erotic fiction is about shrinking men—providing a similar effect (from the males' point-of-view) that the woman is growing into a giantess. More recently, we have added stories about women whose breasts grow to gigantic proportions." More details in the guidelines on their website. Stories are illustrated with black and white line drawings. Wants 8,000 word stories, pays $150 for "work for hire" (the author retains no rights to the story). Query with sample, "at least one entire page devoted to a description of giantess growth and/or breast expansion 'growth sequence.'"

Eros-Noir.com
submissions@eros-noir.com
http://www.eros-noir.com
Eros-Noir is "an online adult magazine that looks at the erotic underbelly of society." Wants fiction and nonfiction, 500-2,000 words. Reprints only for unpaid publication. Pays $50-$150 on first publication for 90 days exclusive internet rights, non-exclusive thereafter. Their guidelines state: "Our focus is on dark erotica, with an edgy quality. The following keywords should give you an idea of style and relevance: noir, femme fatale, obsession, sultry, steamy, gritty, haunting, edgy, evil, perversions, cruelty, seduction, addiction, lust, betrayal, vulnerability, cravings, hunger, naked shadows, desperation, street life, goth, bdsm, domination, mistress, escort, courtesan." Query first for nonfiction. Complete submission guidelines are on their website.

The Erotic Review
1 Maddox Street, 4th Floor
London W1S 2PZ
UNITED KINGDOM
(44) 020 7439 8999
Fax: (44) 020 7437 3528
editrice@theeroticreview.co.uk
http://www.theeroticreview.co.uk
Editor: Rowan Pelling
This ten-times a year magazine describes itself as an "up-market literary magazine for sensualists and libertines." Read the magazine to learn editorial preferences. Wants short stories from 1,000-2,000 words, pays £75 to £150; articles and features 1,000 words, pays £50-£75; and also prints artwork (£50), and cartoons (£40). Website is offline as of 12/20/2005, although they still own the domain.

Exotic Magazine
X Publishing
818 SW 3rd Avenue, #1324
Portland, OR 97204
Fax: (503) 241-7239
vivacide@hotmail.com
http://www.xmag.com
A magazine for people who enjoy the adult entertainment industry. The editors advise that they are "currently overwhelmed with fiction submissions [so] please only send fiction if it's really amazing."
The content of said fiction should be based upon some "'vice' of
modern culture." Non-fiction is needed, specifically "articles about
viagra, auto racing, gambling, insider porn industry, and real sex
worker stories." Both fiction and non-fiction submissions should be
between 1,000 and 1,800 words in length; compensation is 10
cents/word up to $150.

First Hand Experiences For Loving Men
Firsthand, Ltd.
310 Cedar Lane
Teaneck NJ 07666
(201) 836-9177
Fax: (201) 836-5055
firsthand3@aol.com
Publisher: Jackie Lewis
Contact: Don Dooley, editor
Founded in 1980, First hand is one of the longest running gay
men's erotic magazines. Their guidelines state: "We prefer fiction in
the first person which is believable—stories based on the writer's
actual experience have the best chance." Wants 2,000-3,000 word
stories, sometimes up to 5,000. Write to them for complete guidelines and current payment terms.

Fishnet
fiction-editor@blowfish.com or fiction-editor@fishnetmag.com
http://www.fishnetmag.com/
Editor: H. L. Shaw
Fishnet is an online erotica magazine. According to their website,
"Fishnet is a publication of Blowfish, the coolest adult products
company on the web." They are seeking both erotic fiction and photography. Copyrights are retained by the authors. They prefer email
submissions in the body of the email (NO attachments) and ask that
authors first send a short cover letter containing word count and
previous publications (although they welcome first-time authors).

Then, in a separate email, send the story in the body of an email. That way, they'll know if they get the cover letter but not the story that something happened to it. Attachments will be deleted unread.

"We are always seeking quality erotica, up to 8,000 words. We buy first web publishing rights and an option for one-time print anthology rights (with additional compensation of 2 cents per word if selected for the print anthology). We want hot fiction that goes beyond a mere sex scene – give us a good story, let us pant with your protagonist. Good writing is important, as is originality. Tender or melancholy stories are fine, but we're also not afraid of stories that push boundaries, that blur the lines of gender, propriety or even consent (though excessively gross or gory pieces are not to our taste). Challenge our assumptions, but make our toes curl while you do it.

"Reprints and poetry are OK, but will be a very hard sell. We generally prefer stories between 1,500 and 4,000 words, so stories shorter or longer than that will have to rock our world. No non-fiction at this time, please. We will consider other genres (such as speculative fiction, mysteries, sword-and-sorcery, even westerns) as long as it's also erotica. What your story must be, above all, is sexy. And good."

For Women
P.O. Box 381
4 Selsdon Way
London E14 9GL
UNITED KINGDOM
(44) 020-7308-5363
elizabeth.coldwell@nasnet.co.uk
Contact: Elizabeth Coldwell

Published every six weeks, For Women is interested in stories centering on "women's sexuality and relationships" Fiction manuscripts should be between 2,000 and 3,000 words, and the complete manuscript should be submitted. Further guidelines are available via email, but they do not accept unsolicited emailed submissions. The editors are clear in what the do not want: "We are not allowed to print stories which deal with anything illegal, including underage sex, anal sex (unless those taking part are over 18 and in private—i.e. no threesomes!), incest, bestiality, and anything which features extreme violence or appears to glorify rape or the use of force in a sexual encounter." They also recommend that you steer clear of hackneyed plot twists and place a premium on believable plot.

Foreskin Quarterly
See Brush Creek media for contact info
Their guidelines state: "Foreskin Quarterly is the quarterly for fans of foreskin and anti-circumcision activists. FQ uses unsolicited fiction, art (often-but not always-assigned), professional and amateur photography, nonfiction features, and photography of extreme developments and uses of the foreskin. FQ also uses adult-circumcision fantasies and true stories."

Fox Magazine
Fiction Dept.
401 Park Ave. South
New York, NY 10016
No email submissions.
A sister magazine to Gallery, but raunchier and hardcore (Gallery is softcore). Fox does not buy erotic stories, but they do buy letters. Pays $25-$50 for 500-800 words. Their guidelines state: "Fox is pure fun smut. The letters are often humorous in tone, but, as with all successful porn, should be believable. Be as dirty and raunchy as you like while respecting the [usual] no-nos." (Usual no-nos are bestiality, underage characters, and the like.)

Freshmen
fiction@specpub.com
http://www.freshmen.com/
See Specialty Publications for contact info
This gay men's magazine publishes fiction along with beefcake photos. Their guidelines state: "The themes of our stories can vary. They can be romantic, humorous, outrageous, kinky, rough or tender. Of course, the stories should depict characters having sex in a wide variety of places. We need stories that are well-written as well as sexually explicit. The reader should be able to visualize the characters, and characters should have distinct personalities. Authors may choose to write in the first person, third person or omniscient point of view. A story should have a beginning, a middle, and an ending. There should be something explicit on the first page to hook the reader's interest, but a piece should not climax until close to the end. A story should end with something more compelling than, 'And then we moved in together, and we've been lovers ever since.'" Prefers 2,000-2,500 words. Submit via email in plain text to fiction@specpub.com, and enter "fiction submission" in the subject box. Pays $150 per story, plus $25 per reprint.

Gallery Magazine
Fiction Dept.
401 Park Ave. South
New York, NY 10016
http://www.gallerymagazine.com/
No email submissions.
Gallery is a softcore heterosexual men's magazine that has been around since 1972. Erotic fiction should be geared toward a male audience. Wants 2,000-2,500 words, pays $300-$400. Also publishes "letters" (500-8,000 words) which pay $25-$50 each. Their guidelines state: "Gallery letters should be written from the perspective of our demographic men 25-55 with a somewhat pedestrian attitude toward sex. (We do receive the occasional letter from a woman.) Don't be afraid to experiment a little outside those confines, but remember that the pictures in Gallery are strictly of women by themselves; there are no couple or masturbation pictorials. Gallery is home of the 'Girl Next Door.'"

Genesis
Magna Publications
210 Route 4 East, Suite 211
Paramus NJ 07652
(201) 843-4004
Fax: (201) 843-8636
genesis@magnapublishing.com
http://www.genesismagazine.com
Editor: Paul Gambino
Contact: Dan Davis, managing editor
Genesis editors describe it as a "monthly men's sophisticate with explicit pictorials of women in sexual situations, celebrity interviews, erotic and non-erotic fiction, exposé, product and media reviews, lifestyle pieces." They also operate a for-pay website. Nonfiction features run the gamut: Exposé, General Interest, How-To, Humor, Interview/Profile, New Product, Personal Experience, Photo Feature, Film, music/book/etc. reviews, Lifestyle pieces.

Wants 150-2,500 words, pays 22¢/word. Query with published clips or send complete manuscript. Fiction has a wide range, too: Adventure, Confession, Erotica, Fantasy, Horror, Humorous, Mainstream, Mystery, Romance, Science Fiction, Slice-of-life Vignettes, Suspense, etc. Novel excerpts OK. Wants 2,500-3,500 words, pays $500.

Genre Magazine
213 West 35th Street, Suite 402

New York, NY 10001
(212) 594-8181
genre@genremagazine.com
http://www.genremagazine.com/
Senior Editor: Mark Liebermann
"Genre is the complete lifestyle sourcebook for gay men. Every month, the magazine throws a spotlight on the hottest, the freshest and the best-in entertainment, the arts, fashion, home design, automotive, technology, health and fitness, grooming and travel." Query to above address.

Gent
Home of the D-Cups
Dugent Corp.
2201 W. Sample Rd., Suite 94A
Pompano Beach FL 33073-3006
Fax: (305) 362-3120
http://www.gentonline.com
Articles Editor: Fritz Bailey
Appears to have shifted to an online magazine featuring pictorals.
This monthly magazine for heterosexual men puts the emphasis on big breasts. Founded in 1960, the magazine has changed hands a few times. Buys fiction stories up to 2,500 words, pays $200. Story must feature big breasts.

Good Vibrations Online Magazine
submissions@goodvibes.com
http://www.goodvibes.com
The Good Vibrations Online Magazine is seeking articles addressing topics on sex (pleasure, health, gender, culture) and/or erotica only. GV want original and previously unpublished material with a word count of approximately 1,000-1,200 words. They do not accept simultaneous submissions. Email your piece to submissions@goodvibes.com and include it in the body of the letter. NO attachments. They publish on a weekly basis. Complete submission guidelines are available on their website.
    "Accepted contributor payment is a one-time per/article payment of $100.00 for erotica and $150.00 for nonfiction. Accepted articles may be published and re-published in the GV magazine at our discretion and can be pulled by us at any time for any reason. Acceptance of and payment for an article does not guarantee when the article will appear in our pages nor for how long.
    "Contributors can expect to hear from us (whether the work is accepted or rejected) approximately 90 days after we've received the

submission. You may submit a maximum of 2 different pieces (If we love you and your writing we may invite you to submit more articles.)"

Harrington Gay Men's Literary Quarterly
10 Alice St.
Binghamton, NY 13904
(800) 429-6784 or (607) 722-5857
http://www.haworthpress.com
Editor: Thomas Lawrence Long, PhD
"The Harrington Gay Men's Literary Quarterly (recently retitled from the Harrington Gay Men's Fiction Quarterly to better reflect its broader scope) is devoted to new gay men's fiction, writing, and criticism, whether from emerging talents or established writers.

"The Harrington Gay Men's Literary Quarterly highlights racial, cultural, and geographical diversity; rediscovers lost voices, and explores edgy postmodern writing, erotica, creative nonfiction, literary and cultural criticism, and memoir. This journal will help anyone—whether a scholar, educator, student, gay fiction/literature fan or writer—gain a better understanding of these genres."

Harrington Lesbian Literary Quarterly
10 Alice St.
Binghamton, NY 13904
(800) 429-6784 or (607) 722-5857
JPS360@aol.com
http://www.haworthpress.com
Editor: Judith P. Stelboum, PhD
The award winning literary magazine for lesbian writers and artists, HLFQ (Harrington Lesbian Fiction Quarterly) has been renamed to the Harrington Lesbian Literary Quarterly. HLLQ is published by the Haworth Press. Per their website, HLLQ "is an international journal that focuses on lesbian writing, including fiction, novel excerpts, poetry, essays, and drama."

"The Harrington Lesbian Literary Quarterly is a vital and important publishing opportunity for lesbian authors and a valuable resource and reference for lesbian studies theorists. In addition, it appeals to the academic field as an important text for programs in postmodern fiction, creative writing, women's studies, sociology, psychology, gender studies, and alternative cultures."

Hoot Island
submit@hootisland.com
http://www.hootisland.com

This online magazine has the motto "Silly sex, for silly people." Their guidelines state: "Hoot Island is proud to archive the largest collection of funny erotica on the web, and we'd love to see what you have to offer. [We want] stories, poems, parodies, and articles that are funny as hell and have lots of sex. Easy, huh?" Submissions must be both sexy AND funny. They should be included in the body of an email, NOT attached. Fiction or nonfiction, 500-3,000 words. Does not pay, writer keeps all rights.

Hustler
HG Inc.
8484 Wilshire Blvd., Ste. 900
Beverly Hills, CA 90211
features@lfp.com
http://www.hustler.com
Editor: Bruce David
Contact: Carolyn Sinclair
The premier magazine in Larry Flynt's empire. No fiction. No poetry. Buys nonfiction articles, personality profiles, and "sex play" pieces. Their guidelines state: "Hustler wants articles that contain information that is daring, new, different and controversial, dealing primarily with sexual topics. Since Hustler's standards are special, the magazine seldom buys articles on speculation, but gives all submissions fair consideration. The best approach is to submit a written proposal outlining not only the topic, but how it will be presented for the Hustler audience. Tell who you'll talk to, what areas you'll cover, and how it's new or something that hasn't been dealt with in other media. We are primarily interested in sexual topics that are current, of interest to a wide audience, and particularly those that are not being covered openly, if at all, by nonsex media. Social, legal, religious and political topics will also be considered. Query first."

Articles pay $1,500 for 4,500 words. Personality pieces should be profiles or interviews, 4,500 words, pays $1,500. Sex Play are "informative pieces written from a well-researched reportorial standpoint, opening sexual mores around the world. Material can cover cultural pressures, rites of passage, bedroom techniques, new trends in sexual medicine, surgery, therapy, etc." Wants 2,500 words, pays $750.

Hustler Fantasies
Hustler Fantasies, LFP, Inc.
8484 Wilshire Blvd., Ste. 900
Beverly Hills, CA 90211
hustlerfantasies@lfp.com

Hustler Fantasies is a monthly letters digest composed of approximately 15 letters and a fiction piece. They buy all rights. Letters (first person confessional style) of 700-1,200 words, pays $25. Fiction from 2,500-3,500 words, pays $100. Their guidelines state: "Well-written short stories or 'true' experiences written in any style, category or voice. At least two explicit, torrid, steamy sex scenes. Emphasis on plot/storyline." They accept story submission via hard-copy and email, in the body of the email message.

Indulge
http://www.indulgeformen.com
See In Touch for contact info
The big brother of In Touch, "Indulge magazine features more mature, aggressive, muscular men in their late twenties and thirties." They are 80% freelance written, according to the submission guidelines on their website.

Instinct
Instinct Publishing
15335 Morrison St., Ste. 325
Sherman Oaks, CA 91403
(818) 205-9033
Fax: (818) 205-9093
http://www.instinctmag.com
Editor-in-Chief: Parker Ray
This general interest gay men's magazine was founded in 1997 and has a much more humorous and irreverent bent than other magazines. Some call it Details for gay men. Wants nonfiction. Their guidelines state: "We are always on the lookout for exciting, provocative, and timely pieces (especially from our readers). Obviously, any submission must be of relevance to our audience, and should adhere to the following guidelines: Articles must always be fun. Keep the politics and/or any politically charged diatribes to a minimum. Sexually-charged material is, of course, welcome, but some of the more 'extreme' practices are off limits. If you are unsure whether the mention of a sexual act or fetish in your piece is questionable, please contact us for clarification. Offensive language is permitted, although it should not be used in excess." Features run 1,800-2,400 words, smaller pieces 800-950. Their submission guidelines (available on their website) do not mention pay rates, so inquire before you sell to them.

International Leatherman
See Brush Creek Media for contact info.

Their guidelines state: "International Leatherman is the serious bimonthly leather/SM magazine for gay men. IL uses unsolicited and assigned fiction, art, photography, and nonfiction that explores, explains, or builds upon leathersex action. It is uncommon for IL to accept unassigned photography, but it can happen. Remember that the action is the important thing here."

In The Buff
ITB Publishing
PO Box 747
Canterbury CT1 3GX
UNITED KINGDOM
stories@hotspotbooks.co.uk
http://www.hotspotbooks.co.uk/
They describe themselves thus: "In The Buff is a 100 page A5 sized erotic stories magazine which is published every six weeks. It comprises of: a sex diary, erotic fiction, readers' letters, interviews and other items of interest to our readers such as forthcoming events etc." No photographs, "purely" literary. "Most of our readership is heterosexual but we do cover Bisexuality, Slave and Master, Bondage, Cuckold, wife-watching, group sex, threesomes..."

Letters run from 800-1,500 words, pays £10 on publication. Fiction from 3,000-5,000 words. Prefers MS Word documents as email attachments. Well-written in the 3rd person (i.e. "he/she") with a good story line and plot. Pays £20 on publication. Complete submission guidelines are available on their website.

In Touch For Men
Go West Media Group, LLC
3230 E. Flamingo Road #8-171
Las Vegas, NV 89121
(877) 446-8682
Fax: (702) 974-0585
infoman89121@gowestmediagroup.com
http://www.intouchformen.com
Contact: Wes Miller or Raul Mangubat
In Touch has been around since 1973 (recently acquired by Go West Media) and emphasizes young gay men between 18 and 24 years old. Wants "light-hearted, romantic, erotic, provocative and entertaining [stories]. There are no limits on sexual content or explicitness in fiction, although safer sex must be depicted. Please refrain from submitting stories involving fantastical characters (i.e., vampires, ghosts, Tarzan)." Wants 3,000-3,500 words, pays $75-$125. Also buys short humor articles (1,500-2,500 words, pays

$25-$35), and freelance nonfiction (query; pays $50-$125). There's a form on their website for contacting Wes Miller (email may be out of date).

Tips: "Our publications feature male nude photos plus two-three fiction pieces, several articles, cartoons, humorous comments on items from the media, photo features. We present the positive aspects of gay lifestyle, with an emphasis on humor. Humorous pieces may be erotic in nature. We are open to all submissions that fit our gay male format; the emphasis however, is on humor and the upbeat. We receive many fiction manuscripts but not nearly enough unique, innovative, or even experimental material."

Juggs
462 Broadway, Suite 4000
New York, NY 10013-2697
(212) 966-8400
slutsrus@echonyc.com
http://www.juggs.com
Editor Julie B. says "While we do not have a formal set of guidelines for writers, the following is some information that you may find useful: Pay rate: $400 for 2,000-3,000 words; payment 60 days from receipt of invoice. We buy first serial rights." Juggs, in case you couldn't tell by the name, emphasizes large-breasted women.

KUMA: Black Lesbian Erotica
literature@kuma2.net
http://www.kuma2.net
This online magazine focuses on black lesbians and is for the most part written, edited, and produced by women. The guidelines on their website state: "We are looking for erotic stories/poetry featuring black lesbians, whether in love or lust, exploring their sexuality. We'd love to see more of the following: characters over 40 ('cause older women fall in love/lust, too), couples who have been together for a few years (a lover doesn't have to be brand new to be exciting), stories where characters explore sexual boundaries/fetishes, stories set in alternative settings (sex in space, sex at a Baptist Convention)." No mention of pay or compensation.

Leg Show
462 Broadway, Suite 4000
New York, NY 10013-2697
(212) 966-8400
slutsrus@echonyc.com
http://www.legshow.com/

Sister publication to Juggs, but with emphasis on legs, stockings, etc... Same terms as Juggs.

Leg World (aka Hustler's Leg World)
8484 Wilshire Blvd., Suite 900
Beverly Hills, CA 90211
Fax: (323) 651-2741
ethompson@lfp.com
Executive Editor: Ellen Thompson
Ellen says "Right now, we're looking for Feature Fiction. All fiction should be as realistic and sexy as possible, WITH A DEFINITE EMPHASIS ON LEGS AND FEET. Keep in mind our taboos: No kids, animals, shit, blood, necrophilia, David Hasselhoff, etc. Feel free to get really obsessive, as feet and legs are a very specific fetish. Remember, most folks are quite serious about their perversions, so even if a particular act or fetish isn't your thing, at least pretend that it is, or don't write about it. The editorial slant of our magazine is towards feminine dominance and submission, but there are no rules. Just try to express the psychology of your characters. What we're looking for is fiction that evokes the obsessive nature of the fetishism, not just descriptions of A putting it into B. And always remember to MAKE IT REALISTIC—even a fantasy needs some internal logic to work. Here are a few pursuits to consider working into your writing: Foot-sucking, panty-sniffing, shoe-sniffing, shoe-licking, dirty (messy) feet, stockings, corsets, pantyhose, ass worship, women smoking, public humiliation, public voyeurism, rubber, light bondage, spanking, tickling, cuckolding. You could just pick one or more of these and go wild." Pays $450 for 2,000-2,400 words. Query first.

Libido
http://www.libidomag.com
Does not currently accept submissions. This was once the printed "Journal of Sex and Sensibility," but they have gone online, and produce books and videos now.

Literotica
http://www.literotica.com
Literotica is a high-profile erotic fiction site on the Internet, which does not pay for stories but has been a respected center for up and coming erotica hopefuls. You must register as a member to post stories to the site. Wants 750 words and up, submitted electronically. Offers monthly and annual contests/awards. Check the site for the complete submission guidelines and procedures.

Men
http://www.menmagazine.com/
See Specialty Publications for contact information.
See Freshmen for submission guidelines.

Mind Caviar
http://www.mindcaviar.com
Editor: Jamie Joy Gatto
Online magazine of "food, sex, literature, art, and the finest erotica on the Web." Takes originals only, no reprints. Fiction, essays, articles, reviews, and poetry. The guidelines on their website state: "Explicit sexual imagery is preferred. Writing must be sensual, preferably food or sex-oriented, thoughtful, emotion-provoking, dimensional and intelligent. Our focus is on indulgence and sensuality, but we are also looking for gender issues, alternative lifestyles, educational pieces and commentaries." Maximum of 3,000 words, shorter is better. Does not pay.

Moist
99 Fifth Avenue, Suite 335
Ottawa ON, Canada K1S 5P5
subs@moist-erotica.com
http://www.moist-erotica.com/
Editor: Liam Taliesin
Moist is a quarterly print journal of erotic arts and letters, publishing seasonally. Primarily targets heterosexual men and women, but will consider content with BDSM, lesbian, and gay themes. Moist accepts reprints and simultaneous submissions, providing that they are informed in advance. Moist is accepting submissions of: fiction, flash fiction, poetry, photography, and art. For articles of non-fiction and interviews, query first with a brief proposal. Moist is committed to paying artists and mails payment 30 days after publication. Original fiction: $50; Reprints: $35; Flash Fiction: $25; Poetry: $25; Photos: $50; Cover art: $200. Payment includes two contributor copies.

Moxie
emily@moxiemag.com
http://www.moxiemag.com
Editor: Emily Hancock
Submissions suspended for the foreseeable future. Check the website for updates. Submission guidelines are online.
Moxie is interested in vibrant, feisty first-person stories that mirror women's strengths. Twice a year, Moxie awards a $100 cash prize

to the authors of the best fiction, best first-person narrative, and best poem published in the past six months. Length: 500 to 2,000 words. Compensation is one copy of magazine or $10.

Nerve Magazine
Prince Street Station
PO Box 389
New York, NY 10012
grant@nerve.com
michael@nerve.com
http://www.nerve.com
Contact: Grant Stoddard or Michael Martin
This ground-breaking sexy site on the internet has spawned a few books as well. As one of the top online markets, competition for acceptance is fierce. Their guidelines state: "Here is what we do not publish: porn, 'erotica,' play-by-play sexploits and purple fiction (read: overwrought romances in the airport-novel genre). Nerve aims to be frank about sex, but not necessarily explicit." Fiction and personal essays up to 2,000 words, short articles to 600 words. Pitch short articles to Grant Stoddard, essays, fiction and poetry to Michael Martin. Complete submission guidelines are available on their website.

Nightcharm
http://www.nightcharm.com
This online gay erotic magazine is visited by over 100,000 people every month. Their guidelines state: "As purveyors of sophisticated smut, we look for erotic fiction for masturbation and cogitation. We feature stories that combine erotic appeal with beguiling story, characters or mood, or unexpected humor and perspective. We think the best stories explore tension and taboo; the contrast of the flat everyday world with the focused blaze of sex creates the violation of expectation that makes hot shit hot." Fiction up to 4,000 words. Pays $60 via PayPal for new stories, $25 for reprints.

Nugget
Web Entertainment Group
4171 W. Hillsboro Blvd., Suite 4
Coconut Creek, FL 33073
(954) 421-8998
http://nuggetonline.com
Nugget Magazine is a hardcore site featuring nasty kink, bondage, and fetishes. No further information was available from them at press time regarding print edition, terms, or needs.

212 The Erotic Writer's Market Guide

On Our Backs
Attn: Submissions Dept
3415 Cesar Chavez, Suite 101
San Francisco, CA 94110
(415) 648-9464
Fax: 415-648-4705
diana@onourbacksmag.com
onourbacks@onourbacksmag.com
http://www.onourbacksmag.com
On Our Backs is a national, bimonthly magazine for lesbians.
They accept a variety of articles, including erotic fiction of 1,000-
2,000 words. All styles considered. Send them your complete manuscript. However, stories that include men, "first time," and coming
out are discouraged. Payment: $100. They are also seeking nonfic-
tion features: 1,800 words; 300 word sidebar. For nonfiction they
prefer a brief query rather than sending unsolicited nonfiction
work. Payment: $200. Please allow six to eight weeks for a response.
Complete submission guidelines are on their website.

Ophelia's Muse
sexcats@earthlink.net
http://www.opheliasmuse.com/
Editor: Jamie Joy Gatto
This online site describes itself as "a tiny webzine of erotic
tragedies." Their guidelines state: "Tapping into a virtually
untouched market, Ophelia's Muse offers a unique publishing
opportunity for erotica authors. Must be erotic, must be tragic, must
be under 4,000 words." No non-fiction. "Tragedy can embrace the
themes of loss, unrequited love, longing, death, addiction, romance,
co-dependency, unhealthy relationships, suicide, murder, abandon-
ment, mourning, grief, insanity. Erotic means sensual as well as
graphic sexual content." Does not pay. Ophelia's Muse does not
appear to have added new content since 2003 and the submissions
guidelines on the website mention having gone to an annual schedule.

Options
AJA Publishing Corp.
P.O. Box 392
White Plains, NY 10602
dianaedt@bellsouth.net
Associate Editor: Diana Sheridan
Options is a bisexual magazine focusing on the gay side of bisex-
uality. "All stories for Options should be about sex between two (or

occasionally more) men or two (or occasionally more) women."
Seldom use threesome stories mixing both sexes. Also use a TV/TS
story on occasion. Length should be 2,000-3,000 words. Payment is
$100 on publication for trouble-free manuscripts. For problematic
manuscripts they pay $80. They buy all rights but will reassign book
rights on request after story has been published. Manuscripts submitted to Options will automatically be considered for their gay
magazines, including Beau and other titles, if suitable. They are not
buying "letters" at this time. (Google turned up AJA PUBLISHING
CORP Phone : (914) 591-2011 Fax : (914) 591-2017; 1 BRIDGE ST
#125 IRVINGTON, NEW YORK 10533-1552)

The Outbound Press, Inc.
P.O. Box 2048,
New York, NY 10116-2048
(212) 736-6869
Fax: (212) 736-0255
http://www.outboundpress.com/
The Outbound Press is predominantly a gay male publisher. Their
guidelines state: "The Outbound Press is constantly looking for good
bondage fiction, both short and long. That a lot of bondage must figure in a story goes with out saying, but equally important to us is
that the story be well written. The Outbound Press pays $100 for a
story, on acceptance. There is no recommended word length, since
we believe that every piece of writing finds its proper length; in fact,
we are always looking to publish longer fiction and non-fiction that
deals with life on the cutting edge. We have already published two
novels and one non-fiction anthology. There is no fixed method of
payment for long works; we contact the writer on acceptance and
discuss terms." Per their website, their magazine Bound & Gagged
went out of business June 2005. They don't appear to publish anything else? (12/20/2005)

Paramour
No longer publishing. Was a fine journal of erotic arts and literature, driven out of business by a lawsuit.

Peep Show Magazine
Paul Fry
15 North Roundhay, Stechford
Birmingham B33 9PE
UNITED KINGDOM
For general queries: editor@peepshowmagazine.co.uk
Fiction: fictionquery@peepshowmagazine.co.uk

Artwork: artsample@peepshowmagazine.co.uk
http://peepshowmagazine.co.uk/
Horror magazine with forays into erotic fiction and sci-fi erotic
horror. They accept unpublished erotic horror stories only, 6,000
words maximum. Writers should query for longer works. Payment
for now is a copy of issue containing submitted work. E-mail submissions are not accepted.

Penthouse
Penthouse Media Group
11 Penn Plaza, 12th Floor
New York, NY 10001
Tel: (212) 702-6000
Fax: (212) 702-6279
forum.submission@generalmedia.com
http://www.penthouse.com
Rumors of the demise of Penthouse have been exaggerated. The
company recently went through bankruptcy and has emerged with
a new name ("Penthouse Media Group" replaces the old "General
Media" moniker). They still buy from freelancers and have a new
editorial team in place.

Penthouse Forum
http://www.penthouseforum.com/
See Penthouse for contact address.

Penthouse Letters
http://www.penthouseletters.com/
See Penthouse for contact address. Penthouse Letters is the leading magazine of erotic "letters," which are stories told in the first
person, as if true (sometimes they even are), focusing on vanilla
content. Submission is via a form on the website.

Penthouse Variations
http://www.variations.com/
Barbara Pizio, Editor
See Penthouse for contact address.
Penthouse Variations is Penthouse's magazine dedicated to kink
and fetishes. It is a digest-sized magazine which is published twelve
times a year. Variations publishes 3,000-word, first-person narratives
of credible erotic experience, squarely focused within a specific category. Editorial content, which varies per month, consists of feature
stories and reader letters in some of the following categories: Anal
Sex, Bisexuality, Bondage, Casual Encounters, Dominant Sexplay,

Exhibitionism, Exotic Vacations, Erotic Fantasy & Roleplaying, Female Domination, Fetishism, Group Sex, Lesbianism, Masturbation, May/September, Oral Sex, Outdoor Sex, Sex Toys, S&M, Spanking, Swinging, Threesomes, Tickling, Transvestism, Video Sex, Voyeurism, Watching My Wife.

Payment for an accepted, fully revised manuscript is up to $400. One contributor's copy is mailed to each author of a featured story upon publication. Variations does not publish poetry of any kind. No e-mail submissions from freelancers.

Playboy Magazine
Attention: Fiction or Articles Department
680 N. Lake Shore Drive
Chicago, IL 60611
articles@playboy.com
http://www.playboy.com

"Playboy regularly publishes nonfiction articles on a wide range of topics—sports, politics, music, topical humor, personality profiles, business and finance, science and technology—and other topics that have a bearing on our readers' lifestyles." The average length for nonfiction pieces is 4,000 to 5,000 words, and minimum payment for an article of this length is $3,000. They do not accept unsolicited poetry. Playboy buys first North American serial rights only—no second serial rights are considered. Playboy does not accept simultaneous submissions. Their response time is approximately four weeks. Fiction: "We accept unsolicited manuscripts of up to 5,000 words that include stamped, self-addressed return envelopes. We will not consider stories submitted electronically or by fax. Response time is approximately eight to 10 weeks." Pays $2/word.

Playgirl
Fantasy Forum
801 Second Ave. 9th floor
New York, NY 10017
http://www.playgirltv.com/
Editor: Michele Zipp

Playgirl is a national monthly magazine geared towards women, featuring photos of naked men and stories of interest to sexually active women. Often offers sex tips and advice, profiles the latest in porn and erotica, and features the "Fantasy Forum" erotic fiction department. Each month, they choose four fantasies to be published. One of the four is chosen as Fantasy of the Month and the author receives $100, all others, $25. Fantasies need to be in the first person. They must be typed and be 1,500-2,000 words in length.

Complete submission guidelines are available on their website.

Punk Planet
4229 N. Honore
Chicago, IL 60613
punkplanet@punkplanet.com
fiction@punkplanet.com
http://www.punkplanet.com
Leah Ryan: Fiction Editor
Punk Plant is a bi-monthly magazine dedicated to music, culture and politics, and living outside the mainstream. They accept unsolicited submissions and consider all of them for possible publication. Usually publish 2 out of every 50 submissions or so. Article length falls between 1,500 and 5,000 words. One short (700-1,500 words) fiction piece per issue. Interviews pay about $40 each, articles about $60 each, DIY and fiction pay about $30. They do have some submission guidelines on their website as part of their FAQ.

Sauce*Box
GuillermoBosch@guillermobosch.com
http://www.guillermobosch.com/saucebox/sauce_box.html
Editor: Guillermo Bosch
Sauce*Box is an online literary erotic magazine. They are looking for short stories, poems, essays, and novel excerpts. All persuasions/orientations are welcome. Does not pay. They recommend reading through the current and past issues to get a feel for what they publish. Submission guidelines are on their website.

Scarletletters
Poetry: editor@scarletletters.com
Fiction: diva@magenta.com
Nonfiction: hanne@hanne.net
http://scarletletters.com
One of the best established and best respected erotica sites on the internet, Scarle Lletters is sex-positive and non-exploitative. They describe themselves thus: "Since February of 1998, Scarlet Letters has been one of the web's premier publishers of humanist, feminist, sex-positive, original and visionary creative and artistic work of all kinds." Their guidelines state that they are "interested in all types and genres of short fiction except for short-shorts or 'flash fiction,' which just rub us the wrong way for no particularly good reason." Also takes poetry, reviews, creative nonfiction and essays. "Sexual description should support the story or work, not be its primary focus or entirety. Keep it real, make it interesting and compelling,

for the reality of what we do. Don't be timid, shy, or coy in your writing." No poetry. Stories must be published under female byline. Pays small honorarium "bigger than a breadbox, smaller than a dinner for two at a nice restaurant. Until the world changes and someone gives me a MacArthur grant or something, we're stuck with the economics we have." Complete submission guidelines are on their website.

Suspect Thoughts: A Journal of Subversive Writing
gregw@suspectthoughts.com
http://www.suspectthoughts.com
Editor: Greg Wharton
Suspect Thoughts has both a book imprint line and an online magazine. They describe the website as "an online magazine that features exciting alternative writing and artwork that blur the lines between genres and aren't afraid to frighten, cause laughter, or confuse, while perhaps arousing sexual desire." In 2005 they began rotating in "guest editors," so submission guidelines for each upcoming issue will be different. Do not send unsolicited work and check the website for latest guidelines.

Swank
210 Route 4 East, Suite 211
Paramus, NJ 07652
(201) 843-4004
Fax: (201) 834-8636
editor@swankmag.com
http://www.swankmag.com
Editor: Paul Gambino
Contact: D.J., associate editor
Swank is an adult heterosexual men's magazine. Swank will consider stories that are not strictly sexual in theme (humor, adventure, detective stories, etc.). However, these types of stories are much more likely to be considered if they portray some sexual element or scene within their context. All non-fiction submitted must be accompanied by footnotes and references. Although dealing with sex and sexually related topics, these articles should be serious and well-researched without being over-written. Will consider non-sexual articles on topics dealing with action and adventure. The availability of photos to illustrate the articles is crucial to their acceptance. Pays up to $0.22/word. Payment upon publication. All articles paid by length are according to the final edit. Buys 1st N.A. rights. Occasionally accepts reprints. Due to the volume of material received, they discourage phone calls and faxed queries/submissions.

Taboo
http://www.HustlersTaboo.com
Taboo is a national magazine published by Hustler, and focuses on way out fetishes, including bondage, spanking, amputee erotica, and more. For contact information, see the entry for Hustler.

TechnoDyke
articles@technodyke.net
http://www.technodyke.com
TechnoDyke is an online magazine for lesbians. Ostensibly they are still publishing, but ceased to pay contributors in January 2003 in what was called "a temporary setback" but which appears to still be in effect. Still needs 500-800 word pieces, reviews, columns, and the like, as well as "Erodyka" erotic stories. Appears to be adding limited new material.

Tender Chickens
See Young & Hung.

Three Pillows
drew@threepillows.com
http://www.threepillows.com
Three Pillows calls itself "The place for bisexual erotica on the net!" Founded June 2001. "Although we have erotica catering to all kinds of tastes including bi women, our specialty is M/M/F Bi erotica which is of strong appeal to many bisexual men." Pays $20-$35 for columns, articles, and reviews. Pays $15-$30 for erotic fiction. "Material should be of a bisexual/bi-curious nature or of interest to bisexuals." Submission guidelines are available on their website.

Unzipped Monthly
Specialty Publications LLC
P.O. Box 4356
Los Angeles, CA 90078-4356
(323) 960-5400
Fax: (323) 960-1163
http://www.unzipped.net/
Unzipped Monthly is the definitive journal of gay male sex and sexuality. While it does not contain fiction, they do welcome query letters with story ideas. You can also call them with tips and information about any related news or events in your town: video shoots, parties, live appearances by porn stars, etc. Call (323) 960-5400 between 9 A.M. and 5 P.M. Pacific time, or send an e-mail to unzmail@specpub.com.

Complete submission guidelines are available on their website. You may also email writersguidelines@unzipped.net to get a copy. Or you may send a self-addressed, stamped envelope to Unzipped, P.O. Box 4356, Los Angeles, CA 90078-4356, attention: Writer's Guidelines.

Velvet Mafia
editor@velvetmafia.com
http://www.velvetmafia.com
Velvet Mafia is an online gay magazine run by the folks at Suspect Thoughts. They write: "The best gay fiction contains an element of the erotic, the adventure of sexual conquest, and the mystery of unexplored territory. Velvet Mafia seeks alternative gay literary fiction and erotica for future quarterly issues and annual anthologies. We want work that dares to step over the line, fiction with teeth. It can be sensual, dark, sexy, indecent, experimental, hard or raw, so long as the story makes us sit up and pay attention." Wants stories up to 4,000 words, must have gay male focus. Pays only in trade advertising, unless work is included in a print product such as an anthology (negotiated separately). Complete submission guidelines are on their website.

Velvet Park
210 Cook St. #311
Brooklyn, NY 11206,
info@velvetparkmagazine.com
http://www.velvetparkmagazine.com/
Editor: Grace Moon
Velvet Park is a national lesbian magazines focusing on lesbian culture. Guidelines for non-fiction: looking for something original and/or unusual. Nonfiction submissions should be 600-800 words. Velvet Park also publishes short fiction, fiction excerpts from longer works and poetry. Pieces should not exceed 1,000 words. Complete submission guidelines are on their website.

Venus or Vixen?
No longer publishing.

Vice
http://www.viceland.com

Whap! Magazine
http://www.whapmag.com
No longer publishing. Website still sells back issues.

While You Were Sleeping
WYWS Magazine
4919 Cordell Ave.
Bethesda, MD 20814
Fax: (301) 590-3289
nick@whileyouweresleeping.com
http://www.whileyouweresleeping.com
Managing Editor: Nick Weidenfeld
An eclectic pop culture magazine that runs the gamut from porn star interviews to Gen X/Gen Y political rants. Their motto: "Let's get weird." Here's what they say in response to queries. "This is a standard letter, letting you know that we know that you're interested in writing for WYWS. So here is the story: we do use freelance writers and we're always into hearing brilliant ideas. However, be forewarned, they must be brilliant. If the idea/pitch/story is not 'mind-blowing,' we'll be really disappointed and won't run the story. We think that is reasonable." Send detailed pitches by email to Nick Weidenfeld.

Yellow Silk
http://www.yellowsilk.org/
No longer publishing. Editor Lily Pond has collected some work in anthologies from time to time but the magazine ceased publication in 1996.

Young & Hung
See Sportomatic, Ltd. listing for submission and contact details.
Their guidelines state: "Tender Chickens and Young & Hung are about boys 18 or occasionally 19, who should be described in young terms. They may be hairless on the body, look like they barely need to shave, have small balls, use teen lingo in their speech, or in other ways be presented as sounding youthful, though they do not need to be innocent. Do not, however, have your character be younger than 18. The use of such terms as 'boyballs,' 'boybuns,' and 'boycum' may also be helpful. These boys are not the viewpoint character in the story, but rather the viewpoint character (who should be at least in his 20s, possibly older) has an encounter with, and describes, the 'chicken.'"

Young & Tight Fantasies
Bridge St. Publishing Corp.
P.O. Box 392
White Plains, NY 10602
dianaedt@bellsouth.net

Young & Tight Fantasies is a heterosexual publication that uses primarily "letters," with, at present, only one story in each issue. Letters should be as close to 1,000 words each as possible. Stories should be 2,000 words. The main female character in all manuscripts should be a girl of 18 or 19. Story/letter may be told either from the girl's viewpoint or the guy's. All stories/letters written in the first person. Pay is $100 for stories, $20 for letters. All submissions must be electronic (on disk or online). Payment is on publication. Does not consider simultaneous submissions.

Zyzzyva
P.O. Box 590069
San Francisco, CA 94159
(415) 752-4393
http://www.zyzzyva.org

Zyzzyva is a magazine for "West Coast writers and artists only." Zyzzyva publishes a wide range of poetry, fiction, nonfiction, and translations, especially of Latin American and Asian writers. Submissions by snail mail only. Does not read simultaneous submissions. Pays, on acceptance, an honorarium of $50 plus two author's copies for first North American serial rights (and Zyzzyva anthology rights) only. Reserves the right to put work up on their website. They are not accepting novel manuscripts at this time. Complete submission guidelines are available on their website.

Ellora's Cave
submissions@ellorascave.com
http://www.ellorascave.com
Ellora's Cave publishes e-books of erotic romance in many gen-res. They are the only electronic publisher to be recognized by the Romance Writers of America and their site sells 30,000 books per month. The guidelines on their website state: "Send a detailed full-story synopsis, the first three chapters and the final chapter of your manuscript via email as attached files (in .doc or .rtf format). Note: We are an e-publisher and all our work is done electronically; we do not accept paper submissions." Wants novels of over 50,000 words, but some shorter works are acceptable. Pays 37.5% of cover price on all e-books. Note: "All manuscripts must contain sexual content and language that is explicit and leaves nothing to the imagination." But they point out: "Ellora's Cave publishes Erotic Romance or Romantica, not erotica. Submissions for non-romantic erotica may be submitted for our upcoming erotica website" by emailing mckenna@ellorascave.com.

Erotic Titles: *Fantasy Bar* by Trista Ann Michaels, *Cherry Hill* by R. Casteel

eXtasy Books
submissions@extasybooks.com
http://www.extasybooks.com
Ebook publisher
President: Tina Haveman
Executive Editor-in-Chief: Stefani V. Kelsey
The guidelines on their website state: "We at eXtasy Books are proud of the reputation we have earned in the short time we've been in operation for the quality of both our novels and shorter works. This doesn't happen by accident. We are accepting submissions in all the sub-genres: romance, sensual romance, BDSM, G/L/B, interracial, and any and all combinations thereof. We embrace the unusual and original, and are interested in all heat levels. If it's outside the box, feel free to send it." Needs Nuggets (5,000 - 11,000 words), Teasers (12,000 - 18,000 words), Sizzlers/Novellas (22,000 - 45,000 words), and Full novels/anthologies (55,000 words and up). See sample contract on the site along with formatting and sub-mission instructions.

Erotic Titles: *Torrid: A Shounen-ai Romance* by Morgan Hawke, *Daughter of the Shadows: Tasherytakhet* by Julia Kaye

New Concepts Publishing
4729 Humphreys Rd.

Lake Park, GA 31636
http://www.newconceptspublishing.com/
Editor-in-Chief: Madris Gutierrez
Senior Editor: Andrea DePasture
This in one of the original e-book publishers, and they still accept their submissions on paper. Their emphasis is on romance, with sex as one element of a good story. See their website for detailed and complete submission instructions. They prefer a synopsis and sample chapters. They need shorter works for anthologies and longer works, from "love bites" (10,000 words) to novellas (20,000 words) to full novels (90,000 words to a maximum of 120,000). They are seeking romantic erotica, patriotic romance, paranormal, BDSM, and many other categories varying from sweet (mild) to spicy to carnal (graphic).
Erotic Titles: *Orgasmizer9000 and Other Stories* by Angelique Anjou, Jaide Fox, and Marie Morin

Pink Flamingo Publications
lizbeth@pinkflamingo.com
http://www.pinkflamingo.com
Editor: Lizbeth Dusseau
The guidelines on their website state: "Pink Flamingo Publications publishes in paperback and Ebook versions, roughly 36 titles per year. We primarily release BDSM fetish novels, featuring either Female submission/Male domination or Female Domination/Male submission. We also publish some Spanking and General Erotica titles. We do accept a limited number of short story collections." Wants novels 42,000-62,000 words. No lesbian or gay male focused fiction. Pays royalties quarterly, 12-15% of cover price on paperbacks, 17-20% on Ebooks. Also wants short stories for "free samples," but does not pay for them.
Erotic Titles: *Allow Me To Serve* by Alexander Kelly, *Capturing Cressida* by Imogen Edwards

Renaissance EBooks
Northampton, MA
submissions@renebooks.com
http://www.renebooks.com
Publisher: Jean Marie Stine
This e-book publisher has several imprints but the one of most interest to erotic writers is the Sizzler line of electronic books. Sizzler publishes romantic erotica, B&D (bondage and domination), lesbian, gay male, and Scorchers (mainstream erotica). They accept submissions by email only, in a very specific format detailed on their

web site. They pay quarterly royalties based on sales/downloads.
Erotic Titles: *Virtual Slave: A Novel of Marital Submission* by Elisabeth
Nash, *I Want to Die in Drag!: The Transgender Erotic Classic* by Ed Wood, Jr.

Ssspread.com
writing@ssspread.com
http://ssspread.com
Editor: CJ Hammond
Appears to have ceased operations.

Wicked Velvet
lagatta@comcast.net
http://www.wickedvelvet.com
http://www.wickedcastle.com
Billed as "The web's premiere publisher of erotic romance for
women," Wicked Velvet is an electronic publisher of erotic novels
serialized chapter by chapter. They are a subscription site with a
mostly female readership. They accept submissions from both male
and female writers, but with focus on women's erotic fantasies. The
guidelines on their website state: "Use straight sex, spanking, some
BDSM, abduction fantasy, slave fantasy, orgies and exhibitionism—
basically a bit of a mélange. The graphic content should be varied,
not repetitious from scene to scene."
Looking for all settings: historical, western, regency, sci-fi, vampire, contemporary, fantasy, suspense, time-travel. Query with one
paragraph synopsis, first two chapters (up to 13,000 words), and
cover letter. Finished novel should be 50,000 to 100,000 words,
with 4,000-7,000 words per chapter. Pays per chapter as posted,
50% up front, the remaining 50% as lump sum after the entire work
is serialized. Additional 15% royalty paid on downloads of completed work. Also takes print rights for up to three years, with additional payment terms. After three years, all rights revert to author. The
site only keeps books in the process of being published on its site
and moves completed books to the Wicked Castle sister site.
Erotic Titles: Completed: *Web of Lords* by Maria Isabel Pita; In
process: *Arabella Book 3: King's Brat* by k.a. halle

SECTION THREE
Resources

Resources For Writers

As a professional writer, you do not exist in a vacuum. There are many places to turn for help, advice, inspiration, and knowledge beyond this book. In this section, we list some of the ones we have found helpful.

Writers Organizations

There are many organizations for writers. Some specialize by genre, region, ethnic/cultural similarity, or other reasons for affinity and common interest, but here we list some of the more general, national organizations, and the one specialty organization currently in existence for erotica writers.

American Society of Journalists and Authors (ASJA)
1501 Broadway, Suite 302
New York, NY 10036
Voice: 212-997-0947
Fax: 212-937-2315
http://www.asja.org/
The American Society of Journalists and Authors helps professional freelance writers advance their writing careers. Members share candid data on writing rates, publishing contracts, editors, agents and more. Non-members benefit from their Contracts Watch newsletter, annual writers conference and writing resources. The ASJA is for nonfiction writers, and proof of journalistic credentials in the form of clippings from major magazines or books is required to join. But the Contracts Watch, rates, and other services they provide help fiction writers as well as nonfiction writers.

The Authors Guild
31 E 28th St, 10th Floor
New York, NY 10016-7923
Phone: (212) 563-5904
Fax: (212) 564-5363
http://www.authorsguild.org/
The Author's Guild, the nation's largest society of published authors
is a leading advocate for fair compensation, free speech and copyright
protection. Since 1919, the Guild has worked on behalf of its members
to lobby for freedeom of expression, copyrights and other issues of
concern to authors and bring authors the latest news in the publishing
industry via the Guild Bulletin.

Erotic Authors Association
http://www.eroticauthorsassociation.com
mjaye22@localnet.com
This fledgling organization for erotica writers was founded by well-
known erotica writer and editor Marilyn Jaye Lewis. Membership as of
press time is free to interested parties. The organization sponsors
awards, interviews writers on the web site, and is growing.

National Writers Union (NWU)
113 University Pl. 6th Fl.
New York, NY 10003
Phone: 212-254-0279
Fax: 212-254-0673
http://www.nwu.org
The National Writers Union (NWU) is the trade union for freelance
writers of all genres. The NWU is a part of the UAW (United Auto
Workers) and through them the AFL-CIO. They offer contract advice and
grievance resolution, member education, job banks, networking, social
and professional events, and much more. They fight the unfair use of
freelancers works without compensation in cases like Tasini v. New York
Times which went to the Supreme Court and established important
payment practices in favor of writers.

PEN American Center
588 Broadway, Suite 303
New York, NY 10012
Telephone: (212) 334-1660
Fax: (212) 334-2181
http://www.pen.org/
An association of writers working to advance literature, defend free

expression, and foster international literary fellowship. PEN American Center is the largest of the 141 centers of International PEN, the world's oldest human rights organization and the oldest international literary organization. The Center has a membership of 2,900 distinguished writers, editors, and translators. They sponsor various grants and awards programs, publish a magazine, and support many programs for writers.

Online Market Listings

There are numerous web sites and email newsletters online that list markets and which are especially important for keeping up with transient markets like book anthologies which only open for submissions for a few months or weeks before filling up. You may want to check these sites regularly to keep up with opportunities.

Erotica Readers & Writers Association,
http://www.erotica-readers.com

Fiction Factor/Erotica Factor
http://erotica.fictionfactor.com

Gila Queen's Guide to Markets
http://www.gilaqueen.com
Newsletter featuring market listings, $20/year

Tristan Taormino's Double T newsletter
Subscribe at http://www.puckerup.com/subscribe.php
Free monthly newsletter edited by Rachel featuring numerous magazine and anthology listings.

Katy Terrega's newsletter
http://www.katyterrega.com
Free bi-monthly newsletter with articles about porn writing and market listings by the author of Writing Porn for Fun and Profit.

Sex-Writer
http://www.sex-writer.com
Website created by Katy Terrega

For Your Bookshelf

There are many more books beyond this one which you might find helpful to you as an erotica writer. Some of these are reference books, some instructional, others more personal in nature.

The Bald Headed Hermit and the Artichoke: An Erotic Thesaurus by Allan D. Peterkin, Arsenal Pulp Press, 1999

Elements of Arousal by Lars Eighner, Richard Kasak Books, 1994

How To Write A Dirty Story: Reading, Writing and Publishing Erotica by Susie Bright, Fireside, 2002

How To Write Erotica by Valerie Kelly, Crown Publishers, 1992

It's a Dirty Job...Writing Porn for Fun and Profit! by Katy Terrega, Booklocker.com, 1999

The Joy of Writing Sex by Elizabeth Benedict, Revised Edition, Own Books, 2002

The Burning Pen: Sex Writers on Sex Writing edited by M. Christian, Alyson, 2001

Writing Erotica by Edo van Belkum, Self Counsel Press, 2001

Writing Erotic Fiction: How to Write a Successful Erotic Novel by Pamela Rochford, How To Books, Ltd., 2001

Writing Erotic Fiction and Getting Published by Mike Bailey, NTC Publishing (part of their Teach Yourself series).

Subject Index

Bisexual

Books: Alyson Publications, Bi Press, Cleis Press, Red Hot Diva

Magazines: Blithe House Quarterly, Cybersocket, Options, Three Pillows

EBooks: eXtasy Books

Gay

Books: Alyson Publications, Arsenal Pulp Press, Atta Girl Press, Bearpaw Publishing, Cleis Press, Gay Men's Press, Gay Sunshine Press/Leyland Publications, Green Candy Press, The Haworth Press, Idol Books, Palm Drive Publishing, Suspect Thoughts Press, Unbound Books, West Beach Books, Windstorm Creative, Zipper Books and Prowler Books

Magazines: 100% Beef Magazine, Specialty Publications, American Bear/American Grizzly, Bear Magazine, Blithe House Quarterly, Boy Next Door, Brush Creek Media, Cherry Boys, Coming Out, Cybersocket, First Hand Experiences For Loving Men, Freshmen, Genre Magazine, Harrington Gay Men's Literary Quarterly, Indulge, Instinct, International Leatherman, In Touch For Men, Nightcharm, Outbound Press, Specialty Publications, Sportomatic Ltd, Tender Chickens, Unzipped Monthly, Velvet Mafia, Young & Hung

EBooks: eXtasy Books, Renaissance EBooks

Lesbian

Books: Alyson Publications, Arsenal Pulp Press, Atta Girl Press, Bearpaw Publishing, Bella Books, Bullock Publications, Cleis Press, Collective

Publishing, Firebrand Books, The Haworth Press, Limitless Dare 2 Dream Publishing, New Victoria, Red Hot Diva, Suspect Thoughts Press, Unbound Books, Windstorm Creative

Magazines: Blithe House Quarterly, Cybersocket, KUMA: Black Lesbian Erotica, On Our Backs, StoryMistress, TechnoDyke, Velvet Park
EBooks: ArtemisPress, eXtasy Books, Renaissance EBooks

Fetish/BDSM

Books: Blue Moon, Chimera Publishing Ltd, Citadel Press, Daedalus Publishing, eXtasy Books, Green Candy Press, Mystic Rose Books, Nexus, Olympia Publications

Magazines: Behind the Scene, Bizarre, Blue Food, CF Publications, International Leatherman, Nugget Magazine, Penthouse Variations, Skin Two, Taboo

EBooks: eXtasy Books, New Concepts Publishing, Pink Flamingo Publications, Renaissance EBooks

Letters

Magazines: Busty Beauties, Fox Magazine, Hustler Letters, In the Buff, Penthouse Letters, Young & Tight Fantasies

Nonfiction: General

Books: Akashic Books, Alyson Publications, Arsenal Pulp Press, Artemis Creation Publishing, Chronicle Books, Cleis Press, Conari Press, Daedalus Publishing, Delectus Books, Down There Press, ECW Press, Fairview Press, Feral House, Firebrand Books, First Tribe, Green Candy Press, Guernica Editions, Hatala Geroproducts, The Haworth Press, Lonely Planet Publications, Melcher Media, Mystic Ridge Books, Mystic Rose Books, New Age Dimensions, New Victoria, North Atlantic/Frog Limited, On Your Own Publications, Palm Drive Publishing, Park Street Press, Pedlar Press, Persea Books, Really Great Books Inc, Roam Publishing, Sable Publishing, Seal Press, Shecky's, Soft Skull Press, Ten Speed Press & Celestial Arts, Thunder's Mouth Press, Vision Paperbacks/Fusion Press

Magazines: AVN (Adult Video News), AVN Online, Bear Magazine, Bitch, The Blacklisted Journalist, Clean Sheets, Desire, Dr. Susan Block's Journal of Sex..., Eros-Noir, Erotic Magazine, Genesis, Genre Magazine, Good Vibrations Online Magazine, Harrington Gay Men's Literary Quarterly, Hustler, Instinct, Mind Caviar, Moist, Nerve, Playboy

Magazine, Playgirl Magazine, Punk Planet, Sauce*Box, ScarletLetters, Swank, Velvet Park, While You Were Sleeping

Nonfiction: How-To

Books: Chronicle Books, Cleis Press, Down There Press, Greenery Press, Hunter House, Kensington, Mystic Rose Books, Running Press, Swann House

Magazines: Clean Sheets, Good Vibrations Online Magazine, Hustler

Poetry

Books: First Tribe, Limitless Dare 2 Dream Publishing, Manic D Press

Magazines: Clean Sheets, Moist, Sauce*Box, ScarletLetters, Sliptongue, Velvet Park

Fantasy/Sci-Fi/Horror

Books: Chippewa Publishing LLC, Circlet Press, Windstorm Creative

Magazines: Blood Fetish, Cthulhu Sex Magazine, Peep Show Magazine

EBooks: Amatory Ink, Renaissance Ebooks

Ethnic/Multicultural

Books: Atria Books, Aunt Lute Book, Brown Skin Books, Flowers in Bloom Publishers, Genesis Press, Washington Square Press

Magazines: Blackfire, Black Lace Magazine, Black Male For Men, KUMA: Black Lesbian Erotica

Senior Citizen

Books: Hatala Geroproducts

Crossdressing/Transgendered/TS-TV

Books: Alyson Publications, Bearpaw Publishing

Magazines: Blithe House Quarterly, Cybersocket

Feminist

Books: AK Press, Aunt Lute Books, Firebrand Books, Seal Press

Graphic Novels

Books: Cellar Door Publishing LLC, Denis Kitchen Publishing Co., Last Gasp, Soft Skull Press

Foot & Leg Fetish

Magazines: Leg Show, Leg World

Microfiction/Short-shorts

Magazines: Moist, ScarletLetters, Velvet Park

Have an update?
Know a market that isn't listed here?
Want to list your market in the next edition?

Email Updates and Changes to:
"editorial@circlet.com"

Circlet Press, Inc.
1770 Mass. Ave. #278
Cambridge, MA 02140

www. circlet.com

Celebrating the erotic imagination since 1992.